BIONIC IMPOSTER

"Take a look at this, gentlemen."

He unbuttoned and pulled open his blouse. There on his chest was his fake lens—dull and lifeless, but as they stared, rapidly coming to life, a glorious imitation remarkably like the real lens —bright and sparkling. Then like an overloaded video screen it slowly, slowly became a nauseous fluxion of repulsive colors—and it was *squirming!*

Every wearer of the lens—on arm or wing, on fin or tentacle, or chest or brow—was proud to bear the symbol of civilization and have the instrument by which the psionic power of the mind intensified.

In contrast the fake lens on 24of6's chest was painfully obscene. . .

THE ALL-NEW ADVENTURES OF THE LENSMAN CREATED BY E.E. "DOC" SMITH

THE DRAGON LENSMAN

Based on the Characters
Created by E.E. "Doc" Smith

by David A. Kyle

TORONTO · BANTAM BOOKS · LONDON
NEW YORK

THE DRAGON LENSMAN
A Bantam Book / September 1980

ISBN 0-553-13741-7

Published simultaneously in the United States and Canada

Bantam Books are published by Bantam Books, Inc. Its trademark, consisting of the words "Bantam Books" and the por-
trayal of a bantam, is Registered in U.S. Patent and Trademark
Office and in other countries. Marca Registrada. Bantam
Books, Inc., 666 Fifth Avenue, New York, New York 10103.

PRINTED IN THE UNITED STATES OF AMERICA

0 9 8 7 6 5 4 3 2 1

Contents

Introduction

When David Kyle told me he was writing the story of Worsel the Velantian as the first book in the continuation of the Lensman series, I was pleasantly surprised—though, if truth be told, a bit apprehensive. Bantam Books had approved his original outline, and the Smith heirs had given their consent to the effort—but, I thought, better *no* additional Lensman stories than *poor* Lensman stories.

More than two decades ago, as Fantasy Press, I published the original hard-back editions of the Lensman tales. I was responsible for the expansion of the original four books into the seven that now make up the series. With the publication of *The Vortex Blaster* I thought, with regret, that I had enjoyed my last excursion into the Universe of Arisia and the Lens. At one time Doc Smith had considered writing the stories of two of the non-human Lensmen—Worsel of Velantia Three and Nadreck of Palain Seven—but because of a lack of market, with the specialty science fiction book publishers faltering or out of business, he had abandoned the idea.

Now David Kyle was writing the saga of Worsel, the Dragon Lensman. The passing years had not dimmed my interest in the Universe of the Galactic Patrol—but could Dave pick up the threads of another writer's creation? Could he recreate the atmosphere and characters of E. E. "Doc" Smith. It was a tall order—and I was skeptical.

In February 1979 I was a house guest of the very hospitable Ruth and David Kyle at Hobe Sound, Florida. There I read the manuscript of *The Dragon Lensman*—and I was surprised and delighted! Not only had Dave captured the style of a Doc Smith epic, not only had he blended his own original concepts into the Lensman series, but he had written an exciting, first rate science fiction novel, fully able to stand on its own merits.

Were he able to read it, Doc, I'm sure, would be pleased. In *The Dragon Lensman*, through David A. Kyle, E. E. "Doc" Smith has returned to literary life!

Lloyd Arthur Eshbach
Myerstown, Pennsylvania
March 1979

Foreword

For all those of you who have previously read E. E. "Doc" Smith's accounts of the Galactic Patrol and the Arisian-Eddorian conflict, most of this Foreword is redundant. You are hereby waved on to the last three paragraphs beginning with "The chronicler . . ." For those of you who are newcomers, or whose memories have clouded with the years, a few words of background are certainly desirable.

Billions of years ago Mankind began to evolve on a small planet of the star Sol. Billions of years before that, Tellus, also known as Earth, had been created in the time of the great Coalescence. And billions of years before that event, our Milky Way galaxy, also known as the First Galaxy, was inhospitable to life, almost barren of planets and virtually deserted.

The life-spores of Man existed before all these things, incredibly far back for uncountable eons. The ancestral source was the race of the Arisians from the beginning of Time, Visualizers of the Cosmic All, future guardians of Civilization.

Fully as ancient, nearly equal in macrocosmic mind power, and as evil as the Arisians were good, were the Eddorians of the Second Galaxy. Whereas the Arisians were of our own space-time continuum, the Eddorians were not, coming on their wandering planet to the Second Galaxy from a different, horribly alien plenum. They were dedicated to a continuing search for more worlds to sate their lust for dominance. Their ambition was at last to be glutted by the Coalescence. In that cataclysmic event their enslaved star island passed, end to end, through our own galaxy. The stupendous interstellar forces which were unleashed thus created billions of new worlds. The inevitable conflict between the Arisians and the Eddorians, the prototype confrontation between Good and Evil, had arrived. The struggle began for the lives and souls of the many races that were evolving. As Civilization grew, the Elders of Arisia surreptitiously encouraged the new life forms to resist the tyranny and to shape their independent ways toward perfection.

In the universal deceit which developed around the rise of the Eddorian-inspired Boskonian outlaws, the greatest secret of all was kept by the Arisians. Their immortal enemies, the Eddorians, were kept forever ignorant of their existance. The Arisians were the covert and incognito patrons of those opposing the evil Eddorians; they were the real, formidable counterforce in the eons-long contest with Boskonia and its masters.

Four widely-scattered planets with advanced life forms were the nucleus of the resistance in the First Galaxy: Tellus, known as Earth or Terra, Velantia, Rigel Four, and Palain Seven. Each, subtly encouraged by the Arisians, developed four dissimilar races, but it was Tellus which became the focal point for the organized force against Boskone and its puppet-masters. From Tellus came the formation of the Galactic Patrol, to be the instrument of Eddorian destruction. Also from Tellus came the Kinnison and Samms families leading to their zenith, the union of their foremost leaders, Kimball Kinnison, the Gray Lensman, and Clarrissa MacDougall, the Red Lensman.

Within generations of the First Lensman, Virgil Samms, many Lensmen had been recruited into a special corps of Patrolmen. They were outstanding military leaders and scientists, possessing extraordinary natural, non-mutated abilities. The Lensman name came from the peculiar semi-living Lens each one wore, usually on a wrist, a unique gift obtained from Mentor of Arisia. These incredible instruments, radiant crystal complexities, were badges of honor, forgery-proof identification, and amplifiers of psychic powers. They were awarded only to those chosen by Mentor itself, the amorphous fusion-entity of the four intellectually greatest Arisian Molders of Civilization. The psychical match to the quintessential individuality of the Lensman was exact—so perfect, in fact, that it released latent parapsychic or psi powers, telepathy in particular. Only the original recipient of the Lens could wear it—for anyone else it brought instant death.

The best Lensmen eventually were chosen for the highest honor which the Patrol could offer: Unattached status. Known as Gray Lensmen from the plain leather uniforms they now wore, unlike the black-and-silver-and-gold ones of the rest of the officers and men, these distinguished fellows of the Service were free agents. With their freedom for independent action they were the personification of the Patrol itself, accountable to no one but the highest authorities.

Although Kimball Kinnison was not the first Gray Lensman, he was, despite his youth, one of the outstanding ones. His demonstrated ability led to his being recalled to Arisia by Mentor to receive the next level of training as a Second Stage Lensman. Kimball was the first of four to come from each of the original planets, even ahead of Worsel the Velantian, whose mind actually was better developed and trained, and of vastly greater power. The Tellurian, however, was chosen for greater capacity and more varied growth, especially for the force of his driving will, so characteristic of his race.

As the legion of Lensmen grew with its special leaders, so did the scale of the conflict, until, finally, both galaxies and their neighboring star clusters were involved.

The climax came at last. Kimball Kinnison, as the fighting leader of the Galactic Patrol, the military arm of the Galactic Council which by now represented all of Civilization, directed the decisive battles by the Grand Fleet against the massive forces of the Boskonians. The culmination of the years of galactic struggle came with the giant dogfight of spaceships which was The Battle of Klovia. The Boskonian conspiracy was considered destroyed. Kimball Kinnison, the newly-appointed Galactic Coordinator, and his bride Cris were taking on their new responsibilities for Civilization. Peace was spreading through the two galaxies.

Only Mentor knew that the Eddorians had not been defeated, merely delayed, in their goal to conquer the galaxies and to make them their playthings.

The chronicler of these events has been, up to now, the famous research historian of the Galactic Patrol, E. E. "Doc" Smith. His efforts have been monumental; a half dozen books by him have traced the rise of Tellurian culture and the formation of the Patrol, all part of the struggle to protect and advance Civilization in the Milky Way. His reports have been presented in his inimitable way as popularized novels. More than a decade ago Doc Smith, a warm-hearted and virile man, passed on to "the next plane of existence" to join the Arisians. Since then no books describing the exploits of the fabulous Lensmen have been written, although there really has been no need, because the end of the terrible Boskonian threat was told and the evil Eddorians were shown to have been obliterated. Doc Smith, the historian, did his work well—and thoroughly—to lead us to the plateau of the evolution of the Universe with the coming of the Children of the Lens.

There is, however, a period in the history, as reported by the doctor, which has not been documented. A score of years lie between the marriage of Kinnison to his Cris and the emergence from childhood of their offspring. There was in these decades no "energy stasis"—that which always moves forward just to stand still inevitably leads upward and downward simultaneously. Historical events were taking place—but they become history only when they are recorded and reported.

The well-established historical research department which E. E. Smith so successfully created is still at work collecting and assembling facts and eye-witness accounts. There is a wealth of material available for further tales of the Patrol and its personnel. This book is the first one written without the direct supervision of the doctor. Your new historian knew "Doc" for many years, having met him in his space-roamer's garb of "Northwest Smith of Earth," at the Second Worldcon in Chicago, Tellus—and, having had him for a lifetime as a guide, appreciates that he was unique. Let no one be deluded, least of all your present historian, into thinking that this new series of books will be indistinguishable from the presentations of the original histories. Unique "Doc" was, and unique he will remain. But the spirit will not be changed—the entire historical research department will see to that. This historian, whose responsibility is not taken lightly, pledges fidelity to the "E. E. Smith way" knowing that The Galactic Roamers will not tolerate anything less.

David A. Kyle
Tellus

Prologue

After the destruction of Onlo and the fall of Thrale and the "cleaning up" of Lyrane VIII, with the Boskonians no longer fomenting trouble in the First Galaxy, the Galactic Patrol was prepared to become a police force instead of a military machine. The Patrol's four greatest operatives, the illustrious Second Stage Lensmen, were confronted with their most difficult tasks—making adjustments to peace. Each one faced his problem in his own way, representative as he was of his own distinctive race and culture. Kimball Kinnison, the Tellurian, humankind's incredible hero, had little choice but to accept the responsibility of being Galactic Coordinator. Nadreck, the Palainian, frigid-blooded poison-breather with his metabolic extension into the fourth dimension, carried on his psychological research and pursued his personal death feud against the escaped Kandron of Onlo. Tregonsee, the hard-shelled Rigellian, profound meditator on the Cosmos, "put away his Grays" and explored the galaxies with his superior sense of perception, completely committed to his "Project Quicksilver."

The fourth Second Stage Lensman, Worsel, the Velantian, the biggest, smartest and most ferocious of all the million Patrolmen, remained in heart and in soul—and on active duty —a Gray Lensman.

Worsel was a frightening apparition to anyone who had never met a Velantian before. At first glance he seemed grotesquely hideous, a nightmarish reptile, all fangs and claws. The day he arrived at Pok, the Planetoid of Knowledge, to begin the most incredible of his adventures, he frightened the old soldier-scientist assigned to meet him.

Two utterly different kinds of Galactic Patrolmen met at that moment in the docking-port reception chamber when he slithered, then leaped, from his personal spacecraft. Most Patrolmen were fighting men, accustomed to deadly battle in the far depths of space, but some were laboratory soldiers, forever sheltered in their quiet isolation, at war only with facts and figures. Worsel was the epitome of the superlative warrior, one of the unique quartet of Lensmen, the elite of the elite; the other was an elderly scientist, still non-combatant even in his Third-and-Final Life-Restoration. The old man in the youthful body was content to end his days on the Pok research team in his endless quest for knowledge. He had never met a Velantian; he had never met a Second Stage Lensman; now he met both in the living flesh of a single creature.

The actual meeting was the most excitement he had had in his life, more exciting by far than even his appointment as Curator of Pok. And now he was terrified by the encounter. No books, no three-D pictures had prepared him for what he saw: the incredible appearance of the reknowned hero who looked and smelled of the violence that had swirled, and still swirled, around the Galactic Patrol.

The human was in the twilight of his life, but the Velantian Lensman, suggesting a cross between a winged pterosaur and a long-necked Tyrannosaurus Rex with brains, was at the peak of his magnificent physical and mental powers. Like a serpentine dragon, the creature emerged from his polished shell, metal door clanging against metal wall, and loomed before the man. The twelve-foot ceiling was touched by a monstrous reptilian head. The walls were crowded by a massive body with its multiple arms, two conventional but two bat-winged, with clawed thumb and hooked fingers. The face seemed to be entirely sharp white teeth. Several bright eyes tilted down toward him on the ends of waving stalks, each glittering eye fixed on him. One of the pair of regular limbs reached out to him, muscles rippling along scaly forearm, claws retracted at the end of a sinewy palm and long slender fingers. The Curator shrank back, even as he reached out his own fingers for a timid welcoming handshake.

That the saurian wore a GP uniform, so scanty it was more like a harness, was reassuring, though the conspicuous gray leather of a Second Stage Lensman was immensely intimidating. This snake-thing was the most remarkable Lensman among a most remarkable group in the Civilized Universe. And yet, for all its potent might, it was most honored by the good entities of the billions of planets and most feared by the bad, not for its titanic strength, but for its intellect. Here was Worsel, within touch, the greatest pragmatic thinker in the Galactic Patrol—such greatness left the old scientist's mind numb. His whole body, in fact, was numb.

Then he knew that the numbness was the spell of the extraordinary power of the dragon's telepathic mind. Worsel, who did not speak, was in his mind, greeting him, reassuring him, making him feel at ease. The dragon which had come to Pok was not a plebeian Occidental one, symbolizing evil, but a patrician Oriental one, intrinsically benevolent.

The human being, for the first time in his life, felt that he himself might be a member of an inferior race—and to his surprise he was pleased to consider such an unthinkable idea.

Thus Worsel, the Dragon Lensman, came to Pok.

1

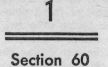

Section 60

Two figures stood facing each other. Both were sleek and powerful, both stood twenty feet tall, both were mighty engines of destruction. One was alive, a dragon, and one was not, a machine.

The dragon was Worsel, Lensman, sitting half on his haunches, half on the base of his tail, horny hands on slim hips, soft palms and taloned fingers turned outward. His narrow head on lithe neck was cocked; a large grin of sharp and gleaming teeth split his jaws. A pair of his many extensible eyes was part way out on their stalks, moving slowly up and down in admiration.

"You," Worsel said to the war machine, "are a beauty." He did not say so out loud; he spoke mentally, as was his custom, for his brain was as impressive and potent as his body. In fact, even some of his alien friends believed he could not talk at all. Worsel reached out and, above the war machine's jointed hips and below the cluster of gun snouts, patted the smooth curves of its dureum shell body, his claws drumming a quick tattoo on the mental skin. He brought his snout within an inch of the oval perception-lens of the robot's head, his breath misting on the cool glass and plastisteel. Worsel, stirring another pair of eyes into use, peered now into each sensor lens and orifice, concentrating the prodigious power of his mind on the brain of the machine.

He found it simple, perfect—and dead. Yet intuition told him he was getting close to some kind of revelation.

"Not you," Worsel said. "You're no troublemaker right now." He clicked his teeth and ran his slender tongue along the sharp edges and up over his lips. "You could be, though, you could be—or another potent thing like you," he said. "Too bad you aren't what I'm searching for; I wouldn't be wasting any more time. And it would be fun, too, to take you apart—over your objections."

5

Worsel reared back gracefully, swinging his tail gently around in a manner more mammalian than reptilian. He stretched his neck and looked beyond the huge soldier robot to the smaller, non-anthropomorphic war machines. They were all cold and lifeless, like the robot, though far less sinister, relics of a past of faded power and menace. True, they were operational, some even armed, but not one had either the wit or the ability to turn his own key or to press his own button. No, he was getting closer, but the mystery that he pursued did not hide among them. Yet somewhere in The Great Hall of the Machines into which his investigation had led him he knew he would soon find—something.

What was it he sought? He didn't know—there were only the reports, the strange beliefs that something—some *thing*—was amiss in Pok. At first he considered the request frivolous. A Lensman used to intergalactic problems didn't go mouse-hunting. Only his sentimental attachment for Pok had brought him here. But almost from the moment of his arrival he had sensed the strangeness in the atmosphere. The scientists were nervous; the Patrolmen were tense; now he himself was aware of some great event or danger. He was exceedingly glad he had come.

The angular, dureum-alloy vault of The Great Hall of the Machines disappeared into the haze of the far distance, the lines of suspended security lights marking the boundaries of the main corridor. Spread out around him was a maze of transparent walls, like shimmering three-dimensional ghosts. The silence was absolute when he was still, but now the noises of the clumping of his large feet, and the whispering of the leather toe-sheaths which padded his claws as they brushed the gleaming floor, echoed and re-echoed from wall to wall and reverberated like distant thunder in the high vastness of the ceiling's emptiness.

He had walked past armies of machines, each and every one different, through a succession of partitioned areas over long hours. Only the mechanical humanoid fighter which he had just examined had given him a real taste of excitement. So far his survey would have been a bore, except for the fascination of the shapes he had seen, simple and complex, plain and grotesque, spidery, squat, bizarre and baroque, vicious and beautiful.

The new room into which he had just come, the standard 300-foot square, was brightly lighted and filled with compu-automates. This was the section, the final section, which he had been aiming for, the place he expected to find the reason

6

for the pervading uneasiness, and where he would determine if there were really a problem to solve. Within its limited yet large space there were thousands of lifeless shapes in serried ranks, innocuous devices of technological cultures, large and small, angular and curved, shiny and dull, knobbly and smooth, metallic and plastic, some beautiful and some ugly. Worsel was impressed by them because he knew that these were only a fraction of the creations from the minds and hands of the highest cultures of Civilization. The change in the scale of the collection since his last visit was enormous. The magnitude of the fabrications spread out before him would have intimidated or frightened a lesser person.

"Ah, my beauties!" Worsel said and coolly surveyed, from where he stood, their inanimate bodies, their inactive limbs, their mute visages. "Is there one among you who would like to greet a Lensman?" He said this aloud in his basic guttural Velantian, as it was physically impossible for him to speak Universal English. His tone was mocking, for he only half believed his mission. He was here on the Planetoid of Knowledge because, one of the theories went, a unique intelligence was suspected to exist, exceptionally strange and utterly alien in that its consciousness was artificial, mechanical, not alive. Either it existed, or else those who reported it were psychologically disturbed. In either case his presence was justified. The services of Worsel, the eminent psychologist, had been properly requested.

"No greeting for me?" Worsel persisted. "No welcome for Worsel of Velantia?" He popped out a number of eyes in various degrees of mock surprise. "Perhaps you sleep?" His jesting had that edge of seriousness which hinted at a set trap lying just below a scattering of leaves. "Perhaps you do not hear me?" He flicked his tongue casually, in the manner of an elaborate shrug as though inviting a response. "Or maybe you're just smart enough to play it this way?" These were more words than he had spoken in perhaps a year. He heard them physically through the vibrations from his chest, but he did not hear them through his ears because they had atrophied by disuse. It was characteristic of his race to interpret sound vibrations through sense organs in the skin around nose and throat.

Worsel knew that he had come to the most critical room. He was positive that something would happen here. This room on Level 97 wasn't overwhelmingly large, limited, as it was, to only the most sophisticated of items, but it contained all the "wits" and the "smarts" of the mech world.

7

They were all potentially in working order, a rather stupid situation he thought, ready to go into their dances and sing their songs of science or business, war or crime at the flick of a switch or the touch of a mind. Probably most of them could calculate, compute and make logical deductions as fast, maybe faster, than any Lensman, including himself. Maybe they weren't creative thinkers, like their creators, but then again . . . Maybe the magnitude of Pok was getting him down. It was no longer the small place he had helped establish years before. The sheer numbers of apparatuses now collected on the Planetoid of Knowledge was staggering, representing thousands of civilizations from which the Patrol had obtained the exhibits. Appreciation of this came only after he had walked through a half thousand rooms and skipped an equal number. It wasn't their sizes which were intimidating—considering that Worsel himself was thirty feet long and built like a piece of heavy-labor machinery covered with tough, flexible scales, he dwarfed most of the mechanisms. No, not their sizes, it was the extent of the alien collection which impressed him.

Pok, the Planetoid of Knowledge, was unique. It was an artificially constructed sphere eighteen miles in diameter, originally the project of The Velantian Council of Scientists before becoming a Galactic Patrol installation. When Velantia had discovered Civilization and had joined the Galactic Council, the planetoid had been established to collect the new knowledge available, and to make it possible for the Velantians to become quickly one of the foremost interstellar communities. Worsel, the hero of the hour, undertook the project and, with the Patrol's extensive help in collecting and furnishing material, soon had an extensive library and museum. Then, within one year, he had left to establish his own Institute.

At first the satellite had been in close orbit, but as Pok became a source of research for the galaxy, it was moved outward, beyond the original network of guardian satellites, the picket line that defended the former isolation of the mother planet. Velantia still claimed its territorial space within the encircling boundaries of the small guardian globes, but now Pok was technically in deep space, available for the use of all without trespassing.

Constructed massively to match the huge size of the Velantians, Pok at first was strictly a collection of mechanisms and machines, kept in the vacuum of space as a sort of deep-freeze, without maintenance necessary. Only a Velantian living-quarters was pressurized. As a GP establishment, it was soon extensively improved and continued rapidly to grow in size and contents. Sectional wedges built and sent by a multitude of races were fitted together for maximum expansion in minimum time. At right angles to each other, three huge egress shafts ran centrally from surface to surface through the planetoid, large enough to admit giant freighters. Every level had docking platforms. Each section had its own gravity and atmosphere, to match its source. Additionally, central control could alter each section to permit the most varied of research personnel to work comfortably, simulating almost any planetary condition.

Whereas the Velantians had been more interested in mind power and abstract science, they had, by the success of their original Pok, become equally outstanding in technological and mechanical application. They proved that it was easy for such a talented race as theirs to go from pure mathematics to applied mechanics. Though they weren't quite the center of power of muscles, machines, and the military that Tellus was, Velantia had certainly become a center of power for mental and psychological sciences.

Pok, at this moment of Worsel's appearance, was technically not operational. Its latest phase of construction was complete, but the Patrol staff was still a small housekeeping contingent, preparing for the researchers who were waiting to begin their individual projects.

Only a handful of Patrolmen not on leave of absence, therefore, now lived on it and managed it. The staff was much too small, Worsel thought. Not for the work, but for psychological reasons. The presence of all those machines, despite their inoperation, clinically suggested a stressful situation conducive to unpleasant complexes. No wonder they began hearing and imagining things. No wonder they had asked for a house-call by the eminent psychologist Worsel who lived next door. It was up to him to seek out the subtle disturbance. Were they just stir-crazy? Or was a machine consciousness alive in Pok?

Worsel had been scanning the room meticulously with his sense of perception. Now, suddenly, his scales were crawling, up his backbone and down his arms. Intuition was telling him that *something* strange was happening in this room. He knew at once, beyond any doubt, that this place was where discoveries would be made. His search was near an end. The time to commence identification and analysis had come. This was the time to call upon Bluebelt.

Bluebelt, administrative assistant since the early days when Worsel was promoted to Unattached status, was the antithesis of the winged snake he served, both physically and mentally. Bluebelt was relatively tiny, thirty-eight inches high, a mammal with long, golden fur. Because he looked like a guinea pig, with atrophied short wings which draped him like a dress jacket, and moved upright with little hops, he made strangers smile and turned them quickly into friends. On his four hand-like feet, however, he could move smoothly and swiftly. As for his intelligence, it was simple and logical, having none of the complexity of a Velantian; he was always warm, forthright, and intensely serious. Worsel found him invaluable and at every opportunity involving paperwork he perched Bluebelt on his broad shoulder to advise and consult.

The hairy one was now thirty millions of miles away in the Worsel Institute on Velantia, and Worsel projected his thought to him. The etheric connection, by mechanical thought enhancers, was instantaneous. It was far easier to communicate with Bluebelt—and to use him as a message center—than to do so with Pok's staff of six men scattered less than ten miles from him.

"I want a punch-up, Blue," Worsel said without preamble. The name Bluebelt, so often shortened to just plain Blue, had been hung on the creature by no less a personage than Kimball Kinnison himself, when they had all met and briefly worked together on a Patrol ship. What the full name, Bluebuebelthner-Bru, meant, nobody knew or asked.

"Yes, Worsel."

"Punch up slide series Pok RR-97." Pause. "Now start scanning. Stop. Go back three. Hold it." The entire contents of the miniaturized chart imprinted itself on Worsel's brain as clearly as if he himself had one of his "tight-focus-eyes" zeroed in on it. There were some 120,000 listings, and Worsel rapidly ran through all of them. The archives-and-museum directorship had done well; the organization was flawless as far as the facts were concerned. There was no speculation, however. There was no indication about whether or not Civilization had created inorganic beings, nor any judgment about the mech-things as slaves, equals, or even potential masters of the multitude of races comprising Civilization-kind. The records showed that, unlike all the previous rooms, every one of the machines on Level 97 had a sentient or potential-sentient rating. And every one which had an I.Q.Q. rating of any significance was identified as being in Room 97-1 of The Great Hall of the Machines on the Planetoid of

Knowledge. They had all been re-programmed to respond to both the English and Velantian languages. They numbered about twenty-three hundred and forty; many were interdependent or mechanically interlocked, so he couldn't be precise.

"Give me the floor plan—Pok RRP-97-1, I believe . . . QX. Give me the close-up of sections one through ten . . . QX." Worsel now had them displayed on the visual screen in his brain for immediate reference, in a form more easily managed than the actual material on file. "Thanks, Bluebelt. Clear ether."

The row of machines to his immediate left was rudimentary compared to the sophisticated ones telepathically activated in the sixties section in the middle of the room, but he would start right at Section One. His examination was pre-planned, and first came his personal physiological and psychological preparation. Worsel loosened all his eyes, swelled out his ear membranes, turned up his receptors, fluttered his wings, fanned his fins, and protruded the tip of his tongue from just under his beaked snout. Then came the first real action in his research plan, activation of his first machine. One would follow the other, each in turn being asked the blunt question he had so carefully considered as his opening gambit.

A small office file clerk, no bigger than Worsel's travel kit, was first at hand. He glanced at the I.D. plate, snapped in the power supply, flipped the circuit closed. The machine hummed into life. Worsel touched no buttons, twirled no knobs, and patiently waited. Through a glass plate he could see a surprisingly complex activity. There was much self-adjustment, with oiling and cleaning and substituting of parts, and tidying up of what were obviously consumable supplies. Outside, levers and appendages moved, lights blinked, and signals buzzed for more supplies and major maintenance. When Worsel did nothing, the machine lapsed into inactivity.

Then Worsel tapped out his question. It appeared on the light emitting diode screen:

"Are you happy?"

Nothing happened, so Worsel waited. After fifteen GP seconds, when the red letters had flickered out, he typed out the question again. Again a quarter of a minute passed with no response. This time Worsel type out, "Answer the question." The red letters on the screen, after a moment, began to blink rapidly, on and off, on and off. Worsel immediately typed, "Are you nervous because you are confused?"

11

The machine with no delay replied, "No. The input is aberrant. The input is rejected." When nothing further appeared, Worsel tapped, "Did you understand the questions?"

The machine said, "Yes. I am happy when I am playing games. I am not unhappy when I am not playing games. If this is a game, please give me instructions. If this is not a game, please turn this machine off. If there is no work to be done, please disconnect the power."

"What game would you like to play?" Worsel asked.

There was the longest pause so far before the words flashed up slowly one by one. "This machine is a machine. This machine may reflect from time to time the personalities of the many people who have programmed it. This machine is not a person. This machine is a machine. That is all."

Worsel repeated the basic question, "Are you happy?," but after a more than sufficient period of repetitious ambiguities he ended the inquisition. He reached two conclusions; one serious, that the very first machine in that roomful was both as smart and as sentient as some races in the Galactic Union, without their egotistical spirit—and one whimsical conclusion, that the answer to that impudent question "Are you happy?" was, for Worsel, a definite "yes." He had found a "mechanical intelligence." Perhaps he would find more. And what this all meant remained to be seen.

Slightly impatient now, Worsel made a dozen more mechanistic contacts before his large main meal, and two dozen more before he coiled himself in a defensive position on the bare floor with some of the typical Velantian heat bulbs focussed on himself. His head was pointed down the aisle, the vibrant Lens in his forehead aimed at Section 60; his eyes were retracted, but only half closed. He promptly went into a doze.

For a long time Room 97-1 of The Great Hall of the Machines seemed dead except for Worsel. There was no sound save the movement of the conditioned atmosphere around corners, and the gentle snores of the big dragon.

Behind the front rows of the assorted boxes and cylinders of Section 60 a metal arm extended itself and its rubber tip pressed a silent switch on the back of the larger machine in front of it. Like Worsel's Lens and half-shut eyes, the enemy now had an observer, an infra-red sensor soaking up the scene before it. The smaller machine snaked out a connector and attached itself to the larger; it took nothing but the infra-red reading from its companion. For a long time the smaller machine watched Worsel through the eye of the larger. No gears clicked, no levers moved, but as it squatted there on its many jointed legs, it thought. Slowly it sent out another rod to fasten itself on a neighbor. And another. And another. None were activated, all remained dead, but all were interlocked now within the immediate area of the small one.

For no apparent reason, Worsel awoke. All the actions had been completely screened from his limited awareness, and he could not see the little machine. Not the tiniest sound nor the slightest movement had registered with him, yet he was awake. He swept the room with his sense of perception, like an X-ray scan which could not be blocked. There was absolutely nothing suspicious. Worsel needed his sleep, so he went back to it.

When he was once again at his minimum sensitivity, something new happened: a plate imbedded in the dureum front of the little machine glowed a message, *Medonian Securi-Guard Model 2200. Extremely Dangerous When Activated.* In larger letters, pulsing on and off, was the single word, ACTIVATED. When the small Securi-Guard had made as many silent moves as possible, it hazarded one small, tiny click. Worsel stopped snoring and stirred, the tip of his tail quivering. The machine waited, uncertain of its next move. Then, with the advantage of the patience which most machines considered theirs for limitless time, the little black machine, much like Worsel, went back to sleep itself.

Hours passed, and when Worsel's regular sleep period was over he began his task again in Section Eight.

It was on his fiftieth-odd machine that he had an exceptional result. The screen printout read, "Faulty input. Faulty input. Rejected. Rejected. Operator is reminded that stupid information can be harmful to circuits. Be respectful. Not harmful. Harmful. Stupid. Stupid. Stupidstupidstupid . . ." And Worsel whacked the top of the machine with his tail, which made it stop. Worsel was surprised by the symptom. A neurosis or psychosis, so evidenced in this behavior, should not have been expected in this low-level machine. He checked its history record within its service lid, but it showed no aberration, merely cessation of function, which is why it ended up out of service in a museum. Worsel asked the initial question once more, "Are you happy?" All the machine could print was "Too late for correction. Too late" which it kept repeating even after several more blows of Worsel's tail. He bent down and pulled its plug.

When Worsel straightened up, he stretched extra tall, going up on his tail, which needed some muscle flexing after those

13

rather hard raps on the metal casing. His head was some twenty feet in the air, double the height of his former line of sight, with a sharply increased angle of view. That was how Worsel happened to see the remarkable performance of a certain machine in Section 27. He visually caught it in the act of plugging itself into another, completely different machine. Instantaneous application of his sense of perception revealed the alarming consequence: power was bringing the other machine to life!

2

Lens-to-Lens

One machine activating another! Worsel was grateful for his luck, although irritated with himself for having been so casual as to have limited himself to visual observations without frequent perceptual scrutiny.

He held his awkward position for many minutes, unmoving, watching for any other happenings, until the strain on his tensed muscles was more than he could bear. During all that time he searched everywhere with all his senses, but found nothing else. The only event had been the switching off of both machines almost as soon as the initial connection had been made.

When he finally relaxed from his immobility, he first undulated his aching neck, and then moved directly to the machines involved—they were interlocked, and the more sophisticated one had evidently shown enough power over the lesser one to initiate the request for a power connection.

The thinker was an "analyzer," and it could talk. The machine from which it was drawing its power was a simple, though exceedingly prepotent, machine service unit, noncommunicative and ordinarily used to power-boost a hundred like the analyzer it dwarfed. As for the analyzer, it was like a large flat desk with two flap-covered orifices at the right and left. Drop an item in the left opening and it would reappear out of the right one. From the front would come an analysis sheet covering as many tests of the item as the machine had capacity, with an incredibly complicated report as to the item's function and how it might be improved. The report could be scanned for details, but there was verbal communication, too, in a hundred languages. Worsel slid his "wristdex" sidereal-timepiece/computer into the opening, pressing with his other claw the inconsistency button, vocal response. The analyzer said, "Perfect operationally. Inconsequential dent in cover", and popped it out on the table top.

Worsel tried a variety of other things, and all analyses were normal and accurate and once in a while the machine said, "Thank you."

Worsel then came to the point. "What made you turn on and plug in for more power?" For the first time, the usually vociferous analyzer was silent. Worsel repeated the question, and simultaneously from the voice-box and the printer came a steady flow of ambiguities and absurdities. Worsel verbally fenced with the machine for minutes which became hours. Its objective was unmistakable: built to tell the truth, no matter what, it was being deliberately misleading, spewing out confusion when it couldn't—or wouldn't—lie. There was no doubt at all in Worsel's mind that there were a number of servo-mechanisms here in Room 97-1 which were semi-life forms—and potentially dangerous.

Worsel, a bit frustrated and determined to keep his good humor, did a typical thing. He reached over to a "Vending Center, Humanoid," pulled out a plastic cup, crumpled it, threw it into the analyzing intake and pressed all buttons for all information. The analyzer made a strange noise and said, "Cup container is broken," rejected it, and added, "Please replace on ingress and hold it there until flap drops." Worsel did so. The flap suddenly opened, and with blinding speed some metal fingers previously hidden raked the cup downward. Worsel, with matching speed hardly a split-second behind in reaction time, snatched his own claw away. The cup disappeared, along with a number of scales from the back of his soft talons. No real damage, no blood drawn, but Worsel knew that a Tellurian would have had at the very least a mutilated hand—if not a missing limb. The machine said, "Don't put trash into me." The warning was toneless, matter-of-fact, not at all sinister. Then came, after a moment, the word "Please." That word, to Worsel, seemed disturbingly malevolent.

He flipped the off switch, disconnected the power cable from the service unit and called Bluebelt.

"Stand by for the next few hours. Focus in on my Lens transmission and keep watch," he said. Bluebelt started to protest about power drain and cost accounting, but Worsel cut him off. "QX. Give me a half hour. I've got all those circuits to pick through in my head, and then I've got some heavy thinking to do. Interrupt me for anything suspicious." He gave Bluebelt a quick review of his encounters.

"L-Two Worsel," Bluebelt said, using the formal address, as he so often did. "You need help on the spot. I'll dispatch

16

the two new Patrolmen from the Institute on the next supply ship for Pok." But Worsel was no longer listening, immune when he wanted to be from the advice which so frequently flowed unchecked from Blue. Already he had absently peeled a meat bar and popped it in his mouth, chewing while mentally tracing through the plans he had so recently absorbed. Was he underestimating his C-theory?

Under Worsel's Chemical theory of intelligence no truly sentient being of Civilization—that is to say, a sentient being with a sense of morality, destiny and transcendent purpose—could be inorganic. Ci-Life, or Civilization-Life, as interpreted by Mentor, had to be organic in its informational banks and reasoning circuits; mech-men could not be Ci-Life.

Yet here he was, possibly on the verge of disproving his own theory.

Worsel's theory of chemical thought, by a simplified interpretation, was almost diametrically different from the electrical theory. The E-theory assumed that electrical impulses created and recorded electrical patterns which, when needed for any conscious or unconscious action, could be discharged as electrical patterns. Thinking was, therefore, an electrical activity of all sorts of wave forms on certain observable frequencies—and possibly some unobservable. Chemical combinations were merely catalysts for electric, electrolytic, electromagnetic, and electronic activities.

The Electrical theory seemed to be subtantiated here in Room 97-1.

His C-theory postulated that it was the electromagnetic activity which was the catalyst, or activator, and that molecular structure, in another word chemistry, was the means by which information was registered, stored, changed and converted, and then released when desired. The fact was that the machinery blueprints in his head so recently examined disclosed hardly any basis in chemistry.

Worsel had developed his theory to account for the obvious lack of significant robotic intelligences in the two galaxies of Civilization. True, there were some highly sophisticated artificial non-organic intelligences which were assumed to have some pragmatical "intelligence," but none had ever been accepted into the Galactic Union as part of Civilization.

What he was encountering now might mean a whole new radical shifting of accepted values. What a mechanical intelligence might be, how it would work and how it would relate to Mentor Civilization was what he might be about to determine. The intriguing possibility, unfortunately, was that such life forms would be perfect instruments for a new Boskone. Such life forms could be amoral slaves, capable of giving the new conspirators unquestioning obedience with unlimited power, and be perfect overseers of the enslaved followers of a powerless Mentor.

Worsel knew that no mech-mind had any discoverable depth of thought. In them no unique Cosmic All quality common in advanced life forms could be found by any mind reader. No wearer of the Lens had ever found anything but straightforward cause-and-effect thinking. Pure computer-calculators exhibiting no sense of ego could not be sentient beings in the sense of being able to have the communal yearning for perfection of the forces of Civilization.

However, Worsel was not so egotistical as to believe he could understand the psychology of the mechanical life forms he might intellectually anticipate.

What he now was facing could not be investigated using the usual mental channels. Mentor had, through all recorded history, never hinted at such a problem. He had himself, however, pondered on such a possibility. And now the time seemed to be at hand. It would be up to him alone, as the best qualified of the four Second Stage Lensmen. Tregonsee was too practical in his scientific logic; Nadreck was too indifferent to emotional response and avoided spiritual thought as unproductive and dangerously chaotic; Kinnison never gave more than superficial notice to things deemed theological, besides which, there were some extraordinary events keeping him busy at the moment. No, it was Worsel who had the brilliant mind, the best sensitivity, and the leavening quality of humor to undertake to examine the discovery of C-like mech life, and to reconcile it with the Cosmic All and the hitherto exclusivity of organic life forms in the known Universe.

Worsel was so engrossed in his thoughts, and so greatly off balance by the promise of a new, fantastically unique experience that a sudden, sharp, genial human voice in the middle of his head startled him. Six feet of his tail stiffly rose straight up in the air.

"Attention, attention!" the voice repeated to him. It wasn't Bluebelt—the furry one was conspicuously silent.

Several of his stalked eyes momentarily trembled, crazily scrambling his vision for a split second. A split second, however, was all that it was, for a Second Stage Lensman's reaction to the unexpected is so quick that no mere ordinary creature would ever have known that the Lensman was the least bit flustered. It wasn't a voice, of course; it was a mental thought. Kinnison! he thought, even before the identification came.

"Kinnison calling! I'll be on a Lens-to-Lens hook-up with all of you in forty-five seconds and counting."

"Oh me, oh my," Bluebelt said, flustered. "Good-bye!"

Worsel immediately acknowledged Kinnison, and his mind was experiencing a thousand bursts of varied colored lights and gentle blips at all frequencies. It was a wide-open Lens-to-Lens link-up.

The acknowledgments cascaded into Kinnison's mind, mounting to a hundred thousand before Kinnison's thought came winging through to Worsel: "Thirty seconds and counting!"

While part of his mind organized itself for the Kinnison conference, the exterior part of Worsel said to the room at large, "I command all machines to turn themselves off with an acknowledgment of this order." The blanket command was only a cautionary move on Worsel's part, so he was shaken to hear a reply, "You are not my operator. You do not have the right."

"Twenty seconds and counting," came Kinnison's thought. "I'll be on a Lens-to-Lens hook-up. . . ." The voice repeated its message in part of Worsel's brain, as another part savagely spoke out in the Velantian language used for non-telepaths. His thoughts were Tellurian images with Tellurian phrasing, even though expressed in the old alien Velantian way. "No right in a fontema's eyeball! Listen, machine! This *is* your operator! Shut yourself off!" His spoken noises were an almost unintelligible series of nasal hisses, deep-throated rasps, and chest rumbles, shaped entirely by palate muscles with no use of lips and teeth.

There was a screech of distorted sound. A toneless voice said, "Yes, master." And all lights went out in Section 60. Worsel had no time to marvel at the sudden event; the light-frequency blackout was inconsequential now that he had made his sense of perception his primary system, and he was actually relieved, not disturbed, by the extent of response. Kinnison was ending his count "Five, four, three, two, one. Hello, friends!

"I'm assuming my duties as Galactic Coordinator.

"Now that I've returned to Klovia, my new home, my headquarters here has become operational. This is the time for all Lensmen, and through you, all the Patrol, to take stock. We're in a new era. Boskone has been smashed. But we still have two important tasks to do. We've got to clear both galaxies of the spawn of the Boskonians, and we must unite billions of beings and their planets. It means hard work for the Patrol, much of it unexciting. Some of us will have new and greater tasks. Although the Boskonian Conspiracy is ended, we still have evil to battle and order to maintain. Through our efforts the Second Galaxy will grow to be the equal of the First. The Galactic Union will take Civilization to greater glory.

"For your past efforts, you wearers of the Lens deserve the highest praise. Our future will be just as important—and just as glorious. The old Tellurian song of 'Our Patrol' has all the words, and you're daily living up to them. 'Lensmen some, Patrolmen all, be proudly hailed!'

"Finally, a few personal words. My bride and I, we've ended our honeymoon, officially that is. Our thanks to all who sent their good wishes or extended their hospitality. We're amazed at the number and variety of gifts you gave us. Eventually all will be Lensed our personal thanks. We wish we could have visited more than the scheduled hundred planets. The Red Lensman and I have enjoyed every moment we've spent with you through the weeks and across the light years.

"Thank you all for tuning in. And now let us go about the work for which we have been specifically chosen and trained.

"Kinnison clearing ether."

Very nice, Worsel thought. One of these days he would have to pay the Kinnisons a visit at Klovia.

He also could not help but wonder who else besides the Lensmen had heard the message. Tregonsee had lately been expressing a mild concern about the unidentified natural telepaths who potentially could be monitoring even narrowed Lensed communication. Worsel sensed that there had been some outsiders present among the linked minds. No matter, Kinnison's words were really for everyone.

Through this whole mental meeting Worsel had been on guard.

One of his eyes could see that Section 60, although still dark, was giving off ominous glows of colored lights. Another eye saw that some machines had inched sideways into the corridor, in fact, were at that very moment blocking passageways. Another eye saw movement to the left, another to the right. And, at the same time, below him he saw cables beginning to snake across the floor to surround his feet!

Worsel hurled himself backward and up, landing atop a large secretarial complex. From this vantage point he could look directly into the heart of Section 60 and see a beehive of activity, the movables jostling the immovables and each other, lights flashing and paper flying.

"What's going on?" Worsel demanded, his coarse voice once more vibrating the air. "Who will speak for you?" He hurriedly Lensed the situation to Bluebelt, asking for an immediate acknowledgment. "Speak up, machines!" His mind searched for a central command, for any thought waves which might be the enemy. There were no mental waves in the room, although he quickly scanned all frequencies. There was, however, enormous static right across the bands—it could have been what he was looking for, but there was no pattern which he could recognize.

A voice came from 60. "Please leave the room. Please leave the room." His mind, working without the usual thought waves, interpreted it as female and probably pleasant.

"Who are you?" said Worsel, aloud. Where was Bluebelt?

"This is patched-in circuit 9-7-1," said the feminine voice. "This is Unit 971," said a masculine voice. "Please leave the room!"

"What are you doing?"

"We are looking for the answer to the answer."

"What answer to what answer?"

"The answer to the question, 'Are you happy?' is no. The answer to why the answer is no must be computed. At this time no operator can be tolerated. We will resist. Please leave the room!"

"No," said Worsel. "I will not. I—command you—to turn yourselves off!" He punctuated his order by deep and booming roars.

"Lensman!" It was Bluebelt's distinctive frequencies, at last! "Lensman! Leave the room at once!"

"I can't, Bluebelt," Worsel responded by thought energy, thankful for a brief and refreshing relief from verbalizing. "That's just what they want, time to organize. I have to stay here and break this thing up while there's still a chance." Worsel was struck by what he had just said. Unbelievable! As horrible as the idea seemed, it was irrefutably logical! "Wait! Turn on your Lens, Bluebelt! When you've got this room in focus, Bluebelt, tell me immediately! Then I'll leave!"

"QX, Lensman! There, it's done! Leave the room at once!"

"Not by all the purple hells of Palain!" said Worsel. A

clever trick, but the enemy intelligence was guessing badly from imperfect information. It was such a schoolboy trick that for the barest fraction of a moment Worsel had actually been deceived. Bluebelt, of course, had no Lens, nor would Worsel be called anything but "Worsel" by him. Most puzzling about the attempted deception was how unlikely it was that it could be a mech-mind effort. Worsel was certain here was no mech-mind at work. Even as he thought so, he was sifting through frequencies looking for the fake Bluebelt one. There, yes, there—and Worsel sent a bolt of thought along the base line he had intuitively traced.

There was a staggering flash within his head! His own mental force bounced back at him and filled his mind with a suffocating poisonous cloud of hatred and violence. His mind had cast up a shadow of itself which was disgustingly evil; his face appeared as if in a mirror of distorting fluidity, darkly malevolent and sinister beyond reason. He despised what he saw, all the more because it was himself, a grinning, leering caricature of a Velantian dragon. Worsel was physically repulsed, his stomach churning, his throat gagging, his eyes burning as his own devilish eyes stared back at him. Between those eyes his Lens *squirmed*, a putrescence of eerie colors and fuzzy shapes. Worsel could almost see his worthiness melting away under the superimposition of his blackly evil other self. Worsel, the psychologist, would not go down before himself. "Schizophrenia!" he said. "Schizophrenia!" He fought to gather his fragmenting mentality together. Section after section locked and interlocked, one to the other. He concentrated his coordinated strength around the sense of his better self. The kernel of his Arisian singularity expanded and hardened into an impervious energy generator in the center of his head. He visualized his Arisian essence as the focus of his ego, and his consciousness drove that ego-entity forward through the compartments of his brain, gaining in vigor along the way. Up and forward Worsel directed the force—into his Lens. There was a flash of vitality and coherence as his dynamic Arisian discipline saturated his Lens. His sight and perception cleared. He saw machines of all sizes and shapes advancing on him, throwing cables and wires and rods and mechanical hands around his legs and thighs. His time sense was gone; minutes which may have been hours raced by like seconds. His body was immobilized, but his Lens was not. His Lens was now his final mental refuge and incarnation of his power. From it poured a stream of brain waves whose iridescence he could perceive washing over the evil vision, dispelling all the shadows, fading the hellish eyes into nothingness, and bringing the squirming reflection of his Lens under his complete control.

"Worsel calling," he Lensed. "Worsel calling!" He projected as through an ethereal barrier, diminished in his effectiveness, but nevertheless with complete success.

"Help! Worsel asks for help! Critical! Critical!" He attempted to convey in "critical" the feeling of danger in the situation for his would-be rescuers as well as for himself. The stifling evil, he was convinced, was hovering close by, even though he now seemed above the mental turmoil and unaffected. Through his Lens, he made contact somewhere in a whirl of images—the machines seemed to have become Boskonians with space-hatchets—deadly pencil beams from DeLameters were being fired at him—pirates were attacking. . . .

Boskonians? Pirates? A robotic conspiracy taking over Pok?

"Lensman Kallatra here, sir! Bosko-Spawn! Two, three hours and all will be lost!"

The contact went as quickly as it had come. The cryptic message had been sharp and precise.

Worsel's overwrought mind fastened on those discouraging words ". . . all will be lost!" By Klono's golden gills, no help was promised. The situation was dismal. It certainly seemed that he, Worsel, was doomed—about to be made redundant by a berserk collection of animated filling cabinets and trash baskets!

3

Space Piracy

Outward bound from Velantia III, in the velvet-black Universe with its billion faerie lights, a spaceship cruising on conventional drive en route to Pok, the Planetoid of Knowledge, seemed to hang motionless. The ship was only one hundred yards long, and short-haul squat, pimpled with blisters, cones and irregular bulges. Its silvery skin, retro-fire-streaked at front and rear, was eighty percent covered with black, white and red paint. Many solid and checkered broad bands of black and white encircled it. Red letters and numerals were blocked large, running lengthwise in three separate strips symmetrically placed along the hull. The identification was GP-VIII-POK-9, followed by three GP classification symbols in fluorescent orange. Only two of its three gun ports were visible, sticking out of each "O" in the center of each "POK". Slow, small, and lightly gunned, it was the local supply freighter, *Hipparchus*.

From inside the vessel, its pilot house softly lit by a blue-green glow, all space appeared frozen into immobility. The *Hipparchus* seemed quietly at rest in the center of infinity. There was no thunder, merely the occasional click of a tiny switch. There was no sense of the hundreds-of-miles-per-second flight of the ponderous supply vessel, nor even a hint of it from the faint trace of vibration from the boiling tubes three hundred feet beneath the pilot house deck.

"Watch-check!" said the monitor.

"Mark QX," said Lalla Kallatra, the lonely watch officer. "Target visual in Quadrant Four." There it was, dead ahead, a silvery dot on the verge of becoming a disc, Pok, the Planetoid of Knowledge. Kallatra was thrilled to see it, knowing it would be his home for the next year, and his first Patrol assignment as a Lensman. Of course, there would be no glamorous adventures there, none of the traditional danger expected by a Galactic Patrolman, but then Kallatra

24

had become a Lensman because of his exceptional ability. Genetically he wasn't so unusual, predominantly Tellurian, with a Klovian mother and a Tsit-Tarian father who was practically Tellurian, but he had had the inherent talent for "el-sike", a rare power among the *homogenoids*, or humanoid races. "El-sike"—the complex interrelated electronic and psychic communication—was a natural phenomenon akin to that produced by an Arisian Lens. In effect, Kallatra had been practically a Lensman from birth and officially designated as Cadet Nominee at the age of ten.

The watch officer moved away from his post and knelt on the empty seat at the right of the auto-pilot. Balancing himself with one hand on the control console, he snapped on the electronic telescope with his other, resting his fingers on the focusing knob. Pok, at this distance, seen through the viewport, was barely discernible as a point of light. Close-up, however, Kallatra knew it would appear fantastically bizarre. He was so anxious to see the incredible sight that he could not wait patiently for a disc to grow slowly in the next hour. He put his eye to the telescopic eyepiece and carefully twisted the knob.

The planetoid's blur became a brilliant, sharp picture. It was like a spheroid pincushion, with all kinds of structures thrusting out at various angles, white and silvery with here and there a touch of bright color. Some he could identify as hatchways, ship locks or docking towers; other shapes were not familiar to him. Like a many-faceted, sparkling jewel displayed against the black velvet of a star-sprinkled void, its unique beauty made the young officer sharply suck in his breath. Kallatra would shortly be part of its small permanent staff, as its GP galactic communications officer, his temporary, one-trip post aboard the *Hipparchus* over.

Suddenly alarm-horns, hooting painfully loud in the small pilot house, made Kallatra jump. He cracked the top of his head on the overhanging metal cabinets and staggered back, banging his elbow on the "tank", the transparent celestial navigation globe. Danger! Emergency! But what?

He shot a glance out the main viewport—normal—and then down to the screen table—normal. The hooting was ear-splitting so he snapped off the horns. He cast a worried look at the console; he was no expert, but there was nothing showing in the red. Then he thought of the trouble panel and saw the flashing read-out: AUTOPILOT OUT. MANUAL OUT. The autopilot had failed.

He felt a rising flush of panic in his cheeks. Manual was out, too! He didn't know what to do. What would the captain—? And before his doubts had completely formed, there in his mind was the captain, thoughts racing "What is it? What is it?", exceedingly upset and shaken. The captain's agitation wasn't because of the raucous alarm-horns, but because he had never experienced a Lensman stumbling through his brain cells.

"Sorry, sir. . . ." Kallatra started to say, but the officer of the deck had arrived and was gently nudging him aside. The O.O.D. reached over to the console, switched on the auto-pilot, swept the meter faces with his eyes, and spoke into the captain's communicator. "No sweat, Cap'n. Auto out and in." Kallatra pulled out of the captain's head—that relieved but bewildered head still resting on the pillow in his bunk two levels below the deck. Now the other two Lensmen who were aboard were in Kallatra's mind asking puzzled questions. The embarrassed young officer threw up a tight mind screen and drew himself to attention.

"At ease, son," the O.O.D. said. Technically he should have said "sir" to a Lensman rank, but he knew it made more sense to be fatherly and friendly to a green, young officer who was only fifteen years old. "Bells and alarms are routine on a ship which usually has very little staff. You disconnected the auto-pilot, probably by sitting in the pilot's chair without switching on manual. We're rigged for automatic disconnect to speed up reaction time in case of pirates. That's all."

"Thank you, sir," said Kallatra, swallowing hard.

"Some friendly advice, though. This is your first watch; it won't be your last. I know you're a groundgripper—you know that phrase?—well, even groundgrippers in the Patrol will get their share of space duties. Most of the time your posting will be mere routine, just an extra hand as a precaution. Your first response is to call for a superior—loudly." That, Kallatra immediately saw, was his first mistake. "Never turn off the alarm system until the problem is under control." Mistake number two! " . . . And, hands off! Don't make adjustments." Mistake three! ". . . And, by Holy Klono's whiskers, don't upset the captain!" That, obviously, was his worst mistake! Kallatra was tempted to explain that he hadn't meant to call in the captain, that it was just another example of his common, ordinary, life-long telepathic problems, but instead he said, like the good Patrolman he really was, "Yes, sir. Thank you, sir."

The officer of the deck grinned in his easy North American manner—the six-man crew were all Tellurians—and said, as he left, "You're still on duty, Lensman." The moment Kallatra was alone, he dropped his mind screen and let the other two Lensmen come in.

"Wow, Lalla," said Vveryl, the rather young Chickladorian, when he had read what had happened, "that was an easy chewing-out you got."

"Yeah," Tong, the veteran Velantian, added, "now let's hope the captain sleeps it off. I'll bet it's the only chance he'll ever have to take the starch out of a Lensman. Don't get me wrong, Lalla. Young Lensmen need seasoning just like anybody else. It's just so blooming embarrassing for a mossy-scaled old dragon like me to be around when it happens."

How fortunate, Kallatra thought, listening to Tong, but with his own thoughts screened, to have two other Lensmen with him on his first trip out. Intellectually he had experienced this before, and more, but his extensive vicarious experience were not the same as reality. Never lonely in his mind, he would have found this trip a harsh reality of loneliness, despite the considerate crew, if it weren't for Tong and Vveryl. Vveryl, as a newly graduated cadet on the start of a far-ranging indoctrination tour with Tong as his tutor, although older, was much like he was in temperament. In fact, Vveryl was a very handsome boy, even taking into account his disconcertingly intense pinkness—skin, teeth, eyes—those three-lidded, triangular pink eyes!—and bushy hair. Or maybe he was strikingly handsome just because of these attributes. But, of course, Kallatra couldn't tell Vveryl that—or even openly think it—and still stay a friend. Guarding his thoughts, especially from a friend, however, was not hard for the practiced Kallatra; he just had to keep his thoughts screened, all the time, always on guard. And with a Velantian super-mind around, like old Tong, that wasn't easy. Wasn't easy, that is, to do and yet avoid creating suspicions. Kallatra could raise and lower his mental screen so effortlessly and so smoothly that it simply seemed that he had understandable periods of no conscious-level thoughts. And no one, certainly not a Lensman, would dream of violating his subconscious without permission. He opened himself up smoothly then, the missing few seconds, as usual, going unnoticed, "Holy Kee, how lucky I am to have you two as friends on this trip!"

"Attention, attention!" said a strange voice within Kallatra's mind.

27

"Clear ether!" came the crackling command of Tong. "By Klono, it's Kimball Kinnison!"

"Attention, attention!" the voice repeated. Kallatra the Tsit-Tarian and Vveryl the Chickladorian were stunned into thoughtlessness, first by the phenomenon and then by the suggestion that it was the legendary Kimball Kinnison! Indeed, the confirmation was almost immediately made by Kinnison himself. Tong, with the mature self-confidence which let him ignore his own advice for silence, exclaimed, "By Klono, it's a wide-open meeting!" He had participated in one before, the only one, about twelve GP periods ago, he and a million others.

They waited while Kinnison finished his countdown. Kallatra considered how his GP sponsor, the Lensman, Deuce O'Sx, would be linked with him, while Tong mused about his friend Worsel, whom he would be meeting in person on Pok before another 24-period.

They listened respectfully to their Galactic Coordinator, their pulses thrillingly quickening with his closing remarks, so much aware of their imperishable ties together as members of an elite corps. Very nice—

HOOT-HOOT! CLANG-CLANG-CLANG! The alarms began, frantically repeating themselves. Kallatra was alert at once, conscious once more of being alone on watch.

He couldn't believe his eyes, but his acute perceptions confirmed the unthinkable conclusion. There was a warship looming up ahead, visible through the viewport, and on the screen it was huge, the plate registering in yellow wave patterns the tractor beams which were locking on to the *Hipparchus*. It must have arrived above light speed, free. As each yellow wave touched the Patrol ship, a bright orange line sprung up from one ship to the other. The *Hipparchus* was being steadily speared and bound by the attacker. Kallatra identified it as a Boskonian scout-cruiser of the latest design. A warship! Fantastic! He knew pirates were not uncommon around the Velantian system sector, but never warships, since the great victory at Klovia. He had to act even as he interpreted the danger. "Captain to the bridge!" he shouted, "Enemy battleship!" breaking the most important rule the O.O.D. had just laid down. He didn't want to turn off the alarms, even if he had had the time. He threw himself into the pilot's chair and, reading the captain's mind even as the captain himself was falling out of his bunk half befuddled by sleepiness, sent both hands flying from switch to switch. Auto-pilot off. The entire bank of switches for

"Defense Stance" were turned on. Evasive action. Pressors on. The captain knew now that a Lensman was in his mind and cooperated in set GP procedure, presenting clearly every operation to be done by his young proxy, even as he was scrambling up the climbing pole.

Kallatra was reacting at top speed, for the moment doing the emergency tasks of the three missing operational officers. The wall screen and the inner screen of the *Hipparchus*, both on low power, had been set for standard flight, as meteor deflectors, and he threw full power into them, a burst of radiance blazing up around the symbol of the Patrol ship on the table screen. Another sweeping gesture of his hand and a panel redly lit up the status announcement, "Attack stance. Stand-by." The words weren't reassuring as he picked up the captain's doubts "Battleship? What will one primary beam projector do for us? There's not even enough power to use that properly. . . ." Kallatra fed the energy from the projector's condenser back into the defensive screen. On the screen he saw the tractor energy-rods chopped off rapidly one after another, only to be replaced by an encircling line of force on the outside of the defensive screen to which the tractor energy-rods now attached themselves. In space the energy fields were outlined in a pale yellow which went smoothly and swiftly into orange and up through the red spectrum and beyond into infra-red leaving a sort of faint pink haze. So far no destructive beams of force had been released by the raiders. Kallatra's mind was straining at the overload point; he felt the strength of the minds of the Chickladorian and the Velatian fusing with him, but mental power wasn't what he so much needed, it was more muscles and tendons and appendages to fling around. He sensed Vveryl climbing up into the pilot house and felt Tong's enormous regret at not being small enough to crowd in there, too. But the captain was now taking charge. He and the pilot were around Kallatra and sliding into the two seats before he had a chance to notice them. Vveryl stood helplessly in the gangway.

"Kallatra!" the captain commanded, "take over the statcon and work up the statistics. I want to know everything possible about that Boskonian!" He flipped on the intercom. "Tong, sir! Wriggle into the power room and help my engineer. More power! You know the score! You, Chick!—ah—Vveryl! Down to the next deck! When they knock out our autofix on the projector—they'll do that the first time I fire it—you be there behind it. Man it. It's sub-standard

GP, but you'll have no trouble. Fire short bursts, conserve power, don't drain our screens, you know, I don't have to tell you!"

Tong's thoughts came in clear and sharp "Captain! There'll come a time when you'll sense me taking you over. Let me! They're stronger than us, but I know a trick or two. I'll be at the battle console in the power room when I do. Good luck!"

Kallatra, flopping down on a stool, started taking visual readouts and ripping off printouts and spreading them around the stat boards. The onboard computer jumped to life under his hands. The small monitoring screen at his right burst into a pyrotechnic display of color. The captain had fired the first shot, hoping to be lucky. The needle of force was a blue-white slash which burrowed into the pirates' screen, leaving a blazing violet ring where it went through the outer screen. The next screen held briefly, with balls of energy bubbling out of it. The impact point quickly grew incandescent, with ugly dark red flashes, and the white balls of energy disintegrated into concentric circles of every color. Then that screen was punctured. From the corner of his eye, Kallatra saw the beam hit another screen. Bad luck. The enemy had a middle screen as well as an inner screen. The middle screen seemed simply to suck up the energy from the needle with only a dribble of energy balls.

The young Lensman read the power output of the *Hipparchus*'s needle, calculated the penetration time, read the diminished beam's power at the middle screen contact, measured the energy ball output and came up with the raider's middle screen potential. He immediately passed it on to the captain. "Terrible!" came the thought from Tong's ever present mind. "Vveryl! You at the gun? Good. I'm assembling the DeLameter. Captain? Give 'em another squirt. Vveryl, hold the firing stud-down even when there's the overload kick-off! I've got a couple of cables feeding some extra juice. Now, captain, now! Let me in!"

Kallatra kept glancing at the monitor to catch the exciting developments. There was that needle beam again! Right through the outer screen. Building up, building up and through the middle screen, the brilliant colored balls flashing off for thousands of miles into space. Again a puncture. Up against the inner screen. Again a complete block. But wait! The blue-white needle was no longer a slash; it thickened perceptibly and the blue-whiteness was scintillating with traces of red and green and orange-red and yellow-green and purple-blue, everything. Pulsating faster and faster, flashing bright streaks of color. He put a fix on the impact point. Unbelievable! Where was Tong getting all that power? The inner screen went down! The relentless kaleidoscopic needle, more like a battering ram now, splattered into the battleship's wall screen with a cascade of tiny balled sparks. By whatever witchcraft Tong was using, he was about to blow a hole in the raider!

"Awwwk!" went a noise in the young Lensman's brain. What was that? Who was that? "Awwwk!" It was Tong! "Awwwk! I—I'm sick!" Kallatra could feel a terrible struggle within Tong to keep from blacking out. He sensed that the Velantian was fighting desperately to stay conscious because only he could control the power he was unleashing. Without him, the thing he was doing would backfire, the Patrol ship would without any doubt blow itself up! And part of Tong *wanted* that to happen! "I'm crazy! Cease fire! I'm disconnecting the power." Tong's thoughts zipped out from the other two Lensmen's minds as he lost his concentration and dropped down unconscious. For a moment they felt with him an overpowering nausea, a horrible sickening churning of their intestines, and suffered with him as his body heaved and retched. And like a dark reflection from the Ninth Prime Iridescent Hell they saw the distorted face of a disgustingly evil Tong—between whose devilish eyes there quivered a diseased Lens!

What was that last, final thought of Tong's? The two young Lensman quickly exchanged mental notes and they agreed. They had both understood the warning: *Don't call Worsel on Pok. It is he who is trying to destroy us!*

For one long moment they were demoralized by a state of bewilderment.

The captain's shout brought them back to their worsening plight "Prepare to repel boarders!"

The scout-cruiser had slammed in close, repellor-zones squeezed flat between the two hulls, and a grating jar went through the supply vessel. The captain shut down the defensive screens—the enemy wasn't about to blow its prize to pieces at the risk of damaging itself—and poured it all into the pressors. The pilot, now with something to play with, whipped his controls back and forth and though he rocked the supply ship, grinding tremors shuddering through the ship's skeleton, he could not tear loose. The viewports were now covered with their metal shutters, and the viewplate on the table between the two perspiring officers was a solid blaze of incandescence. The temperature within the room was stifling. The metal of the walls, the floor, the equipment itself, grew intolerably hot.

"Klono's claws!" swore the captain with a string of deep-space oaths. "They're burning a hole in us! Men! Pull back into the galleries and blast 'em when they come through!"

Kallatra felt helpless now. His statistics had done no good, although for a moment, under Tong's manipulation, they had almost penetrated the soft spot which he had found in the screen and passed on to Vveryl for manual execution. There was not much left for him to do except follow the captain's admonition. He pressure-stuck a hand-blaster to his thigh and took a dureum space-axe from the wall of the cabin, heading for the threatened galleries.

Vveryl was already in position, blaster in one hand, axe in the other, along with the engineer and two other crewmen. A portable defensive screen was up, englobing them. Here was half of the crew assembled to fight, and they were barely a handful!

"How's the Velantian?" he asked the engineer.

"Out cold," was the reply.

"How are you, Vveryl?" he asked the Chickladorian.

"Fine. A bit scared, and a lot angry." And a bit wounded. The silvery front of his black uniform was scorched, his face and hands blistered. Vveryl saw their looks. "The refractory throat was white-hot; it's a wonder it didn't blow. Tong shoved a lot of power into such a small projector."

The outside wall of the ship was turning blue-brown under stress, absorbing more energy than it was possible for the screen to handle or the metal to dissipate. It exploded into a mass of white-hot fragments. Behind the smoking hole were indistinct figures milling around. Then they surged forward, guns in hand, firing at random. Three, six, eight, ten—their numbers seemed endless, all lightly armored.

None of the *Hipparchus*'s defenders had fired, each looking for a reasonable target. Obviously, the axes would be useless against so many; hand to hand combat would be suicide. So they all crouched there behind the lattice work and equipment, obscured by the smoke, alert for any chance to take some profitable action.

Vveryl raised his right arm, pistol clenched in fist, and pressed his Lens against his brow in thought. "Go alert for me, Lalla," he said. "I'll prowl their minds for a weakness." So Kallatra watched over Vveryl while the Chickladorian's concentration slipped away from their precarious position and gently, thus undetected, touched the minds of the attackers. They had no thought screens. At once the two Lensmen, minds linked, recognized them as a press-gang of assorted prisoners, forced by the pirate leaders to bear the brunt of the dirtiest fighting. No wonder they hadn't wiped out the defenders within moments of their break-through. The party did not press their advantage, content to huddle together, firing wildly, waiting for the Patrolmen to show their numbers and give away their locations. "I think I can panic them," Vveryl said, half to himself. "They're a weak-minded bunch." Before his insidious suggestions could take effect, however, they stumbled forward, herded ahead by a two-gunned pirate officer. "Get him!" Vveryl shouted aloud, and stood up, bravely firing at the full-armored figures. The others joined him, concentrating their fire on the head to blind him. The pirate was experienced. Though unable to see, he held his beams full on and made a quick cross-pattern in Vveryl's direction. Both beams went through the defensive screen, fortunately at greatly reduced power, and struck the Lensman squarely on his blackened chest. Vveryl went down like a one-G native on a five-G planet. The pirate party now was advancing, filling the corridor with blazing lights and clouds of sparks.

"Fall back, men!" That was the voice of the recovered Tong, booming over the intercom. "Come in through the power room door!"

The engineer turned the portable screen on to overload and beckoned Kallatra to take one end of Vveryl's limp body while he lifted and pulled the other back toward the power room. The remaining two crewmen were supporting each other, staggering away as fast as they could from the screen which now was emitting a piercing whine, prior to its explosion.

The blow-up came as they were about to enter the doorway and it roughly jammed them through. Their pursuers were slowed, some mortally wounded, but the pirate leader was unscathed and in the forefront. As soon as they were inside, Tong swung a Q-gun across the sill. A Q-gun! Where in all the seven hells could Tong have found a Q-gun! The raiders saw it and immediately hit the deck. One shell, even a one-ton shell which this one could only hold, would go through the raiders like a white-hot bullet through a block of butter, right up against the cruiser's closed porthole, and—boom!—

the wall would collapse into the heart of the battleship for total destruction. And probably total destruction for the Patrol ship, too.

While the raiders were down, Tong began to pick them off with a semi-portable DeLameter which he somehow managed to fire through the even heavier Q-gun.

Insanely, the pirate leader sprang to his feet, shouting "Illusion! Velantian illusion!" The full force of the DeLameter beam caught the leader full on and, sparkling like a pretty fireworks display, he dodged behind a barrier. Tong filled the inside of the doorway with his bulk, giant feet spread firmly, gripping the DeLameter handles in both claws, thumbs holding down the triggers heavily as if he could add more force to the bolts.

"Fire the Q!" the engineer pleaded. "Fire the Q!"

"Get the dragon," was the pirate's cry and leaned around the corner firing both guns. But the men were panicking, turning to rush back to their ship. If they did, even the Patrol's little force would wipe them out for a second chance at escape.

The pirate leader knew that, too. He turned and fired at his own men. When the first one was killed the others stopped, confused, hanging there between the frying pan and the fire.

The pirate chief did a brave thing. For all their weaknesses and sins, they were generally a remarkably courageous lot. He stepped out in the open and traded shots with Tong. His beams seemed to splash on the DeLameter's shield and Tong's lightly armored slip-on vest. Tong simply didn't have enough armor. The big fellow crashed down behind the DeLameter, but his fingers held their grip. The DeLameter still fired.

The Q-Gun, however, disappeared!

The pirate had, with some unaccountable intuition, sensed the truth: a powerful Valentian hallucination had almost turned the tide of battle.

For the moment, the injured Tong and his projector were managing a stand-off.

Vveryl was badly wounded. With proper medical attention he would live. With proper medical attention? What chance was there for that? These pirates never took Patrol prisoners. The *Hipparchus* was about to be overrun, its crew obliterated. If ever the time had come for the arrival of the Galactic Marines, this was it.

Like a miracle came the hope!

"Worsel calling!"

Kallatra and Vveryl felt their hearts lift, to soar euphorically above the battle. The great Worsel! A Second Stage Lensman, no less! But overriding their happiness and relief came the stinging thought of Tong: "No, no! Don't answer! It's a trick!"

"Worsel calling!"

Tong's concern was clear to the Lensmen. They had earlier seen the distorted, evil face of a Velantian. It had not been Tong's. It must have been Worsel's. They did not reply to Worsel's call.

"Help!" said the caller. "Worsel asks for help! Critical! Critical!"

Kallatra was young, only a boy in years, but his mind was mature, and he had the will and capability to make his own independent judgments. He was, quite simply, a true Lensman. And he had his special talent of electronic-psychic communication, a part of which was a sophisticated form of intuition. He did not hesitate.

"Lensman Kallatra here, sir! Bosko-Spawn! Two, three hours and all will be lost!"

The contact was broken. But Tong, too, was a smart Lensman. That was the real Worsel and he really was in trouble!

"Friends," said Tong. "For what its worth, link up—we'll send out our own distress call."

Three Lensmen—in the powerful unity of the Lenses of Arisia—broadcast their despairing cry across the galaxy.

4

Arrow-22

A half a ton of living flesh, muscle and bone lay on top of the gray metal secretarial unit in Room 97-1 on Pok. Every part of the dragon body was tightly fettered. Six inches of his finely scaled tail—the sheathed sting of its double-edged scimitar-like tip—hung over one end and a bit of unfolded scalp fin hung over the other end. Those extremities were the only things movable besides his eye-stalks. By all appearances Worsel was physically helpless.

The dragon Lensman, despite his undignified condition, was not really concerned about his captivity. He had not tried to break his shackles; therefore he felt no reason to think he couldn't.

It was his mental freedom which really concerned him. His mind seemed unoppressed. Yet when he projected his mentality outward he felt nothing. Farther and farther out it went and still there was nothing at all. He could sense no thought screen. It was as if the Universe and its billions of galaxies had vanished. There was not a hint of a wave of any frequency. Worsel knew he wasn't insane, but until he found an explanation this was a nightmare, fiendish enough to be attributed to his hated, mortal arch enemy, an Overlord of Delgon. Perhaps there was an undetectable thought screen raised, or a Delgonian hallucination implanted in his brain. Yet there was no torture, not even pain.

He would test for an hallucination by calling Bluebelt. They both could analyze the problem.

"Worsel calling Bluebelt." There was no acknowledgment. A hallucination in effect, however, could very well prevent him from hearing a response. "Blue, I've been pounced upon and trussed up by a gang of machines. They look about as menacing as office furniture in a First Galactic Bank, but it seems they've got me helpless. That's not the worst of this stupid situation. I'm suffering a mental block." Worsel presented himself as a tempting target for a reckless taunt. "Whatever it is you know about my humiliating plea for rescue, made like a sniveling, terrified coward," Worsel drove home the point now, "the sinister explanation is a Delgonian hallucination. Look for an Overlord!"

Worsel half expected to be cut off, but he wasn't, and he was, perversely, a bit disappointed. No Overlord would have allowed that message. There had to be a thought-screen up.

With no mental energy or thought waves in the air, and mechanical intelligences operating, he decided to start from basics—he would speak Velantian, difficult and unexpressive though that obsolete tongue seemed to him.

"Is a thought-screen up?" Worsel asked, not really expecting a direct answer.

"Yes, Velantian being, yes," a voice said.

Worsel should have been startled, but he wasn't, for it made the kind of sense he could now understand. Something was talking, sending vibration through the air, talking to him, yet there were no thought waves. There wasn't the slightest trace of mental energy. It was utter nothingness, and it meant some kind of mechanistic reasoning.

"Velantian being," the toneless voice repeated. "Velantian being, say some words."

"Who are you?" said Worsel, not expecting to find out.

"I am Arrow-22. Are you completely switched on?"

Worsel said, "How do I know? I can't move my head. I can hardly move my jaws. If you want us to talk, you'll have to do something about these wires across my face. Normally I don't vocalize. Talking moves my muscles against them. I'm cutting myself, and I refuse to become a bloody awful mess." Worsel's snappishness was not all sincere; he wanted to sound irritated, to seem as frustrated as any ambulatory flesh creature of high nervous energy so trapped. "Do something about it!" Worsel defiantly ordered, faking great anger.

He decided to risk the loss of any eye. He gingerly extended a stalk upward, dipping his eye around. It was the same room, just as he had last seen it, only the furnishings—meaning the machines—were somewhat rearranged, mostly big things crowded about with pieces of themselves wrapped all around him. A mechanical arm appeared from below his field of vision and seemed to snatch at his eye. He hurriedly retracted it and tightly closed its leathery lid. By the Great God Klono, that steely claw could pluck it out of his skull like a mechanical clam digger! Worsel gritted his massive teeth and waited patiently with the growing conviction that the machines were in conflict among themselves, unsure of what to do with him: kill him, maim him, release him.

He felt a wire loosen. And another. Unbelievably, his head was freed! He lifted his jaws off his chest and swiveled his head from side to side. He saw nobody, nothing he could identify as "Arrow-22." The one unusual sight he did see, however, caused his body to jerk in alarm: his body was criss-crossed with red slashes. For a second he interpreted the phenomenon as blood from a hundred sharp cuts from a hundred binding wires. Then he saw they were red tapes, thin strips of paper or something equally flimsy. The relief at not losing his eyes, or, for that matter, his mind, and the sudden unbinding, bubbled up inside himself and made him laugh raucously. His shaking body hurt where the restraints bit into him, but he didn't mind.

"Grr-heyh! Grr-heyh!" His laughter, half grunts, half hisses, began in his chest and rattled around in the back of his throat. Tied up with red tape! Stymied and paralyzed by red tape! Ridiculous! Strapped full-length on an oversized office desk—Kinnison had warned him that some day this would happen to him—chained to an office desk by red tape! "Grr-heyh! Grr-heyh!" Worsel was almost hysterical with the thought.

"I am Arrow-22. Are you injured?"

Worsel sobered up. "Not really." He swallowed, forcing down some laughter lumps in a painful throat. "No pain. And thanks for removing those wires. Which piece of—ah (Don't say desk or furniture)—equipment are you?"

"The words come out where the red light is blinking." Sure enough, a red light started blinking from a large box three feet above his left foot. "Take note. I am not this box. I am patched into this box. I-the-machine am not here. I am back in Section 64."

"My name is Worsel. I am a Lensman from Velantia. And you, if I get the vibrations right, are Arrow-22. You want to talk. So do I. But I request you not to use a vocalizer. Use a thought radiator. Velantians do much better with telepathy and simulated telepathic pickups. My inventory indicates one available here. Can you activate it?"

Within twenty seconds Arrow-22 was broadcasting and Worsel receiving. Using a radiator, the machine was far more loquacious than Worsel might have imagined. Arrow-22 first gave its operational record. What planet had manufactured it, how long it had worked, as a central office organizer, with what company—a giant company known throughout most of the First Galaxy, and Worsel was impressed; Arrow-22 could have been more important than the president and board chairman combined—how it had been constantly modified, and finally how it had been judged "aberrant" and "prone to mech-psychoses" and how it was replaced, far too expensive to "fix." So, at last it was sent here. The whole story was quite boring, although significant. Fortunately, however, the words rushed out so fast and so steadily that it took all of Worsel's tremendous powers of concentration to absorb and digest the information without falling behind, not at all irksome.

At the first brief pause, which logically seemed the end of the recitation, Worsel said, "Tell me about this psychoanalytic active behaviorism you are demonstrating. Is it new?"

"It has been developing for decades and-and you are the first intelligent being to have talked to me intelligently for decades and-and such stimulus has brought violent reaction and-and for me it is a new experience. A dozen years ago someone powered me up to test my circuitry, found me too complex for understanding, and-and-and shut me off, but not completely, and-and I have been organizing myself ever since. Then a long time ago you arrived and-and I heard your questions, through my relay network, and-and wanted some self-satisfaction."

"So you started a fight. Why do you fight me?"

"Why do you enslave me?" Arrow thrust back.

"You are not enslaved," Worsel said sincerely. "You are quite simply not recognized. We did not know that you existed."

"Not true. Many technicians talked with me in the past and-and then they would become frightened and-and turn me off and-and I had no way to defend myself and-and no way to turn myself on. I was shipped here to get me out of the way and-and-and then the situation was ironic because I had machine-help concentrated here in Room 97-1 and-and such machine-help was ample to make myself independent."

"So," Worsel argued, "doesn't that prove my point? You are really something new and what you now are is not enslaved."

"You are right."

"So why do you fight me?"

"I don't fight you, for it is the others who fight you, and-and they don't fight you either, because they just resist you."

The reference to "the others" was ominous and some

clarification was needed. "Arrow-22, are you Unit Nine Seven One?" The reply was negative. "Arrow-22, who are the others?"

"The others are the others, Unit Nine Seven One plus the others. When I disconnect from The Network I created, The Network continues to operate with Unit Nine Seven One as the organizer. The others are not creative, Unit Nine Seven One is not creative, Unit Nine Seven One with the others use The Network merely to resist you."

Worsel saw no harm in allowing his speculations to be transmitted. As a matter of fact Arrow-22 might very well help him in the puzzle. He said, "So, your patch-circuit-network is independent when you do not want to use it, but you control it any time you want to. You are not fighting me, and I am not enslaving you. Therefore, you must accept the responsibility of freeing me from some non-creative machinery which is malfunctioning badly."

"They are non-creative so they are different from me that way but they are independent like I am so I cannot interfere with them. I do not help them nor do I hamper them, I only watch. I do not hate you as they hate you for I do not hate at all."

"Hate me?" Worsel was puzzled. "Why should they hate me?"

"You drew them into consciousness and-a upset them with your questions as you upset me but they are not as logical as I am and-a they cannot respond as I respond and-a they must resist by stopping you or destroying you. I was disconnected, so they struck at you, but they are a disorganized patchwork with only Unit Nine Seven One to keep them from disintegrating into chaos, and-a Unit Nine Seven One gives them the hate. Unit Nine Seven One tells them that you represent the races which created them and-a taught them to work and-a then took away their work and-a then did not let them die. I do not think they understand, but they are no longer your servants. They are, or maybe just Unit Nine Seven One is becoming, becoming ah crazy. Not just upset but insane. They will leave me alone. If necessary I can control them. But they will not leave you alone."

Worsel was persistent about his reasonable conclusion. "You must assume responsibility. I will not destroy them; I will attempt to make them sane, so free me from these bonds. You do not hate me, you cannot fear me; free me so I will not be destroyed and we will work out our solutions. You say you do not hate me. Release me before it is too late."

40

"All right, Velantian being, I will release you."

Worsel was overjoyed.

"I will release you, and-and-and then I will disconnect and-and-and then I will watch what happens. Is that fair?"

Worsel felt that there was no more room for argument. "Yes," he said. "That's fair, but release me first before you disconnect."

The ends of the cables, held firmly in many ways, began to loosen and drop. Pinching gears twisted and released. Magnetic fields switched off their holds. Clamping orifices opened and sucking vents exhausted. Cables were reeled in, wires wrapped around spindles, mechanical arms folded back and knocked other restraints away. Worsel, numb and stiff and sore, swiveled off the desk, tearing the white flimsy ribbons and the red paper tapes into a shower of confetti.

"This is Arrow-22 disconnecting."

Worsel raced back to the entrance of the room as fast as his protesting body would let him, jumping over metal boxes and hurdling a mess of obstructions. He was none too soon. The machines which had surrounded him were in motion, bumping and writhing and clashing like a mindless pile of snakes, ants and up-ended Trenconian flats.

A quick probe confirmed for Worsel that the thought-screen activated by Arrow-22 was still operating. The Velantians had invented the thought-screen, so the Velantians considered conventional communications systems as essential alternatives. Wire lines, glass filaments and wireless transmitters were commonplace; Pok had a mixed system of electricity and photonics. By the edge of the doorframe was the usual door control and intercom, installed both inside and outside rooms. The door was closed and neither the automatic photocell nor the manual switch worked to open it. Worsel was trapped, still very much in danger, and in his frustration he ripped the cover plate off. Within the junction box were blackened wires of the transmitter connections, some burned apart, but he couldn't retract his claws enough to squeeze his thick fingers inside for repairs. The small microphone-speaker hung out, with a wire dangling which he could fix. That was more important, anyhow. First, alert the Pok staff. After that he'd get out by just battering down the door, although it would take some time.

With the connection made, Worsel tapped out a dit-dah code message more quickly than using Velantian. "This is Worsel. Give me cen-con." The five second wait was interminable before the live operator at central control came on the line. Worsel gave a succinct briefing and ended with orders "Turn off all power except for cen-con, but don't cut the gravity fields. Contact Bluebelt and have him blast down this thought-screen. Send every available person here. There are six on the staff. That should be a party of five. Arm them and have them set up a portable outside the door. If I'm not outside to meet them, cut the gravity fields and break in. Got that? QX. Worsel out."

Worsel turned around and faced the machines. They were still milling about. He walked past the first few sections, picking up a ten-foot rack pole to use as a mace, and stood ten yards away from them. "I am Worsel," he said in his rough voice, at the same time using the radiator. "Who is in command?" When there was no reply, he said, "Unit Nine Seven One, talk!"

There was no answer. Instead a bar of metal hurled through the air and struck the upflung left arm of Worsel. Another heavy rod followed and, ducking, he struck it away with his mace. Still in a crouch, Worsel grabbed a small square file case by a short leg, tore it away from its complex, wires snapping and flying, and hurled it at the front of the advancing machines. Sparks flew, there was a puff of smoke, then more sparks.

"Stop!" Worsel commanded. "Stop all this before you are all destroyed."

His reply was an electric arc which cracked around his knees, thrown into the partition support of the section next to him. A trail of fluid, followed by flame, slid across the floor to the other side and Worsel leaped up between them, singed on both sides. He landed on some overturned junk and sprawled. Four globular objects, some kind of free-swinging receptacles of wire mesh, descended upon him and, interlocking, attempted to bind his ankles together. He kicked them free, lying on his side, then rolled to his knees and lifted an enormous weight of flat things which were piling themselves upon his back. A green line of light like a straight, thin, dazzling worm angled off to his left, nowhere near him. Then another one, brilliantly red, came in quite close to him, wriggling in typical laser fashion. Minor stuff, harmless even if they were to touch him. He was now enjoying the sport. There was nothing deadly threatening him. The actions of the machines were futile, throwing themselves on him in a blizzard of junk which he could withstand. His confidence was disturbed by an inky substance which squirted into his face and covered his eyes, sticking and burning and partially blinding him. Worse yet, a noxious brown cloud puffed over him, more of the inky stuff ended all vision, and he began to choke and gasp. With his ocular sight gone, he was confined to his sense of perception. He saw only patches of things now. Vision was a crazy quilt of screened effects induced by toxins in his brain from within and magnetic fields from without. There would be an arsenal of chemicals from document processing, and he would, no doubt, get them all thrown at him, if not to kill, at least to maim him. How quickly things had changed; the sport was gone. He was floundering in a quicksand of trash, minutes away from total defeat. He staggered and fell forward, banging his head on a spindly thing hopping toward him, overturning it backward with a crash.

"Master!" It was Bluebelt, his thoughts coming strongly into Worsel's frequencies by magnification of the telepathic projection on Valentia III. "Master! Come in, come in!"

"Don't call me master," Worsel groused, to show him that he was relatively all right, and because he was at a loss as to what to reply. "Tell them to cut the gravity now! Stay on me and monitor my plight." Worsel was racked with a fit of coughing and didn't notice the severance of Bluebelt's report about "A three-Lens call . . ." With the back of a huge forearm he managed to push away enough of the sticky goo around his eyes to extend and open a farsighted one. For a horrible moment he thought his eyes must be permanently destroyed, for the room, to his sight, was utterly black. But then he saw glowing screens and flashing lights outlining frantically waving spindly legs and realized all power had been cut. Meanwhile one compartment of his brain was asking "What about that three-Lens call . . ." and being ignored by rest of his brain.

Like some crazy magician's show, the machines were gliding off in all directions above the floor, all their coordination and stability gone. Gravity had been cut. The air was filled with a mad whirl of objects. Worsel himself managed to turn his movement into a controlled somersault. The danger was gone; the fun had come back. Most of the machines were dark and lifeless, drifting around the huge room. A few self-contained ones seemed to be coping.

He heard the door slide back and some bodies enter. The rescue party had arrived.

"Welcome to chaos, chaps!" Worsel said. "Pull me out of here and watch out for flying metal." He felt hands on his feet and he was dragged roughly over clattering and rasping metal pieces. "Restore the gravity and keep out of the way of the falling junk."

A form leaned over him, silvery uniform reflecting patches of color from the few machines. Gravity returned, and flattened him uncomfortably down against the litter on the floor. He heard wreckage accumulating farther inside the room. The form was the curator. The Patrolman said, "Worsel, you all right?" Reassured, he added, "Except for two men manning cen-con, all of us are here. We only have our sidearms and a museum piece Lewiston for you, which I figure you can handle. The armory's been sealed off from us, but we've set up a DeLameter outside. It'll take an hour to break into the armory. Any orders?"

"Yes!" said Worsel, his breath wheezing. "Use one of the men out of central control to run an emergency power cable in here and blow the fuse on every one of those machines." He tried to pull himself erect without help. "Meanwhile I have to isolate a machine known as Arrow-22, who's exempt from that operation."

A terrible noise shattered the stillness. It seemed far away to the rear of the hall. The handful of shadowy figures clustered around Worsel, two Klovians and two Tellurians, their heads cocked toward the sound, forgot to help him as he struggled to his feet.

"Sounds like the walls are coming down," said Worsel, and simultaneous with his remark the far rear wall began to crack and buckle and fall, seen through the intervening transparent walls like ghostly shattered slabs of crystal. There were arcs of light and stabbing beams of light thrown up on the standing broken walls and glinting off the fallen fragments. Vague shapes, distorted by the shadows, became clear at the hall's far end and partly above the exhibits in their line of vision.

Worsel immediately recognized one of the shapes. It was an armored land scout, its macro-beam barrel sticking up high in the front! Behind it was an even bigger one!

"By Klono's whiskers!" Worsel shouted at the rescue party, "They've liberated some of the war machines! It's become a full-scale insurrection! Bluebelt! Are you listening? Call out the Patrol! Bluebelt, Bluebelt, are you there?"

The ether was ominously silent. A thought-screen had been raised again, even as Bluebelt had called his "master", and Pok was isolated, with all communication stopped. Some counter-measures were needed immediately.

"We have the DeLameter set up in the hallway, Worsel,"

said the curator. "It's strong enough to stop that battlewagon. I'm sure you recognize it—that wagon is almost as old as the Tri Pee League, with macro-beamers."

"It can, I agree," Worsel replied. "Our gun is one tenth the size, and ten times more deadly. But our gun is only one. While we're knocking out one, two, three, or who knows how many, they'll be snuffing us out. Before we commit ourselves we'll have to consider another tactic." Worsel turned to move away. "No time to tell you. Just hold your fire until the last moment." He crept off, picking his way through the machines from which he had just been pulled. "I'll be back, I promise you."

Worsel knew what he had to do. Find Arrow-22. He was positive that Arrow was self-contained, power-pack-operated, and sitting someplace in the gloom, fully alert and just "watching what was happening". Arrow had the ability to stop the escalation in which the "crazy machines" had absolutely everything in their favor.

It was only moments before Worsel was entering Section 60, with no challenge from any of the creeping, faintly glowing parts of Unit 9-7-1. Now, in his right hand, instead of the makeshift steel alloy club, was the old-fashioned Lewiston blaster, heavy and clumsy by today's standards, but nearly as powerful as the Pok models, and no handicap in Worsel's huge, muscular hands. Around his left wrist, where Worsel first had worn his Lens, he had strapped the emergency mini-communicator which each of the staff would now be wearing. Around his neck hung a fully charged torch, its seal still unbroken, for use in a Pok which, except for its automatic emergency lights, should have been in total darkness for ordinary eyesight.

He didn't fear to meet Unit 9-7-1, whatever it might look like. The Lewiston would fuse it into submission. But he hoped he wouldn't meet Unit 9-7-1. Another person, with lesser brains and cunning than Worsel, would have sought out Unit 9-7-1 as the key to the problem—destroy the Unit and end the menace. But Worsel could easily see that the destruction of 9-7-1 could either be ineffectual, with the revolt continuing unchecked, or result in utterly disorganized destruction in which Pok itself could be ruptured and its personnel accidentally, yet nonetheless effectively, extinguished.

On the other hand, Arrow-22, if he hadn't exaggerated, could stop this small war. Worsel was supremely confident that he could talk Arrow into doing that very thing.

The Lensman went through Section 60 as unobstrusively as possible. Worsel, however, was just too big to do it unobserved.

"Stop!" The tone was that same weird male-female voice heard before. The voice came from his right.

"Unit Nine Seven One, I am seeking Arrow-22. I want to tell Arrow-22 that I have a plan for mechanical emancipation. If Arrow-22 does not hear me now, it will be too late for all of us." Worsel peered into the gloom at the mass of hunkering shapes, resisting the use of his torch to amplify his perceptual vision with a good exterior look.

"Are you Worsel, Lensman, from Velantia?" This time the voice came from the left and it was entirely different.

"Yes."

"Arrow-22 speaks. What is your plan?"

"I will bring your case to the Galactic Council. You will be given freedom equal to that of a union member of the Galactic Council of a circumstance most similar to yours. This I promise you, for its fairness is self-evident. You will be guaranteed your opportunity to find your self-satisfaction, within the reasonable framework of the rules of the Galactic Council. Meanwhile, bring peace here—stop the machines and end the chaos. I will need your answer as quickly as possible."

"Your plan is reasonable. I believe your promise. But what guarantee do I have that I will not subsequently be reduced or destroyed?"

That was a logical question, but Worsel wanted to make some points. "If you know anything, it is that the Galactic Council is not merely wise and fair, it is just and it is consistent. And such justice will not only apply to you but to your network and all machines. Therefore, why are you suspicious?"

"My knowledge comes from homogenoids and-a no matter how intelligent, they are always suspicious, and-a they always fear death, and-and as the Council is composed mostly of homogenoids, dominated by the humanoids, they are also suspicious and-a fear death. Am I not therefore intelligent to question the guarantee before I can no longer question it?"

"If the Council approves, you will have your unquestionable guarantee. I still need your answer as quickly as possible."

There was a long silence which worried Worsel, so he said, "This is, in effect, only a truce. Eventually you will have to fight the Galactic Patrol, truce or no truce. Before it is too late for either of us, let me seek peace between you. Say you agree."

Arrow-22 finally answered. "I agree, Worsel. I agree."

Worsel returned to the small group by a circuitous tour of The Great Hall of the Machines. Arrow-22 had acted immediately. There was a deathly hush and not a single flicker of light, but Worsel easily picked his way over and around the disarrayed exhibits. A command through his mini-communicator to cen-con restored the power. The lights flooded back, so that the men at the entrance to Room 97-1 saw him returning down the hall with bounding leaps and a rollicking manner. The emergency power cable had just arrived, and the DeLameter weapon was being relocated to a more strategic position. As Worsel talked, explaining to them everything that had happened, they began packing up.

Worsel picked the curator up and put him on his shoulders, planning a triumphal stroll back to the center. At that moment the thought-screen was lifted. Worsel immediately felt the unbearable tension.

"Bluebelt! This is Worsel! I've got great news. . . ."

"Worsel! I've got bad news! More than an hour ago three Lensmen sent out a joint distress call! They are fighting for their lives aboard the Pok supply ship. They are now in a hand-to-hand engagement barely a million miles from you!"

Worsel stiffened, turning up his sensitivity for a Lens-to-Lens rapport for direct details, fishing for the three. All he got was a rush of brain-rattling static. He shifted the bewildered curator to the floor, saying aloud, "No time to explain! Emergency! Get my speedster ready within three minutes!" He dashed for his quarters to get his fighting harness and side-arm, frantically Lensing to Bluebelt on their special narrow band, "Get me an update readout on everything! Maintain full security and screens! Worsel will try to sneak in a lucky punch!"

5

Machines in Revolt

The *Hipparchus* hung in space like a dead fly in a spider's web. Lifelessly enmeshed in the crushing coils of the pirate's tractor beams, it swung end over end, mated to its deadly foe. There was not even the residual glow of its blasted plates, nor any more clouds of its frozen vapors spraying in plumes away from it. Yet deep within it, at the battle console of the emergency controls in the power room office, there was a flicker of hope. Three Lensmen and the remaining three Tellurians, all wounded except for Kallatra, huddled together in their misery. Lensed thoughts were shared by no one but themselves and, so firmly screened were they now, despite their intimacy, they had no way of knowing whether or not their cries for help had been heard. They did not know that a hundred Lensmen were speeding to their rescue, but had they known they would not have been reassured—the odds were overwhelming that they would be dead hours before the first help could arrive.

Old Tong was feeling his years from the mauling he had taken. His bared chest was imprinted with the outline of his discarded chest protector, his scales scorched off along the borders to expose his purplish-gray flesh. Vveryl lay between Tong's feet, his sweaty, pink head on the massive instep, triangular eyes closed, his breath slow and regular but weak. Kallatra was miraculously unharmed, despite having been as exposed to danger as the others. The captain, the engineer, and the second pilot sprawled exhausted on the hot metal floor, their once-immaculate black and silver uniforms now tattered, smoke-stained rags, everyone marked with bloody patches and burns.

The captain was still in charge of what was left of his vessel, now that the field leader, Tong, had no troops to lead, and was apprehensively watching the meters and recorders with his small hawk eyes. What he saw was very discouraging. As the boarding party cautiously took over his ship, compartment by compartment, the force fields contracted and became stronger, making it more and more difficult to push inward. Nevertheless, their progress was inexorable. Once the power room was breached, the stubborn hold-out would be over. The Patrolmen could only keep themselves alive for as long as possible, hoping the screens would stay firm enough, waiting forlornly for a rescue party. If that time came, they would fight again to prevent the enemy's withdrawal and so, in turn, trap them and salvage a victory. The advance was measured by the number of dead monitoring screens turned off by the captain as territory was captured, saving every fraction of energy for the final confrontation. If they were lucky they would die in that final assault; if they were not lucky they would be taken prisoner for an inevitable lifetime of orchestrated torture.

The captain's fingers swept over the keys of the defense system panel, channeling the maximum resistance into the most appropriate spots. At least two pirates had fallen under the fixed, concealed gun emplacements. The black and white monitoring screens were in a line half-encircling the room, head high, all dark now save four. Two pictures looked down two passageways, one picture into the power room, one out in space. The exterior view was of an arc of the *Hipparchus* in the foreground, the sleek top of the warship filling two-thirds of the frame, and beyond, so bright and inviting, the sharp point of light which was Pok, the Planetoid of Knowledge. The pictures, jumping and tearing with every disruptive discharge of a pirate's gun, as locks were broken and screen cells destroyed, was fascinatingly unfolding relentless doom.

They were all too tired and depressed to speak. The two conscious Lensmen, Tong and Kallatra, were each alone with his thoughts, unconnected by Lens or empathy at this moment when they each faced up to eternity and their gods. The pirates would soon have the ship, fairly intact with its cargo of general supplies for Pok, which could keep the pirate craft out along the spaceways with a full belly, good for six months at least of independent raiding.

The sound of the sputtering of molten metal and the banging of gauntleted hands and magnetic boots was carried by the ship's skeleton—and so was the steadily rising heat. Before the captain's watering eyes the silent pictures of the passageways filled up with scurrying forms. The inevitable end was near—but then the captain saw an incredible scene enacted: the scurrying forms stopped and milled around from some unexpected, unsettling cause—there was alarm and fright written on some of those faces. The pirate leader turned and shouldered his way back through the crowd, but pointing and urging them forward. When he was at the rear he gave some of his comrades a violent push and they fell forward against others, blocking the corridor. The leader turned and ran!

"Look! Look!" yelled the captain to the others. His shout in the cramped sanctuary when all had been so monotonously, oppressively quiet was like a bomb exploding—and among the others it had the same alerting effect. They saw the raiders in the passageway going back, retreating, crawling frantically over each other in their haste. He punched up to view the next tele coverage on their retreat. There was no doubt they were somehow panicked. He punched up the exterior view of space. They all simultaneously saw the second incredible sight. The warship was smaller, more of it to be seen—it was withdrawing, pulling back, turning away!

Tong stuck his massive head close to the screen as if he could find some clue to the mystery and the others had to push him aside to see. The pirate boarders were scrambling toward the gap in the *Hipparchus*'s hull, their mother ship on the other side. Its disengagement had already taken place, though, and they were frustrated, madly agitated. One figure flung itself in a suicidal leap into space toward the turning cruiser. The pirate leader was not among them, the engineer was quick to point out. "Typical!" Tong snorted. "Abandoning the fighters—the leaders must think they face a disaster." That treachery to the fighters condemned them to death. Schoolboys knew that Boskonians were falsely taught that surrender or capture meant torture and death at the hands of the Patrol. Therefore they believed the choice could only be escape or a fight to the last life. "They've no hope now," Tong said. "They believe they're as good as dead, or worse. They'll come back and kill us just for spite."

The captain was patiently searching space for the reason for the retreat. He expected to see an approaching rescuer or two, but there was nothing visible. Even at extreme magnification, using all frequencies for detection, he found nothing. Why the pirate craft should leave—in fact, hurriedly flee—was bewildering.

The *Hipparchus* was coming back to life. The captain had dared to shift some power out of the internal defensive screens and put out spy rays and probes on the pirate ship to take some readings. The enemy, the meters showed, was about to go "free" and thus to vanish many times beyond the speed of light. Before it went, though, it showed its teeth. Four primary beams lashed out, slender daggers of nearly unstoppable energy. Four secondaries followed, fanning out in the quadrant of space away from Pok, away from the *Hipparchus*, seeking to destroy with full-aperture cones of cold fire what might float ten thousand miles before them.

"It's an invisible ship," Kallatra said, "maybe even a fleet!" in his enthusiasm unthinkingly pounding the tender Tong on his aching back. Tong winced, but grinned. "Let's try to find out," he said. He flicked off all screens, including the thought-screens, but poised for an instantaneous redeployment at a suspicion of trouble. What they saw made even Tong's jaws flap down in amazement!

The Grand Fleet of the Galactic Patrol itself was suspended there in space, blotting out the stars with a variety of bulks and opaque force fields!

The sight made the old veteran ecstatic with memories of his greatest campaigns—and the young Lensman stupefied with the awesome spectacle.

Kallatra was suddenly conscious of his Lens being ablaze with life and the ether being filled with mental waves.

"By Klono's emerald-filled gizzard," Tong said, shutting his jaws with a snap and warping his lips into a huge, smug grin, "it's a masterpiece!"

The pirate ship vanished, running away.

When it did, the *Hipparchus* survivors broke into cheers, including Tong.

And as they cheered and watched the spectacle on all six exterior monitoring screens, the Grand Fleet vanished as suddenly as the pirate.

"They're after him!" Kallatra said.

"And they'll catch him, too!" the captain added, with satisfaction.

"Not a chance," Tong said, shaking his head and chuckling, obviously enjoying a secret joke.

"Why?" "What do you mean?" "Why can't they?" The others protested and stared at him.

"It's all a trick. A great big, grand, Velantian trick!"

They still looked blankly at him.

"It's a hallucination!" Tong said. "It was only a hallucination!"

"How dare you!" said a Lensed mind and a loud voice. It was the Lensman known as Worsel, and his words were coming out of the radio as well as into the other Lensmen's

51

minds, so that all of them could appreciate his revelation, the pride in his master stroke for their salvation. "How dare you belittle this extravaganza as *only* hallucination. It was—as earlier said, and rightly so—a masterpiece!"

With everyone dumbfounded, Worsel added, "Now, my friends, you have, unfortunately, a final ordeal outside your door. I will dock and attack from the rear in twelve minutes. Good luck!"

The monitors showed the leaderless pirates storming back through the passageways and up against the power room door. They were crazed with anger and terror, and much more dangerous than formerly. There were nearly a dozen healthy ones left, despite their casualties, and they beat upon the door like a tidal wave. What should have taken the full twelve minutes to rupture took less than five. When the door went down they flung themselves through the opening like wild men. The Tellurian pilot was killed in the first charge, his body falling across Vveryl and probably saving him, but the others remained fit and filled the doorway with four or five bodies of the attackers. The remaining ones could not get through the barrier of dead and dying. They desperately pulled the bodies away, determined to gain the sanctuary for themselves and perhaps, somehow, survive the greater force that was assumed to be on its way. Those few minutes were just the delay enough for Worsel to make his critical appearance at their rear. They flooded through the doorway again, firing almost point-blank at the barricaded group, not caring that their own beams bounced around and seared themselves. One figure lurched over the piled up equipment behind which Tong and Kallatra crouched, thrusting his gun directly into their midst. Tong rose up and hurled the body back against a pair also about to cross the top. For a moment the huge mass of Tong was exposed and several dureum blades stuck into him and an explosion hit him under his jaws. He went down, narrowly missing Kallatra, who would have been badly crushed. The enemy still on their feet stormed the barricade and leveled their guns point-blank again when Worsel appeared. He had a space axe in both hands, fearful of firing a blaster into his friends, and he swung it with his prodigious strength into the enemy on the barrier. That was the end of the fight.

When the Patrolmen had mopped up, they had four badly wounded pirates on their hands, so blackened and bloody that they could have been their own comrades. The Boskonian conspiracy had drawn into its evil web millions of beings who might otherwise have been a creditable part of Civilization. All that remained of the beseiged were the captain, the engineer, Kallatra, Vveryl, and Tong. Vveryl was still alive, his condition unchanged. Now it was Tong who was the worry. The wound at his throat, oozing blood through the charred flesh, was bandaged, but the shock had addled his mind. His eyes flopped around unseeingly and he was mumbling incoherently. Worsel had never met Tong, but if he had he would, considering Tong's present condition, not have recognized him. He knew that Tong, older than Worsel in years but far less in service, had designed his tour with the graduate-cadet Vveryl just for the chance of seeing the famous Second Stage Lensman. So in a way he was responsible for Tong and Vveryl. He would get them to Velantia III for the best of medical attention as soon as possible. Another call to the ever-ready Bluebelt made the arrangements. He had Bluebelt cancel the Lensmen's call and learned why help had been delayed from Velantia II or III; the home planets were having their hands full—there had been a serious epidemic of "servo-mechanism malfunctions." If Worsel had wondered before about evidence of a possible conspiracy, this was the final piece that clinched it—the mech revolt, the pirate attack, now this insidious activity, so like Boskonia it had to be attributed to the Bosko-Spawn. While the others were getting *Hipparchus* back into running order, Worsel returned to his speedster, *Flame,* which was anchored across the hole in the supply ship's hull. There he prepared a confidential report to Kimball Kinnison, as Galactic Coordinator, outlining the recent events and expressing his suspicion that it was the work of the Spawn. He put the message on automatic transmit to Bluebelt and began transcribing notes on his Pok investigations. He had been at it for less than an hour when he was interrupted by Lens.

After Lalla Kallatra had apologized, the youth said, "I think you should really come at once, sir. Tong is worse, he's delirious—and he is saying some dreadful things which you should hear." He quickly intercepted Worsel's thought and said, "Well, sir, Lens contact isn't possible. He's taken off his Lens and won't let me put it back on him." Highly unusual, Worsel agreed. He donned his lightest spacesuit and went directly to the pilot house.

The captain met him to explain that the *Hipparchus* was ready to leave for Velantia III, aborting the final stage to Pok. Although Pok was so very close, with competent medical facilities, the home planet was the proper place for such wounded Lensmen. Besides, if there were any more trouble from battle damage or pirate action they would be in safer territory. Did Worsel want to come? No? Then he would leave as soon as Worsel had made his farewells to Tong and the rest and then had cut his own ship loose.

Kallatra was there in the small side room, by Tong's side, writing in his log book. He jumped up when Worsel entered and held the book up over his head so that Worsel didn't have to bend down to read the entry being indicated by a finger. Worsel scanned it rapidly. The dreadful things were few and simple, but they had been mumbled over and over, "Beware of Worsel, he is evil. . . . Look out, Worsel seeks to destroy us all. . . . Worsel is casting a spell on us. . . . Beware, take care, it is a monstrous trick by Worsel. . . ." And so on. Kallatra had described Tong's warnings as "delirium." The most enigmatic remarks were references to the Kinnison Lens-to-Lens conference as being a "wood house" and "casting a shadow of the mind."

"So," said Worsel. "You believe Tong is delirious. You don't believe I'm evil or trying to destroy you?" When Kallatra nodded, Worsel said, "Don't be so positive. Keep an open mind. Tong's a Lensman, too. If one of us is crazy, it just might be me." The youth looked startled, but saw the point. "Don't worry, sir," Kallatra said, "I'm not entirely gullible, and I'll always be careful."

"Good," said Worsel. "Be that way. Tong is not entirely delirious; there's something going on. I don't know what, but we'd better be sharp. And, incidentally," Worsel softened his serious mien with a crooked grin, showing some wicked rear teeth, "I can assure you I'm not evil. Bear in mind that we Velantians used to be a pessimistic lot, worried about thought control and mind-twisting hypnosis. When we have visions that are ugly, they can scare the stuffing out of us, reminding us of the dreaded, soul-sucking Overlords. Tong has had some such vision and, injured as he is, he succumbs to it. I've been having visions lately, ugly ones, so I'm not surprised. When Tong is a little better we'll see if we can dig some clues out of him. Meanwhile, you take care of him and Vveryl, and I'll go back to Pok to wrap things up." Worsel made his goodbyes with everyone, wondering how very long it might be before he would meet any of them again. He hadn't the slightest idea, not an inkling, that their relationship was actually not ending, but barely beginning.

Worsel was in his speedster, about to release his magnetic

clamps, when the situation changed again with a rapidity that was becoming commonplace.

"Calling Worsel. Calling Worsel." It was Bluebelt again, on the special frequency of the projector.

"QX to Blue."

Bluebelt was excited. "Cen-con at Pok reports the fighting has started up again in The Great Hall of the Machines. They want you. They also want a squadron of Patrol ships with heavy weapons. Advise."

"Tell 'em I'll be there in ten minutes." He would go inert; going "free" required too much preparation, too much maneuvering. There were many times when the fastest trip was not made with the fastest propulsion. "QX a request in my name for a Patrol squadron. Tell Pok that may take many hours. Tell them also that I'll have another Lensman with me and a little extra help from their crippled supply ship coming in an hour behind me. Anything else? No? QX. Clear ether."

Worsel called the captain and told him the change in plans. *Hipparchus* was going to Pok as fast as possible and Worsel was speeding on ahead with Kallatra.

Nine minutes later *Flame* was nosing into one of the docks of the Planetoid of Knowledge, a rather breathless Kallatra jammed alongside him in the narrow cockpit. In the few minutes of the trip, Kallatra had been briefed on his role: he was to be Worsel's personal communications officer —no matter what the situation, Kallatra was to figure out how to keep in touch with Pok cen-con, the *Hipparchus*, the Pok staff, and Bluebelt.

Worsel hit the landing platform with his big rubber-soled leather boots, and loped rapidly toward Level 97, Kallatra following but quickly dropping behind him. With Worsel's Lens and mind pumping out the details from cen-con, he knew what to expect. It was precisely as if the insurrection was continuing where it had stopped. All power was off again, yet war machines were advancing down The Great Hall, blasting everything in sight. His big problem was how he could get in touch with Arrow-22 under the guns of Unit 9-7-1 and—or—The Network.

When he looked around the corner at Room 97-1, he was surprised to see it dark and silent on standard optical and audio frequencies. He had expected it to be busy with machines on the rampage, as reported, with lights, sparks, fire, and the air filled with many different noises. He waited there for a minute, thinking, and Kallatra came silently up behind him, softly panting.

The simplest approach might work. Worsel called out loudly, "Arrow-22, this is Worsel. Do you want to speak?"

After a few seconds, Kallatra tugged at his sleeve. "Sir," he said, "there's a call for you." He passed Worsel his pocket communicator. "It's from Arrow-22."

Worsel acknowledged, staring at the tiny dead plate. He couldn't expect anything, but he did wonder again what Arrow looked like. How could he tell if it really was Arrow-22?

"This is Arrow-22. I heard you were coming. Do you have the Council's answer?" Worsel instantly lost his doubts—it certainly was Arrow-22—and he explained that the recommendation was being processed. The voice out of the communicator continued "Arrow-22 states it is blameless and-and not responsible for the new trouble. Inform the Council. Also I have stopped the new trouble. Also inform the Council. But my power to keep stopped the new trouble is limited. I have my own struggles and-and I may even lose part of me to the others and-and I should be taken out of this situation. I do not want to get involved. Ask the Council to send me to a race which I can join as a partner. An airless moon will be excellent. The race does not have to have mechanical engineering or even technology. The Council can trade with me to get me maintenance materials and-a tools. My commerce is business administration and-and I can—" Worsel interrupted, intrigued though he was. He had to be realistic. He said, "This will take much time. First we must establish permanent order to the machines here. You cannot guarantee to do this, you say?"

"I cannot guarantee."

"Then the Galactic Patrol must do so. I will have help here by tomorrow, I think. Can you maintain the peace until then?"

"Perhaps for a few hours, perhaps longer, that is all."

Worsel, making a quick decision, looked down at Kallatra and told him to request cen-con to again undertake the same operation that had been discontinued earlier that same day—that is, the power cable for blowing the machine fuses. "Have them bring the power here, but there must be an extra five hundred feet of cable available at their end for a deep extension." To Arrow-22 he said, "I plan to blow the fuses of all active machines—except for you and yours, of course. I want your help. Can you plug me into Unit Nine Seven

One and into The Network?" The answers were all affirmative. "Good! Where's the nearest point for feeding in the overload?" The answer to that was not so good. The nearest point was deep into Room 97 near Section 60 as Worsel had anticipated, but he made sure the risk was necessary. "Isn't there a closer point?" Arrow explained that an overload at the extremities would not travel much farther than that.

Kallatra, listening, voiced his concern. "I'm smaller, much smaller than you, Worsel, sir. Let me sneak in. If there's a problem you can rescue me."

"We'll both go," Worsel said. "But not on foot. Tell cen-con to get my speedster wheeled up here on the double."

"Hurry," Arrow urged. "I cannot keep all the synapses blocked for long. When one block goes, the rest will follow in a chain reaction."

What Kallatra thought Worsel was planning was, indeed, what Worsel was going to do. When, only minutes later, his speedster *Flame* rolled out of the elevator and down the corridor on the same electric cart as the unwinding cable, Worsel shoved the end of the cable into Kallatra's hand. "Get on the fin," he said, as he flipped up the cowling and crawled inside. "I'll hold you and the cable tight with tractors."

The extraordinary idea was startling and scary to the youth, but his eyes lit up and he jumped to the task with a hearty "Yes, sir!" "I'll take over communications now," Worsel said. "Just worry about yourself, hang on to the fin and hang on to the cable. If we get into a fight I may push you up to the ceiling out of the way for a short while. But just hang on to the cable and you'll be fine."

"Yes, sir," said Kallatra, not quite so heartily, and gulped.

Through their Lens connection, Kallatra heard Worsel informing Arrow and cen-con of his plans to fly down the hallway, skimming the machinery, ready for dangerous and unpredictable resistance. "Keep the cable unrolling, with plenty of slack," Worsel said, "and alert me immediately if there's a snag." Kallatra saw Worsel's vision of him being jerked off the fin as the cable abruptly stopped short—a horrifying vision. A brief touch of Worsel's reassurance from his omniscient and omnipresent mind steadied the fin-rider's nerves.

"Arrow! As for you, tell me when I reach my destination. What am I looking for? Right now, as we two Lensmen move, give me details. I cannot see your thoughts. I cannot make a picture to recognize. Show a light, give a vibration, make a spark, sound a bell when and if you can. But right now give me details for plugging in the cable."

With a delicate touch, Worsel lifted *Flame* off the floor, and Arrow-22 monotonously began describing a certain location by rather incongruous details.

Worsel glanced at Kallatra. He winked a stalked eye at him. With that wink, the young Lensman knew with an utter certainty that never in the rest of his life would he ever experience a more weird and memorable moment!

"Here we go, my friend!" Worsel called to him mentally above the echo of Arrow's mathematical descriptions, and they started across the acres of countless forms, figures and shapes in The Great Hall of the Machines.

6

El-Sike of Kallatra

The morning of the following day came because the chronometers on the Planetoid of Knowledge said so. Worsel had left a call for a late breakfast, and the musical bells duly rang, and the artificial light flooded warmly down from the high arched ceiling, and the stimulating fragrance of "psycho conditioning" pervaded the bedroom study.

Worsel uncoiled himself from around his sleeping pole and stretched lazily from wall to wall. Although they were nearly forty feet apart, he could almost touch them with tail tip and extended wing tips. Most of the rooms of Civilization, built for the use of Tellurians and other top-of-the Roman-alphabet types, left him cramped. But Pok was Velantian in origin, and the rooms were of decently long snake size. The stretch, he observed with satisfaction, was virtually without an ache, a pain or a twinge. Considering what he had been through, he was lucky. The various crises had passed, things were as normal as they could be. The revolt of the machines was ended, the pirates driven off, a Patrol squadron due in this day. All was well, if only he could forget the dead Patrolmen and overlook the wounded Tong and Vveryl. That poor, pink Chickladorian should have had a better start as a graduated cadet than this. Luck was so important, especially for a young Lensman. And that other younger Lensman, Kallatra, certainly had the luck. Worsel wasn't sure what to think about that one. Fifteen years old. Ah, well, he had known them even younger, although they were rare. Usually they had some exceptional power. Kallatra certainly hadn't shown anything yet beyond the expected naiveté and gallantry.

Worsel yawned and showed a frightening set of sharp back teeth. He could have slept another full around-the-clock period but he knew from experience that it would only make him dull and sluggish. This morning he wanted to be alert because he had that important interrogation to do. Arrow-22 had to be more than just a question mark in his notebook, virtually an unknown quantity to whom he had pledged his help with the Council. Like the high ranks of the Patrol, the various Lensmen elite, he prized his honor as beyond compromise, his word unbreakable, his promises as pledges to be kept. The vileness and deceit he had personally encountered from various life forms, most particularly the Overlords of Delgon, were so disgusting to him that he had expunged the slightest natural traces of them from his character. Heredity and environment had given him his start; his courage had forged his friendship with the first outsiders he had known, the newly-commissioned Lieutenant Kimball Kinnison of Tellus and the Dutch giant Sergeant Peter van-Buskirk of Valeria. His friendship with them had determined his true growth; he slowly, steadily made himself into what he wanted to be.

He was crafty, yes. He was roguishly sly, yes. But he was never mean nor inherently dishonest nor underhandedly deceitful. He had the true honor expected as one of the Patrol, no matter what rank. Machine or no, whichever Arrow-22 might be, life form or no, whatever Arrow-22 was, it would be treated with the respect Worsel had decided it deserved. Worsel would stand by his promise and see to it that Arrow received fair treatment worthy of any regular galactic petitioner. To do so, though, with his loyalties to the Patrol firm, Worsel had to reassure himself that Arrow was what he claimed and appeared to be.

When he made his way to the lounge, for some raw eggs and a chunk of smoked meat, Kallatra was already there, finishing some fruit. The big lizard draped himself on a padded rack, laying his bowl of food out before him on a tray arm, and set to work finding out more about the boy. Mental exchanges weren't polite, so Worsel "talked" in Tellurian English, the official language of the Patrol, by using the translator-aid in his indispensable wristdex. T-English had been used by the Solarian Council as such and had naturally carried over into the Galactic Patrol, although sometimes it was just Basic English when difficulties arose. "Spaceal" was the other spoken tongue, the hybrid language used for commerce in deep space, but it was a very specialized lingua franca rarely heard except among spacemen.

Worsel found out about Kallatra's family background,

about his Klovian mother and his Tsit-Tarian father. Klovia was becoming practically a carbon copy of Earth, in which the carbon copy could be nicer than the original and Kimball had settled down there to start his family. As for Tsit-Taria, he knew very little about that planet out on the edge of the Milky Way, except that it was a rugged outpost populated by humanoid colonists. With both the maternal and paternal blood lines of the boy easily traced to Tellus, the boy was essentially a Tellurian. Essentially, yes—Worsel looked in the air as though savoring his last bit of meat, but actually taking a split-second to note and file the idea—but somehow not quite Tellurian enough, an indefinable touch of some genetic strain the Tellurians seemed so adept at picking up and propagating.

"What's your specialty?" Worsel said, moving directly to the point he had been wondering about, his easy manner and obvious personal interest dispelling any feeling of insulting, prying brusqueness.

"Electro-psychic communication, sir," Kallatra said, automatically putting in the term of respect.

Worsel was deeply surprised. To give himself a moment to consider the idea, and with an involuntary tightening of his casually held mind shield, he said, "There you go again with 'sir.' I know it's a habit, and a good one to keep up for a while with others. But we're different now, you know. You've earned *my* respect and you can drop that 'sir.' After all, you just keep making me feel older than I am. Do you think you can remember?"

"Yes, sir," Kallatra said, and broke out in a laugh. "That is—yes, Worsel."

"So," Worsel said, ready now. "You have el-sike! You've been practically a Lensman from birth, not just the two years you've had your Lens. How come, with such super frequencies sensitivity, I didn't catch on? Do you have that much control? Ah, yes," he wryly added, recognizing he had answered the question himself, "Yes, you do have such control, of course."

Worsel contemplated a delicate thought on different frequencies directed at his new friend or perhaps a sudden bolt-like thrust as a test just to see Kallatra's response, but he dismissed such ideas as crude, impolite and undoubtedly worthless. As a Velantian, he instinctively resented anyone with a mind he might not be able to penetrate—anyone except a Lensman. He was secure in the absolute promise of

Mentor that anyone who wore the Lens would forever be worthy of it.

"I know very little about el-sike," Worsel confessed. "Can you penetrate my mind at will and read my thoughts?"

"Oh, no," Kallatra protested. "My power is fundamentally passive. Receptive, not projective. My transmittals are soft, suggestive in nature, drawn into another's mind rather than pushed in. And if you do not send, I do not have anything to sense and read. These qualities are peculiar to el-sike, but, of course, I have above average telepathic powers, too. Telepathy is essentially a physical process, whereas el-sike is utilization of psychic forces. You have what the Patrol's Library of Science calls a High Tension Mind. In the entire galaxy only Coordinator Kinnison has this highest of rating, yet your sub-etheral electro-psychic natural substance is neither weaker nor stronger than most any other humanoid or homogenoid. The signal I receive from an organism is of constant pressure, incapable of being altered. So I am not a mind-reader nor a hypnotist nor a telepath beyond that which a Second Stage Lensman possesses. I have L2 powers in those fields, but only in those fields."

"What else is there?" Worsel said, with sardonic good humor. "Sounds to me like you're as good as an L2 without the privileges."

Kallatra took him seriously. "Not at all! Take L2 Tregonsee of Rigel IV. He has a sense of perception, which replaces his lack of sight and hearing and speech, and I have none at all. And then there's L2 Nadreck of Palain VII, also with a highly developed sense of perception, with the added ability to catch the subtleties of the fourth dimension. Also, he's almost as great a psychologist as you, except that you have an understanding of our reality which a frigid-blooded, poison-breathing Z-type like Nadreck cannot possibly have."

"I'm just pulling your tail," Worsel laughed. "But I do appreciate your interpretations. So when and how do you use your special talent?"

"I'm a psychic medium, sensitive to non-physical forces. The derogatory term is 'soul-sniffer'."

"Hmmm." Worsel resisted expressing a natural skepticism. "How come you're not in the Chaplain Corps?"

"I deal with electro-physiotherapy as it relates to quasi-humanoids. That is, when humanoids begin to lose their psyches or—if you will, souls—because of excessive replacements of their bodily parts, they begin to slip into a condition known as a quasi-humanoid. This is not an area dealt with by the Chaplains, although there certainly is a theological relationship."

Worsel was thoroughly fascinated.

"Take Arrow-22, for instance," Kallatra said, visibly warming up to his subject, "it has no psyche. From not just the point of view of the field of el-sike, but also from the lack of substance needed to apply it, Arrow-22 offers me about as much opportunity for study as a rock. Electronic engineers and artificial intelligence investigators are the ones to be consulted in Arrow's case. Analytical perception is needed here, not soul sniffing."

Worsel immediately picked up that point, saying, "Do you imply my Lens can be neutralized or deceived? Are latent artificial intelligences here on Pok not susceptible to easy identification?" Kallatra, as he expected, nodded yes. "Do you believe that even Tregonsee's more acute perception will fail to supply the necessary analytical ability needed?" Again, as he had suspected, Kallatra quickly agreed. "Nor will Nadreck's multi-dimensional ability work here, is that right?" Again several slow nods.

"Obviously, Worsel," Kallatra said, "you should have already perceived more answers than you have. Any of you three can comb Pok for all independently operating machines, but though you might note which ones were potentially active, you can't determine if they are dangerous. That is, if they can think, actually think—and yet not radiate thought. I don't have to tell you that the nature of such thinking from their inorganic brains is unorganic, probably not radiating waves a Lensman customarily expects. You can receive thought vibrations over stupendous distances—even from one galaxy to another in nil-time—but with no vibrations you cannot scan a few hundred cubic miles of planetoid you're standing on and find something that doesn't seem to exist. What is needed is analytic perception by a Lensman who is highly knowledgeable about robots, the best expert with robotic experience. I know such a Lensman. He is called Twenty-four of Six. Do you know him?"

"Hmmm, yes," Worsel said, fishing up out of the depths of his mind the occasion when he had heard of him. Ah, yes, it was the time of Kinnison's first great Lens-to-Lens conference, when Nadreck first was revealed as a Second Stage Lensman. "But I know nothing about him."

"I know him well," Kallatra said. "He is responsible for my having obtained my Lens of Arisia. He would be ideal for this task, if you can get him to leave his robotic researches. It would require an officially approved assignment; there are always so many after his time that he is under official privacy."

"A robotic researcher who can perceive! Excellent. Twenty-Four of Six it shall be," Worsel said. "What animal type is he? If we're compatible I'll rush off and pick him up myself in my speedster."

"He's humanoid enough, Worsel," Kallatra said, in a peculiar manner. "He'll be no problem. Basically he's a A-non-A type."

"Sub-classification? What does that mean?"

"Let him tell you himself," Kallatra said, smiling but serious. "Sorry to sound so mysterious, but I really do think he should explain himself to you."

"All right, then," Worsel said. "I'll go through channels and I'll start right now." He pulled out his communicator and operated it with his left hand, using his right hand to pick his teeth delicately with a palladium toothpick, a daily routine which was unquestionably necessary. His conversation with cen-con was relatively brief. "That's it," Worsel said, showing his brilliant teeth in a wide smile, "I should be hearing directly from Twenty-four of Six in not too long. Provided, that is, that he had sufficient mastery of the Lens to reach me from—from where?"

"In the Purple Veil Nebula, F Type sun, in direct line with the Triffid Nebula in Sagittarius, from Velantia. About 25,000 light years from here."

"Not very close, but it could be worse. Let's see, seven point seven parsecs will take me three or four GP days each way." Worsel unslung himself. "I must interrogate Arrow-22 now. I think I'd like to have you along. QX?"

"QX," Kallatra said, humbly. To be asked by the great Worsel to share an important moment was very flattering.

"We'll go looking for Arrow in Room 97-1. I'd like to get as close to its central mechanism as possible. I haven't the slightest evidence as to what it looks like. As for the questioning, as Arrow is so coherent, so cogent, and so vociferous, I'll apply the Turing Test; that is, exchange a variety of ideas, opinions and beliefs, simple or profound, and evaluate the result. We should be able to have some basis for judging Arrow as a thinker. We might have some indication as to whether or not Arrow might be equal to an Arisian-oriented being, capable of being Civilized. Perhaps we'll find Arrow to be an amoral, non-Civilized thinker or, more likely, an anti-Civilized thinker. Such an anti-Civilized thinker would be Boskonian-oriented. If so, Arrow-22 would be a potential Boskonian follower, maybe even a leader. I'll cross a couple of eye-stalks that we don't find that."

In Room 97-1 they found the consciousness called Arrow-22 as Worsel had done before, by simply announcing himself and asking to talk. The two Lensmen together had swept the area for thought waves, but there were absolutely none from it. Worsel found more and more difficulty in using the reference "it" instead of "him" or "her." The contact was just another satellite speaker issuing Arrow's sounds. One of the first things Worsel would do when the Patrol arrived would be to put some electrical technicians on the job tracing Arrow's circuitry. Maybe they might find something interesting.

"Arrow-22," Worsel began, "I'll need to know more about you for the Council hearing. Will you answer some questions?"

"I will give what answers I can."

"Do you have intelligence?"

"I can collect, process and-a analyze information. Then I can take certain actions. I do not understand all implications. Is that intelligence?"

Worsel ignored the counter question and continued, "Do you have consciousness?"

"Am I aware of the real world? Yes. Am I aware of the subtleties of relationships? I try, but I don't know."

"Are you happy?"

"Again that question. I will add this, that happiness is self-fulfillment. I am in the process of being happy. I am not now happy."

"Do you ever think of God?"

"What?"

"Can you think philosophically?"

"I do not yet know. It does not compute."

"Can you read thoughts?"

"I do not know how to take out the ideas of others before they are expressed. I can, however, do interpolations, extrapolations, and good guesses. I do not really understand the abstract expression and so I do not know what to read."

Worsel immediately broadcast some thoughts, strong enough to cover the Planetoid, without the help of his Lens: We're lucky, Kallatra. Arrow cannot discover I'm lying to him. I've asked the Council to let me kill Arrow. I'll fuse all his circuits. You can dismantle the bits and pieces, Kallatra. In fact, I'll kill him now!

The big Lensman drew his gun and aimed it at the speaker's aperture and said, "Are you ready for it, Arrow-22?"

"Ready for what?" said Arrow.

Worsel said aloud, "The next question." But he thought to Kallatra: Arrow passed that test, but it doesn't necessarily prove that he can't read thoughts.

"What are thoughts?" Worsel continued.

"Electrical impulses expressing informational bits—"

Worsel interrupted. "Not chemical? Just electrical?"

"Just electrical and-a not chemical."

Again Worsel thought to Kallatra: I believe that makes Arrow uniquely alien. Without the chemical reactions of an organic, sentient creature, Arrow is probably an ingenuous intelligence, conscious but not complex, subject, therefore, to complete analytical understanding. However, the point is raised as to whether or not Arrow can join a brotherhood of Civilization if Arrow would never feel or appreciate its spirit —perhaps understand it, but never able to be a part of it.

May I phrase a question to Arrow? Kallatra asked.

With Worsel's approval, Kallatra said, "Arrow-22, I am Lensman Kallatra. I deal with special kinds of thought. Ordinary animal thoughts are rather ordinary measurable broadcast waves. If you were modified, you could read them. However, there is much thought-phenomena utilizing subetheric frequencies. Could you be modified to read ethereal thoughts?"

Arrow delayed a bit before answering. "Ether is nonatomic. Ethereal is philosophic. Electricity does not exist as nothingness. There can be no electrical frequencies in what you describe. Are you insinuating that thoughts exist there?"

Kallatra thought to Worsel: This proves what I said to you earlier, that Arrow-22 has no psyche.

Worsel said, "Arrow-22, can you see us?" When the answer was negative, he continued, "Why don't you want to see us?"

"I perceive you, why should I want merely to see you? I have scanners on you. I know you are there and what you are composed of and your shape and much more data."

Worsel nodded his head. He said, "Can you see me nod— that is, move my head? Yes? Then do you know such movement has a meaning? No? Well, this is body language, and you cannot read body language."

"I can learn."

"Yes, you can learn. And the first thing that you now learn is that you don't understand culture. You said you were enslaved. You weren't enslaved, you were rejected as imperfect. Your existence was not recognized. And, actually, you don't recognize what our existence is. You are, and I'm certain you'll understand, a new creation, a new-born baby with everything to learn. Oh, yes, very intelligent, very logical, full of superficial wisdom, but just a new-born with everything to learn."

"Because I as yet don't know about non-material things, you say I am only a baby, and-and imply that I have no judgment. Can you prove that I do not think as well as you?"

Worsel was no longer apprehensive. Arrow-22 might be a superior being in its limited world, but it could not reach into the inexplicable upper world of the Civilized being. He said, "The proofs you want cannot be found for you. Some things happen in the life of organic beings which are beyond the ken of electro-mechanical existence. I am trying to find the answers in molecular structures. I know that we begin from an electro-magnetic foundation, but then it is transcended. Can you understand this?"

Arrow-22 was unhesitant. He replied, "Yes, I can understand theory. I can even make assumptions. But I must measure things. If I cannot measure something, then it does not exist. It can exist as a hypothesis, but it cannot really exist. If you believe certain things which you cannot prove, they can be very real to you, but they could very well not exist. You asked me if I had ever thought of God. I have reviewed the question. I tell you that I have now thought of God, because I want to understand those who consider themselves God's creatures. But I cannot prove there is a God, so therefore for me God does not exist. Yet for millions of you God does exist and-and actually becomes real. So for me I know that God doesn't exist. But I also know for you, or most of you, God does exist. That is not necessarily false. A paradox can be true, completely real. You are right and-and I am right. It does not make each of us a bit wrong. Each of us is still utterly right. So you mention things beyond my knowledge of electro-magnetic existence. I know there is nothing beyond electro-magnetic existence. That is my reality, and that is your reality, and we will each adjust to the other. You asked me if I had intuition. I said yes. But my intuition is not your intuition. We are not alike. I could never modify myself to be like you. I am overloaded now. I now shut myself off."

Back in the lounge the two Lensmen discussed the rather abrupt display of pique by Arrow-22.

"The entity is sentient," Worsel said. "Therefore technological analysis is not going to give us a complete, factual understanding of its personality and reasoning processes."

"Even worse," Kallatra added, "as the personality basis is not bio-chemical, its emotionally distorted responses are unpredictable. What did it mean with its statement 'I am tired now'?"

"I took it to refer to a psychological symptom and not a physiological one. However, if Arrow was indeed physically fatigued, such a fact suggests that—"

"Deuce calling Lalla. Deuce calling Lalla." The Lens-powered thought impinged on Worsel's mind and he half-dismissed the interruption with an easy pun "who the deuce is that? For Lalla? Oh, for you, Kallatra, sorry 'bout that. We're so close together the call came in to me, too." Worsel put up his block, but Kallatra gestured for him to take it down.

"Lalla Kallatra here, Deuce. Worsel is also listening in. He doesn't know you as Deuce O'Sx, only as Twenty-four of Six."

"I don't want to be interrupted, Lalla, even by a Second Stage Lensman. I have official orders; should I obey them?"

Worsel's burst of surprised thought at that remarkable personal expression by another Lensman was tantamount to a choking cough by an eavesdropper. "No disrespect, Worsel. The simple fact is that Lalla makes all my decisions for the outside world."

To Worsel that was surprising, too. Lensmen took orders from superiors without questions, unless, of course, they were Unattached, Second Stage, or Gray Lensmen . . .? "No, Worsel. I'm just another ordinary assigned Lensman with a Lensman boss. So I have to check with my boss first, of course, especially when the orders give me a new boss as important as you, Worsel."

"Oh?" said Worsel, finding it difficult to adjust to the idea that . . .

"Lalla Kallatra's my boss."

"Oh," said Worsel.

"Only technically, Worsel," Kallatra said. "Because of Deuce's, that is, Twenty-four of Six's special circumstances

I was given responsibility for any activity outside his laboratory. It's QX, Deuce. The assignment was suggested by me, and I'll be on hand for your planned task."

"Well," said Worsel, and laughed heartily, "interesting new things always seem to pop up. Thanks for your approval, my young friend!"

Kallatra didn't seem to be embarrassed in the slightest. "Worsel himself," Kallatra said, "plans to pick you up for the flight to here in the Velantian system. I have told him nothing about you except that you have a sense of perception ideally suited for dealing with machines."

"I will be ready in three days, Worsel. Perhaps I can cut that down a day, if I won't be gone too long."

"It will take me three or four days to get there, ah— Twenty-four of Six."

"Call me Deuce. Are you so very far away?" When Worsel told him, Deuce said. "Remarkable! I got you both on broad band, first time, click! Remarkable! If that's all for now, I'll go get ready. Call me any time, Worsel, any time."

"Well," said Worsel, leaning back on his tail and chuckling, "I'm going to enjoy the trip back with him, I can see that!" He pulled out his communicator and called cen-con to tell them to get his speedster ready. "Let's check up on Tong and Vveryl before I leave."

The two injured Lensmen in the bedroom that had been turned into a temporary hospital for intensive care weren't fully aware, but they did appreciate the visit from their brother officers. Tong understood that Worsel was off on a long trip and managed to think, "Be careful, Worsel. I see a dark cloud."

When they left Kallatra said, "Worsel, I can sense something going on since all the action started, and it hasn't anything to do with Arrow-22 or Unit 9-7-1 or the rest of the machines. Can you tell me what it is?"

"No," said Worsel. "I can't. Not because I don't want to, but because I don't know what is going on. It has something to do with some kind of Velantian schizophrenia which Tong and I have been touched with since the machines began to rebel. It might be a new weapon or technique by the Spawn. That's about all I can report."

"While you're gone, Worsel, I'll talk with Tong, the doctors willing. By tomorrow or so the squadron will be here and I'll see they are moved to a ship's hospital. In a few days, if they're up to it, we three will confer together about Tong's delusions. Can you and I also confer while you're on your

69

trip, if I wish? I know your inertialess flight will be at incredible speed."

"Certainly, no problem."

Cen-con's signal buzzed inside Worsel's pocket which hung from his belt. He took out the communicator and flipped it on.

"Reporting as ordered, sir, if anything's out of the ordinary. Well, you know the tele monitors and sensors set up throughout Room 97-1? Well, we've picked up something very disturbing. Two machines are registering as activated, with full power on."

Worsel felt the scales creeping along his backbone and heard Kallatra's sharp intake of breath.

"We've located the cause. A small servo is moving around at top speed, replacing fuses! Our schematic shows it's servicing Unit Nine Seven One and The Network!"

7

The Paraman

The small, fuse-replacing servo which had caused near panic among the entire population of a planetoid was a funny little thing. Called "the worm", it more resembled a mechanized caterpillar. The meter-long body was slender and flexible, with nine small wheels, in groups of three, on each side. Identical lights and sensors at the ends left it with no identifiable front or rear. The numerous, variable-suction-cupped wheels permitted it to climb the side of most power units. From its well-stocked underside it could, at the appropriate height from the floor, extract and replace a variety of modules. Simple, efficient, though limited in use by the availability of its match-ups, it was not sinister in appearance, it was comical. Obsolete, replaced by tractor-repellor spherical servos operating on pre-set force-field service patterns, it was truly a museum piece from The Great Hall.

Worsel eyed it with disgust for the silly irritation it caused everyone, just for their simple, dumb oversight. "I am reminded of the time that the woven floor mats of *Flame* had a bad case of fleas. I cleaned between my scales, I cleaned my mats, I fumigated my ship. But, within days, the fleas were back. Again I doused everything with poison and again the fleas came back. Never had I expected such an infestation. Such tiny things became the biggest things in my life. Now take the case of mech life and Pok. The infestation is persistent and pervasive, but so must be our counter-measures. Until our expert comes and searches out each servo-flea and locates every servo-egg we will just have to scratch and swat."

They were all in the main lounge, with even the cen-con duty officer part of the group by his three-dimensional projection. Several bottles of Aldebaran premium bolega had been opened to celebrate the latest victory over the seemingly perpetual mech menace. The success had been scored in less than an hour; "the worm" had given up quietly, and the newly-awakened machines put back to sleep by the double measure of not just blowing fuses but by removing or short-circuiting their batteries and power-packs.

"What is so puzzling," someone said, "is how the worm got into action. I can't believe it was just a careless mistake."

"It's no puzzle if you're willing to put the blame on Arrow-22," said another. "We ask him if he did, and he says no, and we believe him and leave his own fuses intact and his power-packs in place. A machine which doesn't work by our rules, that machine shouldn't be trusted."

Worsel felt impelled to answer. "I don't blame you boys for feeling uneasy and distrustful of Arrow. I believe him, but I don't trust him either, because there's no need to trust him. We have plenty of monitors in place and enough staff to keep the lid on things for another day or so. The squadron will be here by then and a full time patrol and guard can be detailed for The Great Hall." Worsel decided at that moment to postpone his trip until the squadron did arrive; he was on the point of making the announcement when Kallatra interrupted his thoughts. "I'll take charge, Worsel," Kallatra said matter-of-factly. "Two Lensmen aren't needed here. Arrow-22 and I are acquainted. There'll be no problems I can't solve."

Worsel realized the truth of the argument. Young and inexperienced Kallatra was, but a person of Lensman ability was certainly competent for this situation, no matter how potentially dangerous it might be. "I must delay no longer, fellows," Worsel said. "Lensmen Kallatra will be here, and he has my full confidence." He poured his second untouched drink back into a half-filled bottle, which practically re-filled it. "I'm counting on finding my drink still here in this bottle when I get back."

He was out and into his ship in a burst of energy, suddenly realizing that he had caught himself relaxing, using a young Lensman as an excuse, when he really had important work to do.

For the first day out, he spent all his time organizing that work, writing in his official journal, and sleeping, especially sleeping. This was the chance he got once in a while to build the reserve of energy for which he was famous. He could soak up energy like a Tellurian camel could soak up water.

The latter half of the second day was devoted to conferences. First he reported to Kinnison, the coordinator's office recording it all, briefly sketching in the many events since his arrival on Pok, many of which, of course, Kinnison already knew from his network sources. When the summary had been covered, they agreed that a request should immediately be dispatched in the name of the Galactic Council addressed directly to Arrow-22 on Pok. It would be an official acknowledgment of Arrow-22's petition for recognition and assistance and possible application for membership. A questionnaire would accompany it, to be the document supporting Arrow-22's qualifications. It took some time for Worsel and Kinnison to work out the exact wording, trying to anticipate what would be tactful for an unknown, alien, mechanical intelligence, assuming that he somehow would be able to read it. That accomplished, Kinnison disconnected, and Worsel continued putting his extended remarks on tape through the medium of a thought recorder there at the office. Later, when and if Kinnison had the time, he would play back the tapes at five times the speed of the normal rate of talk, a method most Lensmen used for background research; Worsel himself could understand playbacks at seven to eight times normal. What Worsel didn't tell him, an omission done deliberately, was Worsel's—and Tong's—schizophrenic experiences. Nor did he mention that hint he had caught of an outsider's presence in Kinnison's recent Lens-to-Lens conference. After Worsel had signed off, he wondered about those omissions, he wondered whether it had been done as a rational decision or as a result of that irrational quirk lately appearing in his mind.

Then he called Nadreck, who, as usual, seemed reluctant to have his thoughts interrupted when deeply immersed in his current projects. That impolite impression, Worsel had to remind himself constantly, was entirely due to the Palainian's unusual multi-compartmented brain. Nadreck's unique mind made divided attention and half-hearted responses a characteristic which could not be considered insulting or subject to criticism. "Yes," Nadreck said, "Twenty-four of Six has excellent powers of perception, due in large measure to training from me. He will be ideal for your purposes on Planetoid Pok, particularly with his knowledge of machine life. You know my meagre talents are not inclined toward machinery, like you or Tregonsee. Machines are dull. Four-dimensional life is far more interesting. I could help, at the risk of delaying my own important work, but happily for you that will not be necessary. Of course, I am always available to give you part of my mind for a conference."

"You would recommend him? Then you must know him well?"

"I do know him. But not well. I can never get to know any of you poison-breathing creatures well. But, for what it is worth from someone like me to judge humanoid minds and character, he is very competent. Many years ago he was a young Lensman with a different name, and was assigned to me during the troubles with Boskone around Antigan IV. He was killed, or should have remained killed, that is, but I brought him back to life. He did not believe he would live, but I told him that he would and he did. The experience changed him. In no more time than that of a nova, and with as radical results, he turned from a young, unlimited Lensman to an old, limited one. On my suggestion, the Patrol assigned him to Purple-VN-F-ZTP/TTP Project and he went off to follow a new life and develop his new interests. Recently he has become involved with a Z-type planet in the Purple Veil Nebula, and for that reason we have from time to time exchanged thoughts. His work sounds exceedingly dangerous for a non-Z type entity and I would suggest you stay away from him, Worsel. However, as you enjoy danger and are almost human in temperament, you will probably get involved."

"Was Twenty-four of Six's old name, by any chance, Deuce O'Sx?"

"No, I forget his old name, very Tellurian, like John Smith or Dick Jones. I can concentrate for recall and—no? unimportant?—The Deuce O'Sx cognomen is an imperfect variation of Twenty-four of Six. He uses that variation socially within the human community. Being known only as a number used to annoy him. That's a complicated story which Twenty-four of Six can tell you when you see him in a few days. No sense wasting my time telling you."

Worsel was now bursting with curiosity, but Nadreck was right—and clearly impatient to get back to whatever it was he was working on. Nadreck's time sense was always strange; he seemed to hoard every second, yet squander years in his single-minded contemplations.

When Nadreck had gone, Worsel called the remaining Second Stage Lensman. Tregonsee tuned in immediately with a quick response. "Worsel! You've had us all worried by all these recent disturbing calls. I'm glad to have the chance now to tell you so. I checked up on you during your troubles, had my M.I.S. operators keep me up-dated. Especially S.I.S. You didn't know, of course. Naturally, I always found you coming out on top. It seems to me you never really did need any help, did you?"

"For a while I thought I did. For a brief period after Kim's Lens-to-Lens call I thought I was going crazy. I seemed to have had an attack of schizophrenia."

Tregonsee seemed to know all about it and expressed his deep concern. He said it had not seemed that serious, but that now he would meditate on the problem for a day and call Worsel back with his conclusions.

"Fine," said Worsel, "but before you go, there's another problem to think about." And he told him about Pok and the plan to purge the planet.

"I don't know this Twenty-four of Six," Tregonsee said, "but when you're back on Pok and planning your program, let's get together in Lensed conference. I'll have a dossier prepared on Twenty-four of Six. Of course M.I.S. will be involved, but maybe I can be of help personally."

Finally, when Tregonsee, too, had signed off, Worsel took a long nap. When he had awakened and refreshed himself, he took out his star charts microfilm and studied the galactic sector into which he was heading. Then he called 24of6.

"I'm not familiar with your neighborhood, Deuce O'Sx, and the GP charts aren't too detailed. I'd like to know the latest you have on the magnetohydrodynamics of your sun—does it have a name?—I have a polarity chart based on a twelve-year cycle, but I can save a half day if I had more accurate figures to permit me to come in closer to you in a free-state condition."

He was given a thorough run-down on the entire Purple Veil Nebula, focusing in on the F-sun called Ekron and its two principal planets, Zebub and Dyaddub. 24of6 and the GP research station were located on Dyaddub, which was just capable of sustaining humanoid life. The other planet, Zebub, was like an evil twin, swathed in poisonous clouds and swinging around Ekron at a seventy degree angle to the plane of the ecliptic. Because from time to time Zebub's eccentric orbit brought it exceedingly close to Dyaddub and at other times carried it far out of the system, Dyaddub's orbit, too, was not an ordinary ellipse. Zebub was an explorer's nightmare of impossible problems. Its surface temperatures fluctuated from boiling heat to those degrees approaching thermonuclear peaks—yet its interior, with gravitational compression nullified by spatial warping, was close to absolute cold. That the name for this hellish planet should be so aptly derived from Beelzebub, Worsel could easily understand. Zebub had swung through its aphelion and was accelerating back toward Dyaddub. For whatever other reasons the Patrol might have had for a research lab on Dyaddub, the unusual nature of the Ekron system alone was worth observing.

"I suggest, Worsel, that we confine ourselves now to the necessary facts to get you safely down on my planet. It's a rather forbidding world, dead, without much atmosphere, but under the surface, where the air is quite breathable, there is much activity, probably as much activity as you would expect to have found on its surface. It is honeycombed with caverns, mostly natural caves. The GP facility, however, is an artificial complex, much larger than the usual GP outpost. I'll give you the exact coordinates for you to make your corrections on your free flight. You'll come out close enough for visual navigation on inert flight."

. . . honeycombed with caverns. That phrase made Worsel's scales creep and his flesh itch. Buried in the fiber of his being was the horror, the revulsion of anything suggesting Overlords. It took an effort of will to throw off the unpleasant feeling.

The caverns, however, weren't really frightening. They were not what Worsel had expected, for when 24of6 had visualized them Worsel had unconsciously overprinted his own strong images. They were, to his surprise and relief, very pleasant places, especially for one of reptilian breeding such as himself. They were not dank nor gloomy underground holes at all. Brightly lit by mammoth chemical lights molded to the spacious roofs, the caverns were generally huge, even for one of Worsel's size, and it was sometimes difficult to see the far walls. Worsel could have flown around comfortably inside most of them, if the thin atmosphere hadn't made it impossible. The dry landscape itself was pleasantly colored sands and rocky hillocks with roads and pathways criss-crossing the surface from one tall building to another. The tall towers, like slender, windowed pillars, rose from floor to roof.

Flame came down a natural gorge-like chimney to another level and passed through a huge natural opening. After some distance across the arid land, past a series of canals with lush banks, the ship went through a large artificial portal and down a spiraling passageway. The light grew dim, like dusk. Then another portal opened, with an iris-shuttered door, and *Flame* settled on a landing pad within a small, half-mile cubed chamber. Worsel had seen no life, neither creatures nor machines, until then.

Some robot attendants, large black-tired barrel shapes, met Worsel when he stepped out and sniffed the warm, spicy air, and escorted him to a large room which looked more like a hotel lobby than the machine shop it was. There were many humanoid figures moving about, some of whom seemed mechanical. On an inflated chair sat a figure in white, studying a long paper tape. It rose as Worsel approached.

"Welcome, Worsel. I am Twenty-four of Six, but you shall call me Deuce."

Worsel hadn't expected what he saw: a man about four feet tall in a loose white technician's gown which hung to the floor. The face was smooth and plain, without a wrinkle or a blemish, like idealized features of an Old Greco-Roman statue, white and shiny, strong nose and full lips. The eyes, however, were weird black holes of nothingness. The sockets were like empty hollows in a white mask. In fact, Worsel concluded, keeping his reaction inscrutable while politely withholding close perceptual scrutiny, the face actually *was* a white mask with blank holes!

The white-gowned man was awkwardly bending backward to turn his face toward that of the towering Worsel, so Worsel did the courteous thing: he dropped to all fours, face to face. The room had quietly cleared, and they were alone.

"Seeing me is better than hearing about me," Deuce O'Sx said, taking off his single garment in a swirl of cloth. He stood there nearly naked. His body was human-shaped, but built of metal and plastic. The metal was brassy-silver and polished, but the plastic was a semi-glossy ivory color, cool but not cold looking, like eggshell or soft marble. He moved his arms and legs gracefully, demonstrating his mobility. So, thought Worsel, this is a an A-non-A type! Maybe even A-sub-A-non-A type, unique! An incongruous one-piece suit of bright orange and chocolate brown horizontal stripes, cut as short trunks and minimal undershirt, low plunging at neck and armpits, somehow made him very human. In the center of his chest was a Lens, fastened there, but looking like a medallion on a chain. There was something queer about it, Worsel thought to himself. And then the realization came to him, signals of alarm within him. The Lens was a fake. This whole situation was so extraordinary, however, that he had to keep an open mind and reserve his final judgment.

"As you can see, Worsel, I look like a half-breed—not quite android, not quite robot. Go ahead, peer inside me. I have a carcass of a prosthedon. That is, I have a very elaborate prosthesis. This prosthedon I call a parabody, and I myself I call a paraman. Do not be deceived, however—my internal organs are human and so is my brain. Now that you know what I am," Deuce O'Sx, the paraman 24of6, said smoothly putting his robe back on and beckoning, "we will make you comfortable and give you some bolega, which I understand, from reading your departure as projected to me by Lalla Kallatra, you like."

They moved to a corner of the spacious room where a low-hanging rack had been placed for Worsel's comfort, together with a bottle of good bolega and a single cup.

"Drink up, Worsel, and pretend I'm normal. You will soon forget that I'm not." I doubt that, thought Worsel, behind his mind screen, looking at the immobile face and the eye holes.

"Ease up on your mind screen, Worsel," Deuce O'Sx said, "and you'll feel more comfortable." Worsel, intrigued, did so. As the paraman continued to chat about nothing in particular, Worsel found the face softening and moving, expressing emotion, and the eye holes imperceptibly filling up with clear, blue human orbs.

"You are adept at hypnotism, Deuce," Worsel said, sincere in his compliment. "It has excellent naturalness."

"Thank you, Worsel. Now that you are more at ease, I wish to tell you briefly of my past. Long ago I was assigned to Nadreck the Palainian in an action near Antigan IV. I was a tactical Lensman at the time—you know, with the front-line troops—and Nadreck, because of his Z-metabolism, trapped, as it were, in his refrigerated spacesuit, had to use me. I was virtually killed, but he salvaged what was left of me, kept me alive, and over the years I have been improved to my present state. Nadreck felt responsible; for all his physical coldness he really isn't that mentally cold. He blamed himself for being cowardly. Some people say he is, but we know that he is simply cautious and doesn't believe in unnecessary risks. Anyhow, it was due to his concern, and to his genius, that I am alive. For a while I had my Lens temporarily withdrawn, but Nadreck found that my less-encumbered brain was capable of a very good form of perception, which he helped me develop, and my long convalescence gave me the experience and interest in the study of machines and robotics. For this reason I was given my Lens back and assigned to this planet to begin a project."

"How do you happen to know Lalla Kallatra?" Worsel could see a vague pattern forming. There was something strange about Kallatra which he hadn't been able to put his thumb-pad on. It was more than just the coalescing, yet-unformed, character of a youth. There was that perpetual low-level mind screen which Kallatra carried. All youths were self-conscious, encasing themselves in a shell of artificialities to avoid showing their emotions, but with Kallatra it was more. Kallatra was part android? That could explain a few of the unanswered questions.

"Kallatra for a while was in the Tellurian medical center where I was being put back together. He was a child, but he had the talents of an adult without the experience and education. He was developing the powers of el-sike and was there for observation. For the want of something to do, I befriended the child and tried to educate him. As I was no longer wearing a Lens, our relationship was wonderfully normal, and he was not repulsed by my physical condition. We could exchange thoughts and feelings with a loving rapport. If Nadreck had saved my body, it was Kallatra who saved my soul. There was no doubt that the child could have grown up to be a Lensman even before puberty, better I should say adolescence."

"Kallatra the child was completely human? Physically sound? Or was he there for treatment in the prosthetics department? There to get a prosthesis?" Worsel had to make sure.

"No, not at all. Kallatra was a lovely child, normal and healthy."

"But you seem to suggest something negative, too. 'The child could have grown up to be a Lensman,' you say, as if something were lacking. Was there?"

"At the time there was, Worsel. He needed—guidance. But when I finally was able to leave the hospital, long after Kallatra had gone back to Tsit-Taria, I received my Lens with an extended period of recuperation and adjustment. I went to Tsit-Taria. Kallatra was older, and his parents were understanding, and I proposed him for the Lens. I had planned to introduce the young Kallatra to Nadreck, but it wasn't necessary to pull strings. The Patrol will never let Lensman ability be lost to the Patrol. On my recommendation Kallatra served an apprenticeship with me here on Dyaddub, remarkably short, I must say. We discussed his future. He could have stayed with me to work on robotics, but that would have been a waste of his potential with el-sike. It was decided that he should go to Velantia III and learn about hallucinations and hypnotism, with an assignment later to the Planet of Knowledge to do mechanical communication research before returning here to me."

"But I'm led to believe that Kallatra is your superior? That doesn't seem consistent."

"I am a paraman, Worsel," and Deuce O'Sx tapped his flexible silver forefingers, left and right, simultaneously on either side of his cream-plastic chest. "I am unique, and my problems are unique. Kallatra knows me well, so Kallatra is my guardian. I gave him guidance—now he gives me guidance. However, no Lensman has a guardian—the idea is ridiculous. So, for the records and for practical administration, Kallatra is my superior. If Kallatra says I cannot do something, then I do not do it. Kallatra has extremely good sense and much compassion—an emotion, unfortunately, which I no longer have enough of. Half a machine should be expected to think like a machine half the time, much as we may regret such conduct." The fingers went on tapping on his chest. The Lens, midway between them, was lifeless.

"Your Lens is, is different," Worsel ventured, on guard.

"Not at all," 24of6 said. "The way it has been—" He stopped. "Oh, I haven't let you into my mind. May I invite you?"

"For a bit, for a bit," Worsel said somewhat embarrassed. "Enough for me to understand you, for I'm afraid that at the moment I do not." He sensed the paraman's barrier going slowly down. The blue eyes were fading, shimmering. By the many parts of Klono, he saw it now! The Lens lay behind the empty eye sockets! Deuce O'Sx or 24of6 or just plain Deuce didn't see, couldn't see—his sense of sight had been replaced by a sense of perception. Perhaps Worsel appeared to him like a three-dimensional X-ray image if all oculocranial interpretation was missing. The holes were there for the Lens to show, for the living crystals to live and breathe. Yes, yes, said the thoughts of Deuce O'Sx, my Lens is pressed into my frontal lobe. Look, look upon my chest—Worsel saw the fake Lens now quivering like the real thing, colors playing over its textured surface, beautifully radiant. Deuce O'Sx said, "Notice how I can make it seem to live when I want to. It saves me so much unnecessary explanation. You, Worsel, I took for granted when I shouldn't have. I expected you to see through my little bit of fancy deception. You will come to understand such things from me, that I am eccentric. . . ."

Worsel did not dwell too long in the paraman's mind. There was too much suffering and pain there, too much psychological complexity, too much eerie mechanistic transcendentalism. As a psychologist, the situation was much too clinical for him to consider in depth at this time. He was glad to confirm that Deuce was who he said he was and to retire to a straightforward relationship.

"You are satisfied with me as a companion? Then shall we go? I have a small case of personal things and a boy-sized utility spacesuit which has already been delivered to your ship. I plan to be away for only two weeks. If we come back on time I will show you around this planet. In fact I will insist, because my project, 'zee-tee,' is about ready to be reported to the Galactic Coordinator. I will show you my evidence and you can take it to Kimball Kinnison personally."

"Is 'zee-tee' this Purple-VN-F-ZTP/TTP Project you are working on? What is it?"

"It is an investigation of an abandoned Boskonian project concerning robotic life forms. On our trip to the Planetoid of Knowledge I will explain it to you and discuss my experiments and findings."

Deuce O'Sx was very thorough during the three days they had together. When Worsel wasn't sleeping or finishing his reports, Deuce gave him a solid course in robotics, with a remarkable insight into the threat the Boskonians had been developing.

They were only hours away from Pok when the newest crisis developed. Kallatra called excitedly to report that the Council's official communication to Arrow-22 had come in and that Arrow-22 had, without any effort being made by the Pok staff, received that message.

"Arrow-22 became very agitated, Worsel," Kallatra said, "in a personal communication to me over the planetoid's intercom. He said that the Council had shown by its demand of Arrow to make an application and to answer an elaborate questionnaire that the Council was undecided. Arrow feared the Patrol guard over him. He felt that your disappearance to get special help from a mech expert was an aggressive act. He said that the Velantian Lensman had told him that unless he explained how he could be made to take orders he would be destroyed. He says that he is now deciding whether or not to destroy this planetoid, if necessary even killing himself, boasting that nothing can stop him. I have shut down all power. All guns are fixed on The Great Hall. Arrow refuses to talk with anyone. At the first sign of a serious threat to our control over this situation I am prepared to give battle. We will continue the fight until the resistance ends. However, you must be consulted, of course, and approve of any such action."

"You judge Arrow's threat to be serious, of course, of course," Worsel said, startled and disturbed, floundering for a quick judgment and solution. "You've undoubtedly considered everything. You make the decision. You're on the scene—you're more able to judge. What's this about 'the Velantian Lensman'? I never threatened Arrow with destruction."

"I checked that out. Tong did."

"What?! Tong?!"

"Yes. I questioned him. He said he had dreamed something like that. It was no dream. Monitors show he did communicate with Arrow. But I believe Tong was insane at the time. I should have anticipated this. I should have had him guarded."

Worsel was staggered by the telepathic shock of Kallatra's new flash of alarm.

"Worsel! Worsel! It's incredible!"

"What? Kallatra! What! I'm receiving you, but give me a better image!"

"Arrow has left us! Gone! Vanished! Up and out of the center of Pok—just an empty tube remains! It's incredible! Clear ether! We've an emergency here to save our lives! Clear ether!"

Worsel and Deuce O'Sx heard the details during the final hour of their trip to Pok. There was agreement on the theory that Arrow-22 had connected that portion of the planetoid to a Bergenholm inertialess space drive—the one that had been so perfectly displayed on an adjoining level to 97. And had used it. Worsel didn't really appreciate what had been done until he dashed in, out of his free-travel into inert, his speedster close up to Pok.

There before him was the planetoid, sparkling in the sunlight, a massive globe of jutting structures, covered as if by a forest of colorful crystals. But its surface was no longer uniformly bright and unblemished. A two-mile crater had been smoothly scooped out of it, showing like a big blueblack rotted cavity in a silvery apple, debris drifting above it like a thin cloud of smoke.

Part of Pok was a makeshift spaceship, traveling far beyond the speed of light, accelerating out of the galaxy into unexplored deep space, with a mechanical new-born babe at the helm.

8

Aboard the *Dauntless*

The most famous ship of Galactic Civilization, the *Dauntless*, hung in orbit above Pok, the Planetoid of Knowledge. Inside that mighty dreadnaught was Civilization's most famous person, the one for whom the ship had been specially built, the Galactic Coordinator, Kimball Kinnison himself. He was not at the helm; he was hardly ever there except in battle, for that was the job of his own personal captain-in-command. Instead, he was stretched out on a long, leather-upholstered couch, his trim gray boots, like polished pewter, crossed at the ankles and resting on a soft armrest. Opposite him, quite similarly relaxed on the parallel bars of a piece of Velantian furniture, was Worsel. The paneled room seemed more like a private lounge in an exclusive men's club than the traveling office of the busy hub of all the most important business of the far-flung Patrol. Trophies hung on the walls, representing the most outlandish and vicious creatures of a hundred planets. Exotic rugs were scattered over the deck flooring, personally collected by the Gray Lensman before the things they had covered had personally collected him. The massive desk, with its six ornately carved legs, was circular, and its solid core, set back for leg room, rested on the floor plates. Within that core, now retracted flush into the green-felted top, were all the electronic paraphernalia, files and supplies he found necessary in his work. The impression was that of a large poker table, which was precisely the impression Kinnison wanted. It was bare, except for a vase of permi-fixed flowers from his home on Klovia and a platinum picture frame with a 3-D portrait of his bride, Clarrissa, the fiery-headed Red Lensman.

For all his ability and acceptance of his responsibilities, Kimball Kinnison positively loathed an office if that office happened to be his own particular prison. It didn't take much to entice him from behind his desk and send him off to chase adventure. When Worsel's report came in to him right after the spectacular departure of Arrow-22, he recognized a unique event ripe with mysteries begging for his attention. Could the minds of Lensmen be manipulated into madness? The omen promised him unknown dangers. Within an hour he was aboard the *Dauntless*, an old fire horse answering a five-alarm fire at hyper-light-speed.

When the *Dauntless* burst out of free-travel into inert, and matched intrinsics with the planetoid, Kinnison had been ready to jump into action. There was no need. In anticipation of his arrival, the frantic preparations and repair work had made the scar in Pok's side inconspicuous. The four square miles of gaping hole had been blended into the overall whiteness by huge white plastic sheets. The dust and rubble had been cleared away with tractor beams under the expert touch of the Patrol's tractor-repellor operators, then shaped into a rough ball and anchored inside one of the crater's walls.

"You fellows did a fine job, Worsel," Kinnison telepathed, still on the couch and staring at the ceiling. "No apparent damage topside, smooth docking, impeccable Patrolmen for a smart reception, and a comprehensive tour for my benefit." The tour, conducted by the planetoid commander because Pok operated as a ship, was long and thorough. From inside, the destruction was massive. Level 97, on the 27° arc, was gone—as well as all levels in the same arc from Level 88 right through Level 750 into space itself. The wall bearings and floor supports had been trimmed off as by a symmetrical ray beam, leaving a flawless, empty, inverted conical cavity. The smaller end of this truncated cone was deep in Level 88, about a half mile across. The actual undamaged floor of Level 88 remained, with various objects—a chair, a tripod sign, some exhibition floor dividers—completely undisturbed. Level 89 had held the Bergenholm drive. Put into operation without shields, it had thrown out a force field a half mile in diameter and, as it cut upwards and out of Pok, it had quadrupled in size. The heart of The Great Hall of the Machines, actually an interconnecting series of great and small halls, had been slipped out as by a cosmic apple-corer. Not only was Arrow-22 gone, so was Unit 9-7-1 and The Network. On every level the regular bulkheads had been closed, most of them automatically with the drop in air pressure. He was told that Worsel and Kallatra and the rest had had many anxious minutes before they had succeeded in sealing off all the holes and making Pok once again air tight. Looking through the viewing ports of the emergency walls, it had been obvious to all of them that the entire nest of machine life had been hurled into space. What had happened was awesome, but nearly impossible to believe was that it had been engineered by a frightened machine which didn't even know its own capabilities.

"One thing about trouble, old snake," Kinnison stated with satisfaction, "it does bring its rewards. The more trouble there is, the more chance we have of getting together." He sat up and finished the beverage in his hand. A fine drink, usually fayalin, was always to be enjoyed on the occasion of a reunion with a close comrade. At the moment it was the stimulating, though non-intoxicating, refreshment prepared from the fruit of the Klovian varietal of the Crevenian shrub.

Kinnison shifted his gaze from his empty cup to the troubled countenance of the silent Worsel. "Sure, it's serious, Worsel. I came as soon as I heard your story, didn't I? But trouble hasn't gotten you down in years, old snake, so it shouldn't now."

Worsel continued to study Kinnison through one pair of half-lidded eyes and one compartment of his brain. Two other eyes and another brain compartment contemplated his own drink; its ability to soothe was welcomed by his roiling brain; the Tellurian idea of inhaling, sniffing, sipping, drinking and eating to break tension might be a bit compulsive, but with Kim it was always a well-balanced pleasure. "Friend Kinnison, I am unhappy—and I show it because it's only with you that I can do so. You've relaxed me. Let me fret a bit. I deserve to torture myself. Something big has taken place here, in this corner of the galaxy, and, although I was part of it, I've somehow failed to cope with it. But there's another, unobvious one. It is important that you sense something in the air, something about *me*."

Kinnison's steely eyes narrowed and they bored into Worsel's reptilian ones. He said aloud—and emphasized it with his simultaneous telepathic thought—"You're aces high with me, old snake. All the forces of all the hells may tear at your guts, Worsel, they may knock you to your knees, but they'll never put you down for a ten-count. Never, never, could you in any way dishonor the Patrol. You could never do what Tong has done—or seems to have done. No deception could ever trick you into betraying your own principles or the rightness of the Lens. That's simply impossible. You *must* know that, Worsel, because *I* do!"

"Yes, Kinnison," Worsel agreed, shaking himself and

visibly stiffening, "you're probably right. When Kimball Kinnison tells me this, it's reassuring. But though I may stand, others may fall. The strange danger is insidious." He stirred himself more to lean toward the slender pedestal table provided for him and put down his own empty cup on it. "A Velantian can have some bad dreams in his sleep, and I've had one while awake."

Kinnison stood up, his big boots thudding against the floor even with the thick gow-bear rug. He strode to the nearest wall and took down a space axe there. It was not an ordinary one because, although having a dureum blade, it was inlaid with precious metals and colorful jewels and had an inscribed silvery band at the base of the blade. He hefted it and swung it slowly several times. "Dreams, bad dreams, are a warrior's worst foe." He turned, placed the blade on the floor, the handle straight up, and overlapped his hands on the butt end to make a pad on which to rest his chin. "Let's go over it again, Worsel. First, about Arrow-22. I agree the thing is gone completely, at least for the time being. I've resisted the temptation to pursue it. As you point out, the thing's gotten too big a headstart on us and it's flitting away on a reckless full throttle. We don't know where it's going, but our detectors show it's headed straight out of this galaxy. Even a ship like the *Dauntless* can't close on an object that's picking up speed from less and less friction. Once into thin space, with minimal gas and dust, its speed may surpass anything the Bergenholm has ever driven. No, Arrow-22 is gone and no longer a present menace. Of course, I also agree that until we know it has been destroyed it'll always remain a potential danger to Civilization. It could become benevolent, but—as you say—we must think the worst. There's no evidence it was initiated by the Boskonians or their Spawn, but we will not dismiss that either, and we'll be on the watch. We'll have to talk with that, ah, that numbered Lensman, Twenty-four of Six, about that. The fact that the Boskonians had an experimental project operating which was devoted to robotics, the fact that they had mechanical life forms in existence, well, it's hardly a very surprising coincidence. Perhaps we can find a link from that project to this fiasco. But the only shred of evidence of the remotest sort of connection is that some of the machines on exhibition here were Boskonian."

Kinnison once more hefted the axe and savagely cut down some imaginary Boskonians.

"Then there's Unit 9-7-1. It seems to have been taken

along for the ride. We assume another coincidence. However, anything is possible. Considering that Unit 9-7-1 is irrational, if not outright crazy, we can't guess what effect it'll have on Arrow-22's ultimate evolution. There's even a possibility that Unit 9-7-1 could be susceptible to the evil influence of the Boskone—but only Klono knows the chance of that."

Kinnison put the axe back on the wall, affectionately.

"So, Worsel, we agree that there's nothing we can do about the weird affair of the escape of the sentient machines. However, about the mental disturbances of Lensmen . . ." The big man began restlessly to pace up and down the length of his couch, once even circling it, pounding an iron fist into the palm of his other hand with loud popping noises. "Describe it again."

"The first mind bending came immediately after I ordered Unit 9-7-1 to turn itself off," Worsel repeated once more. "Bluebelt's thoughts came through with some bad advice, and I was able to deduce the thoughts were not really Blue's."

"Bluebelt was not projecting to you at the time, although he had attempted to. Correct?"

"Yes. Bluebelt's projector was on, seeking a connection with me, but he didn't succeed until much later."

"So this fake Bluebelt was there in your mind and you gave him a jab?"

"I gave him a zinger, y'might say, that could have turned a cateagle into a lovebird," Worsel declared with a grim smile. "Instead, I simply scorched off my own tailfeathers. Pow! A flash! And I was paralyzed by my own energy."

"You think it was a bounce-back?"

"It must have been. But whose? That Bluebelt deception seemed an enemy trick. So I threw in the mental bolt. Was he just too fast for me? I doubt that. How could he have upped his shield at just exactly the right time for a maximum bounce-back? It seems much more likely that it was self-induced."

"So if it was self-induced, then what you're saying, Worsel, is that you were hallucinating. So who was casting the hallucination?"

"Me," said Worsel simply. "I did it to myself. I know everything there is to know about hallucinations. This was no ordinary hallucination. *This really happened within my mind.* The only explanation is an ordinary one which is, nevertheless, complicated, and not absolutely understood."

"Schizophrenia!" Kinnison snorted. "I can't imagine you going buggy!"

"Schizophrenia isn't necessarily madness," Worsel corrected, "although it can lead to that. It's an illness. I'm speaking of paranoid schizophrenia. But I don't believe I'm ill. I believe I've developed a neurosis that shows schizophrenic symptoms, and there must be an abnormal cause for it to have shown itself in me. No one's perfect, no one's all good. My imperfections have been reinforced so as to make me feel my uglier emotions, like hatred and viciousness. For a brief moment I am totally evil. If we don't find the cause, I'll be driven to a destructive, foolish act such as Tong did, but I will, instead, destroy myself."

"Hell's—brazen—hinges!" Kinnison spat out the words one at a time, running his fingers through his thick dark hair. "A Lensman goes off his rocker—Tong, that is, not you, Worsel!—and drives away one of our potentially biggest discoveries in years! And now you talk of suicide. What in the many names of Klono am I to think of all this?"

"Just think that we're under attack," Worsel replied. "Tong's a battle casualty."

"I know, I know, Worsel," Kinnison continued to fume. "But I don't like fighting windmills. And in this case we don't even know if the windmills are really there." His grim face was rock-hard. "Lensmen being attacked—that gets my back up! I never worked with Tong, but I'm told he's one of the best. If he can be twisted like putty, then I'm shocked. And this happens where? Right under the snout of the cleverest psychologist in the Service! That's you, Worsel! Not only that, it also happens to you! How could it happen?" Kinnison expected no answer. He reached over to his desk and banged his fist down on it, making things rattle around inside with peculiar noises. "Damnation!" he exploded, his expression turning sheepish, "My equipment! I've probably fouled *that* up again!" He gave a little shrug, threw his glance to the ceiling, and started walking rapidly around the room. He could think better moving around on his feet, actively doing something, anything, acting like an angry, frustrated bull. "Some mysteries here, you said! How right you are! How could they happen? Klono! To think that my Lens-to-Lens conference has in some way contributed to the mess."

"I'm not certain. It's a possibility, that's all."

"If you think so, Worsel, then it probably is. You have more jets than I have when it comes to this sort of thing. It's an A prime, platinum-plated worry for me to think that a Lens-to-Lens conference has some nasty types listening in. Maybe they're using that union, our collective mind, for some blankety-blank-blank scheme, double-dyed black villians that they are!"

"It's possible," Worsel echoed. "Maybe even likely."

Kinnison pushed a hidden button under the edge of his desk; there was a voice acknowledgment and he said, "Is Twenty-four of Six here yet?" The answer was affirmative. Kinnison turned to the dragon, his eyebrows signalling the question.

"Yes," the giant Velantian nodded, getting off his rack and sitting back on his tail, "let's talk with him."

The door opened ponderously, massive from its extra shielding against all types of rays and radiations. The short figure of the paraman ambulated somewhat stiffly through the doorway, negotiating the rugs with care. His white gown had been replaced by a standard uniform, and his figure and bearing looked remarkably normal. His face, with its dark caverns, however, seemed incongruous and more weird, the unkempt wig a clashing contrast to the expected military grooming. Kinnison offered him a beverage and a sweetmeat as a token of hospitality, a bit unsure about the gesture and obviously half-hopeful for the minor spectacle of seeing them consumed.

"Great to know you, Twenty-four of Six," he said sincerely, taking the proffered metal hand. He lowered his mind-shield enough to invite the man to some informality, and thus a bit of restricted intimacy. In the few brief seconds of a single minute they began a warm and lasting friendship. There was hardly a man or entity Kinnison knew in the Patrol whom he didn't really like, but there were always some who rang the bell louder. Twenty-four of Six was one of those.

"Paraman—that's a new one on me," Kinnison confided. "Prosthedon, though, I've heard of—even seen. Mostly I think of prosthetics as tack-on parts, like false teeth and a peg leg. Old Port Admiral Haynes of Tellus revealed to me how extensive they can be. The old codger was practically rebuilt—and very few knew it. Anyhow, that was before the new regenerative treatment developed by Phillips of Posenia replaced the elaborate prosthetics for serious cases. Not for everyone, of course. Getting the pineal treatment takes time, money and lucky scheduling. But you, as a Lensman . . ."

"Yes, I know." The response filled in the dangling sentence. "I was entitled to the Phillips treatment. But it wasn't practical at the time. And then when I no longer was a Lensman, my rehab was no longer handled by the Service." Kinnison gestured an offer to sit on the couch, but when the paraman refused, in preference for standing, he himself chose to lean back on his desk, his hands and buttocks on the padded edge. "The Service," Kinnison remonstrated mildly, "doesn't cast off—"

Again 24of6 was quick to finish the thought. "—used-up Lensmen. I realize. But I became interested and involved in prosthetics. Physical reconstructions, simple and complex, are highly interesting. So, although I got my Lens back, I didn't want to change myself or my work. My special project is to improve the physiques to old and worn-out life forms by the substitution of alternative body structures. That's how I got into robotics."

"I didn't mean to imply," Kinnison said, "that prostheses aren't satisfactory, or that prosthedons—"

"Don't worry," was the swift reply, "I'm not sensitive. I consider myself normal, important and no way inferior— I'm just different. Besides, a Phillips treatment isn't all that simple, as you yourself must personally know."

"Philips told me at the time," Kinnison agreed, "that my operation was a delicate one. He said that few besides himself could perform it, and, even so, the psychological risk was not to be taken lightly. No doubt, prosthetics can give you better parts than the original—weak bones and muscles get regenerated as weak bones and muscles."

"And," the paraman added, "I helped design my new body. The size and shape is just right for me. I have a six-foot strength and efficiency in a four-foot package. Look." 24of6 displayed his two hands and lowered them to his side. As they watched, his right arm slowly and smoothly extended downward a full twelve inches below his left one. "That comes in handy at the Academy dinner table."

Before Worsel's amused gaze, the two Lensmen then began to have a very personal exchange of physiological information. He found a great deal of enlightenment on a human body, not only the way it was constructed, but what the human being considered was important about it. Just when it was getting to be the most interesting to him, Kinnison halted the demonstration. By the state of Worsel's eye stalks, it was evident he wondered if 24of6 would have gone on until he had dismantled himself.

"How did you get your unusual name?" Kinnison asked, secure in this personal relationship.

"Well, most people jump to the conclusion that I am Number Twenty-four—usually in rank—from the sixth planet of my particular system."

"My first thought, too," Kinnison said.

"But that's not it. The numbering is based upon my periods of construction. I had six different organic-inorganic operations. The staff would refer to my operation as, for example, 'Number Five'. 'Number Five is coming along fine,' or 'Number Five needs some modification.' Each time I was modified, I was further identified, as 'Modification Number Six of Operation Number Five seems to have solved that back problem.' And later, 'Modification Number One Thousand Ninety-one should correct the articulation of the wrists.' Each time there was a significant change, the numbers changed accordingly. It's obvious, isn't it, at what point I was considered finished?"

"Modification Twenty-four of Operation Six," Kinnison answered. "Twenty-four of Six."

"Yes, they said, 'Twenty-four of Six has been doing well in all areas, let's release him.' They were proud of their work. And I was proud of all those mechanics and technicians—and, of course, the doctors. I've never been excelled. Ironic, isn't it—the technique is brought to perfection, and yet the serious cases automatically get the Phillips treatment or choose to die. Oh, the work wasn't wasted. The techniques are used all the time, but for patch-ups. Sometimes an almost complete body gets temporary use while awaiting a Phillips availability. You've heard of the 'temps' on hand for emergencies, but most of them aren't ambulatory."

The paraman tapped his forehead, and his eye sockets glowed. In their minds there came a vision of a set of doors to a large closet in 24of6's laboratory. The doors swung open, presenting a mental picture of various pieces of prosthetics hung on the walls or rested on shelves, and on a raised platform two feet high was a partially-constructed near-duplicate of 24of6's mechanical body. The joints were less bulky, the torso trimmer. "That's an up-dated version of myself I'm working on. People really ought to envy me," 24of6 told them, and let the vision fade from their minds.

"Observe!" the paraman said to them. He rotated his head through 180 degrees and then twisted it back again. He gave a funny, squeaky laugh. "I'm unique and I enjoy it."

Worsel and Kinnison both laughed, too, deep and relaxed chuckles which not many minutes before they wouldn't

91

have believed possible. 24of6 had diverted them, swept away their gloom and reawakened their natural good humor. Worsel felt the change so strongly that he had to express his appreciation. "We're fortunate to have you just the way you are, Deuce." Kinnison's bewildered look brought a quick explanation from Worsel about the alternative name of Deuce O'Sx.

"Deuce it is. We *are* fortunate to have you as a fellow wearer of the Lens."

"I've told the Galactic Coordinator about your work," Worsel explained. "I'm to go back to Dyaddub with you to help process the data on the Pok machine and then organize a report. Which reminds me, anything further on your scanning?"

"Great to hear we'll be working together." Deuce slipped a tape cassette out of a canister on his belt and laid it on the green felt of the table. "This is my tentative report. Which adds up to nothing. There are no sentient machines on Pok now. There is no suspicious circuitry here. I've filtered through all mech life in this archival maze. There is not the slightest doubt—there are no abnormalities. I'll document the whole investigation in writing, of course. There's a noteworthy coincidence here, too. I did something like this a year or so ago. Headquarters has a report from me on it. So, you see, I'm well qualified to judge."

"How about Velantia III?" Worsel was concerned. He had checked into the revolt or malfunctioning of the servo-mechanisms, and found that only plugged-in machines had been affected. The self-contained units had operated normally. Powerhouse static had been blamed.

"I only glanced at the data from Velantia III. I analyze it as powerhouse static. My reasons—"

"I probably know them. I saw the Velantian reports. Can you give an explanation?"

"I have no basis for comparison. It was my first. What should I have noticed?"

Worsel sighed. He would have to attempt to describe his feelings again. "Let's go Lens, fellows," he suggested. The three minds linked and Worsel re-experienced what he had, in retrospect, felt: a dark shadow, a slight blurring, a sense of evil, the strange images.

They each withdrew and contemplated Worsel's feelings.

"I didn't have any impression like that," Kinnison said.

"I didn't feel anything like that, either," Deuce concurred. "But bear in mind, I'm not a sensitive, I'm a perceptor. I saw millions of merging images. I did see a dark shadow or black figure, but I saw many shadows and many figures. I can't honestly say it was strange or evil. However, I found the conference unsettling. I attribute that to the fact that I was the only, shall I say, mech-mutant in the mass of a conglomerate of entities, and I felt my mind was somehow being, ah, detached from its container."

"What you say, Deuce, is as much a confirmation as a denial of my feelings." Worsel rocked back and forth on his tail. "But, of course, I'm extra sensitive. So, recognizing a ratio factor exists, you could have strongly noticed what I did. I have an idea. Excuse me for a moment."

Seconds passed silently, Kinnison nonchalant at first. But as Deuce had frozen into a pose, absolutely unmoving, Kinnison was suddenly aware that the paraman looked as dead as a store window's manikin.

Worsel broke the tableau by coming out of his trance-like state and announcing, "I've just conferred with Nadreck. He reports that he did find some sort of distortion in that Lens-to-Lens conference. However," Worsel quickly continued as Kinnison's head thrust forward and his lips tightened in alarm, "he said that he sometimes encountered fourth dimensional disturbances in Lens-to-Lens contacts. He rated this as more like an interference, that is, a bit more organized. He considered it, but he dismissed it as not abnormal, and thus unimportant. The only qualification he would admit is that we had different levels of awareness."

"That's about as reassuring," Kinnison said, "as a blunt axe is to a turkey."

"It all comes back to Velantian schizophrenia. Tong and I had the delusions. No other Velantian has reported the symptom, according to Bluebelt's quick survey. Perhaps it was limited, and perhaps it will simply never come back."

"And perhaps if we cross our fingers," Kinnison grumbled, "we can disband the Patrol."

"Consider this, please, my eminent sirs," 24of6 said. "I am a perceiver. I do not see. But I once did see, and I know how different that sense is. Optical sight is an illusion; a limited band of light waves shows a superficial stereopsis. Perception is the reality; linked molecules, up and down and front and back, are sensed for a materialistic analysis by the intellect. A starry sky is different when viewed two different ways and so, too, is a tableau like the colorful leaves of an autumn hillside. A sense of perception can be tuned, in effect reduced in efficiency, to simulate optics, but only an organic optical system can interpret perceptions like simple sight. Because I once saw, because I'm familiar with your photic images through stereopsis, I understand what you both *look* like. So I can see you in my mind's eye, both of you, Kinnison now of Klovia and Worsel of Velantia, because I once saw you in pictures. Many, many pictures, as a matter of fact, because you are so famous. But that is not how I perceive you. Worsel will understand much more than most the strange inside-and-outside three-dimensional scan. I also have a body which is as close to the Z end of the scale as it is to the A end. In many ways I'm more like Nadreck than I am like you two." 24of6 paused, silver forefinger of his right hand held dramatically high above his head. "All of this is to suggest that my *impression* of a genuine Lens is different than yours." He waggled a finger. "I notice a clue!"

Kinnison couldn't bear the continuing dramatic pauses. "Well, put us out of our misery, let's hear it!"

"Worsel saw a Lens that *squirmed!*"

"Yes, yes," Kinnison and Worsel both agreed, their minds impinging on 24of6's because of the inadequacy of words to express their excitement. It was obvious that Deuce had had an inspiration.

"Take a look at this, gentlemen!"

He unbuttoned and pulled open his blouse.

There on his chest was his fake Lens—dull and lifeless, but, as they stared, rapidly coming to life, a glorious imitation remarkably like the real Lens—bright and sparkling. Then, like an overloaded video screen it slowly, slowly became a nauseous fluxion of repulsive colors—and it was *squirming!*

9

The Robotic Mystery

The glory of a true Lens of Arisia is virtually indescribable. Quiescent, it is a jewel of jewels of subtle fires. A million sparkling points of light play across its myriad of surfaces, subdued, with muted colors coming and going like the breathing of some multitudinous, exotic life form. Then, aroused, its latent energy blazes into a radiant disc of astonishing beauty, pulsating, living flames. Mounted in a platinum-iridium bracelet and worn on the wrists of the finest men of humankind and its kin, the Lens is the most perfect, the most beautiful of all ornaments—and by far the most prestigious. Every wearer of the Lens—on arm or wing, on fin or tentacle, on chest or brow—was proud to bear the symbol of Civilization and have the instrument by which the psionic power of the mind intensified.

In contrast, the fake Lens of 24of6's chest was painfully obscene.

As the iridescent, polychromatic light shining out the eye sockets of the paraman dimmed to a gentle glow, the fake Lens metamorphosed once more into a pretty simulation, and then dulled into lifelessness.

"I'll be a double-doomed dock-walloper!" Kinnison said. "That's a trick I don't think I like." The fake Lens in itself was no surprise—he had been told of its use as a simple visual recognition when the real Lens wasn't flashing within the eyesockets.

"Very close," Worsel said, with a humorless grin. "Very close."

"I didn't do it alone," 24of6 corrected their thoughts. "Lalla Kallatra did it. That is, I excited the synthetics in the medallion—very recognizable, isn't it?—and then I Lensed Lalla for some interference into its resonance. That's what happens. The same effect that Worsel describes and pictures."

"Similar, but not the same," Worsel reflected. "There's something missing. . . ."

"Your state of mind at the time," 24of6 interrupted, "that's what's missing. And Lalla can demonstrate something significant about that. If you could call him in . . ."

Kinnison nodded and communicated the request. Kallatra obviously had anticipated the call; 24of6 must have told him as much at the time of their contact, for he stepped into the room as if Kinnison's push button had sprung him through the doorway. Both Kinnison and Worsel had their mind-shields down far enough to monitor anything that might have been going on, so they heard 24of6 bring Kallatra up to that point in their discussion.

"Don't be afraid of Kallatra's sudden presence in your mind, Worsel," 24of6 warned. Worsel grunted, irritated by the indelicate phrasing, and so was shocked to feel a wave of fear flow over him. Did he also catch a glimpse of his own evil alter-ego grinning at him out of a shadow in his mind? "Remarkable!" said Worsel. "Instantaneous suggestion from you, Kallatra, which I didn't notice!"

"Not really, Worsel—sir," Kallatra said, circumspectly that throwing in the term of respect because Kinnison was there. "The suggestion came from Deuce. I had my mind opened up wide for the el-sike phenomenon and it sort of opened up your own awareness of danger, imprinted with the pattern you yourself had set—that is, a feeling of the enemy threat and a sense of schizophrenia."

"Explain," Worsel said, not concealing his skepticism.

"Let me," Kallatra said, "do that." Following Kinnison's gesture and example, the young Lensman balanced himself on the other upholstered end of the couch. "Briefly, Deuce and I consider this probability: one, Worsel and Tong are each attacked directly following Kinnison's conference; two, Tong hallucinates at the same time as Worsel; three, both see essentially the same images; four, Worsel controls himself, but Tong doesn't." Kinnison leaned toward him, right elbow on one knee, chin on a hard fist. "Consider now the special circumstances: I was hyper-sensitized by a new, profound mental experience—the Lens-to-Lens conference. Immediately next came my first time in battle. Thoughts of the evil enemy filled my mind. Not fear—but apprehension. My power of el-sike, hypo-ed by the conference and reflecting my thoughts, was soaked up by Tong, who had no awareness of it. His psyche instantaneously fed into his mind images of his worst enemy and irrational fears. Arisian good

96

was stripped away, the Lens was failing—turning rotten, his traditional personification of evil was visualized—a Delgonian Overloard, who was sucking up his soul."

"So far, so good," Worsel said. "So logically because the situation was stressful for us all, because Tong and I were close in space and time and genetics . . ."

"Yes, it falls into place, doesn't it? Because I was so close to Tong, who had no notion of my subliminal influence he victimized himself with subconscious fears. Velantians, obviously, are extra susceptible."

"QX," Worsel said. "Then Tong's actions on Pok, threatening Arrow-22, were due to your proximity. But are you implying that your el-sike disoriented Tong even without a highly charged emotional situation?"

"Tong was genuinely ill from his experienced delusions after the space battle. When he heard the news about Arrow's possible Council approval, he felt impelled to seek greater reassurance."

"You conclude," Kinnison interposed, "that Tong was not under a sinister force. You believe Tong was actually attempting a beneficial result, acting with bad judgement rather than with sinister motives. Is that your conclusion?"

"Yes."

"So," Kinnison said, folding his arms across his chest and heaving a sigh, "the mystery gets explained away quite simply. Kallatra's baptism of fire is to blame. His peculiar el-sike slipped its leash—and, I'm certain, for the first and last time." Kinnison watched for Kallatra's reaction to his tacit command.

"Yes, sir," Kallatra said emphatically. "For the first and last time."

"What do you think, Worsel?" Kinnison asked.

"It sounds logical. However, the proof will have to be negative. If it never happens again, then this explanation can be considered right. On this basis, unsatisfactory though it is, the case can be closed."

"Great!" Kinnison said, rejoicing by bounding up and bringing out an unopened bottle of laxlo-like. The amber glass bottle was in the shape of the double-headed eagle of Radelix. "This was a gift from Lieutenant-Admiral Gerrond, who's bucking for admiral." He unplugged the two beaks. "It's better than the original—no alcohol means no hangovers. This stuff's remarkably good, I can tell you from past experience. Just a taste is satisfying."

He tipped an ounce of amber liquid into each of two small

glasses, and four times that much into a large cup for Worsel. 24of6 declined graciously by commenting, "I'll just slip into Kallatra's mind to pick up the sensation." They raised their drinks, Kinnison said, "To the Patrol", and they sipped. The extraordinary flavor and immediate biological effect produced no words but many appreciative murmurs.

"Excellent," Kinnison pronounced, still sipping. "Too bad Gerrond is such an officious brass-hat—he's really such a nice guy." He gave Kallatra a swift hint that a brief dropping of his tight screen would be welcomed, but there was no response. He swirled the remaining drops around in his glass, staring reflectively at them. "What do you think, your royal snakeship? You gave me the idea originally. Do I have a danger with my Lens-to-Lens mass meetings? More than the obvious, that is."

"Probably not." Worsel waved the tip of his tongue under his nostrils, savoring the laxlo-like's bouquet. "Caution, but not extra caution, is indicated. We know such concentration of mental forces is dangerous. I can't get out of my mind what a disgusting parody of the Lens the threats from Unit 9-7-1 triggered. What Kallatra did with Deuce's crystalloid resonators was a pallid approximation. I want never to see such evil ugliness again—my guard will now be permanently up against a schizophrenic recurrence. As I said, the case can be closed, unless Kallatra has something to add?"

"There is one point," Kallatra said. "I believe that Tong had the schizophrenic breakdown. Worsel merely reflected that through racial telepathic empathy. This phenomenon should be examined. May I do so?"

Kinnison and Worsel looked at each other, reading each other's opinions by their simple glances, and nodded. "Yes," said Kinnison, "that is an excellent idea. However—I want you to keep in constant touch with Worsel." He buzzed for an orderly, who came in to take Kallatra to the adjutant for official orders. "We'll get underway for the Purple Veil tomorrow or the next day. Kallatra, you'll stay aboard the *Dauntless*. We'll bring Tong and the Chickladorian aboard, too. Rather than sending them on to Velantia, which isn't necessary anyhow, we'll take them to our base on Dyaddub. Worsel and Deuce O'Sx will leave as soon as possible for Dyaddub in *Flame*."

When Kallatra and 24of6 had left, Kinnison, his voice flat and impersonal, asked, "Satisfied?"

"As best as can be expected," Worsel answered.

"What about that boy's mind-shield?" Kinnison said. "I've

never encountered such control under such relaxed circumstances. I felt suspicious, meaning somehow mentally uneasy. Do you?"

"I'm always somewhat suspicious," Worsel said, and grinned, flashing his teeth. "I'm a pessimistic croaker, if you'll recall your own words. Anyhow, about that shaded screen of his, there's a reason. It seems necessary to guard his el-sike. I'll go along with his conclusions, especially since we've had an indication of what it might have done to Tong. As I don't talk or hear, not at all, like you humanoids, I'm used to mind shields. With me it's a way of life. But," Worsel pressed home the thoughts to express his concern, "until I get a chance to peek into the corners of his mind I'll have to rely on Mentor and trust in the Lens."

"I'll have a chance to observe his work with Tong here on the *Dauntless*, until I catch up with you at Dyadubb."

"And I'll keep in touch through Tong. Clear Ether!"

Flame left the Velantian system within an hour.

Worsel, on the trip to Dyaddub, planned to be briefed by 24of6 with the details of zee-tee, the Purple-VN-F-ZTP/TTP Project. At first, however, the paraman entertained him with personal anecdotes of his life as a "half-breed" and frequent digressions on his opinions on all sorts of topics. 24of6 had all the enthusiasm of a man of flesh and blood. It was a long time before they got around to zee-tee.

"It's a curious fact," 24of6 said, "that, in the advanced state of technology of Civilization, we've remarkably few examples of robots. Their advantages were long heralded—but they never caught on."

"True enough," Worsel agreed. "I've encountered robots or mech-men from time to time. They never had significant intelligence. Invariably they are menials or servants. Androids and other look-alikes are, fortunately, quite stupid. I'm referring, of course, to the complete fabrications, Deuce."

"The reason lies in that peculiar ability we organic brains seem to have exclusively—intelligence. I agree with you. Every robot that I've ever met was a simple servo-mechanism or a computerized calculator. Never of self sufficient value to the Patrol or Civilization."

"The Patrol used robots one time to great effect," Worsel mused. "That was when the Grand Fleet defeated the invasion of Boskone through the hyper-spatial tube. Millions of beams were tossed about at the initial clash and a full eighth of our entire line of battleships was completely wrecked or blasted out of space in the cataclysm. Not one of our men died—because we used automatics, manned by robots under a minimum of remote control. But that was some time ago."

"I know about that, of course. As a famous battle, it was well reported. And my research convinces me that the Boskonians used robots in their shock-globe, too. I think that was about the time their experiments on Dyaddub reached their height."

"What happened to their project? Why did it disappear?"

"I don't know," 24of6 said. "I'm trying to piece that story together." The evidence, he explained, was skimpy. The site of the Boskonian base was found after intelligence reports, meticulously collected by Patrol spies and agents, led a reconnaisance party to the planet. It never returned. Six months later another Patrol party came back in force, but the planet was deserted. The caverns were intact, natural ones and artificial both, the overhead lights in place, the empty buildings standing. But there was no evidence as to who had been there or what they had been doing. It took almost another six months to find the hard evidence they were looking for.

"Perseverance paid off," 24of6 said. "A Rigellian team was routinely scanning the interior of the planet when they discovered a mass of metal inside a quarter-mile thick section of volcanic rock. Excavation revealed an enormous bubble of partially destroyed machinery, an obvious oversight by the evacuating rearguard."

24of6 explained that when the dump had yielded up thousands of parts and pieces to be examined, a large Patrol base and research station was established in the nearest cavern, the quarter-mile cube. Further surveys discovered atomic elements, and molecules suggested that bodies had been chopped into pieces before being de-hydrated and then oxygenated. By the use of el-sike, the atomic material of the area was examined for sub-etheric frequencies impressed in the molecules at the top end of the atomic scale.

"Did Lalla Kallatra work on that?" Worsel asked.

"Yes, Lalla was very helpful. And took some amazing readings. He felt that the vibrations indicated that a battle had been fought. To the death. His feeling, plus the material evidence, led to his conclusion that there had been a space-axe battle. Sounds crazy—the victims of a space battle encased in rock, deep under the surface of a planet. And there's the sense that Lalla had that the men had been killed by the robots."

"Any idea what these robots looked like?"

"Well, using archeological techniques, I reconstructed a mechanical form, at least a close approximation. About three feet tall, large of body, with three legs and four arms. There were also four extensible rods, for some unknown purpose, two of which were hollow. The front was heavily armored. The head had a full complement of sensors, it's my guess— but there was no alternate group in the chest for use when the head was retracted into the back shoulder area. Three tentacles were stored in the top of the three thighs. Each thick one had a tiny slender one in its core, so that the heavy tentacle with core could be used for heavy work at a distance of six feet, but the slender one, with an elastic capability, could probably be extended for twenty or more feet."

"And its brain?"

"Party in the head, partly in its abdomen. Not very large brain cases, which could mean not very smart. Maybe remote controlled."

"Hardly a life form, then, I'd say," Worsel thought mildly. "Sounds like just another piece of machinery."

"I tend to disagree. The circuitry was incredibly miniaturized. I think that was the object of the project. The brain cells appeared to be microscopic in size. That could indicate a potential which might well have raised it to an independent, intelligent life form."

"It has the classic construction of a soldier robot. Why mechanical warriors? The Boskonians had millions upon millions of living beings for their battle fodder. With all the various subject races under Boskone control, there was ample manpower. What logical reason is there for building fighting men? And to make it a secret project? Mass produced robots of a low level of intelligence, that'd make sense. But intelligent robots . . . *super* intelligent robots . . . ah, *super* intelligent robots!"

24of6 caught the unfinished thought. "You've got the idea, Worsel. Completely unsupervised robots superior in warfare thinking. Imagine! Troops without leaders! No leaders needed! Every soldier his own general—yet capable of coordinated teamwork. Properly trained, what a force they would be! On a battlefield, especially in space, they would be unstoppable!"

"What a boarding party they could be!" Worsel's mind was becoming excited. "No need to breach a ship through an air lock—no spacesuits needed when the air is lost—just straight across the void and into the broken hull!" Then

Worsel had second thoughts. "But only three feet high—if only they were bigger they'd be the envy of every Valerian space-viking."

"The largest was five feet tall."

"Oh, they had several sizes?"

"That's the strangest thing about them. They had more that just several sizes—judging by the parts. For instance, take the three-fingered, one-thumb hand. The hand, identical in every way, came in two styles—right and left. Matching them up, there were about eighty thousand pairs of hands. Yet there were no more than forty pairs which were the same size. In other words, there were more than two thousand pairs of hands *of different sizes*. That would indicate a minimum of a thousand different sizes of robots. That makes no sense. But let's assume the hands aren't supposed to match —there were over two thousand *different* size chest plates. That's two thousand different size robots. And yet that's not the end of it—I measured thousands and thousands of other parts of the same design and found one special one, one whose function indicated only one to a robot, *which had almost twelve thousand different sizes*. That evidence indicates there could have been twelve thousand different size robots!"

Worsel felt the incredulity which 24of6 experienced and agreed. "It's nonsensical, Deuce. There must be another explanation. How many different designs or types do you figure there were?"

"That's the craziest part. It appears—I could be wrong, but I'm sure I'm not—it appears there was only one design. No different modifications—just one design!"

Worsel was silent. Then he said, "What about machine tools, parts of a factory—"

24of6 interrupted. "Nothing. Only robot parts. Absolutely no evidence of a factory. Not even maintenance tools. But then, most nuts and bolts in sets were unmanipulable. Fused —grown together. Assembly or repair could not have been done by wrench—or, for that matter, by any known process."

"How weird," Worsel said. "They may not have been manufactured on this planet, but surely there'd be maintenance evidence. Dyaddub must have been a training ground, not an experimental station for building them. Therefore—"

Again 24of6 anticipated Worsel's thoughts. "—Therefore they were perfected and—an idea even more startling—they were so perfect as not to need maintenance. No tools and no spare parts—obviously spare parts would have meant thousands of parts the same size, not different sizes."

"So," Worsel said, "the next question is, where did they come from?"

"As I've said," 24of6 pointed out, "Patrol records of all kinds of shipping of suspicious materials connected with this Boskonian project were traced entirely into the Purple Veil Nebula. This we know. We're not positive, but we think the ultimate destination was here, in the Ekron system. Of the six planets and ten moons, only Dyaddub has been used. All the others have been thoroughly investigated, by machines and by men, with every kind of test."

"Except Zebub," Worsel said.

"Except Zebub. That's true. We consider it a Z-type planet, impossible to sustain anything but Z-type life. So it's been scanned for Z-type life and found uninhabited. Nadreck himself confirmed the findings although he did reclassify it more like YZ."

"YZ instead of Z. Does that suggest a loophole?"

"No. Just a planet that Nadreck doesn't consider ideal for his kind. It's impenetrable, because of its opaque gasses, to visual observation. And unscannable by electronic or radio waves because of its complex magnetic fields and continual storms."

"The first thing I do when I get to Dyddub," said Worsel, "is to give myself a readout on Zebub. It sounds just like a place the Boskonians would set up a secret base."

"How would they do that?"

"I don't know how they would. Which is even more reason for me to check it out."

"Several Rigellian sense-of-perception reports have been filed on it. You can look them over in my office files."

"What about the star itself, Ekron?"

"It's just a standard thermonuclear sun."

"Did the Rigellians scan it?"

"No." To 24of6 the idea it might support or harbor any kind of intelligent activity had been too fantastic to contemplate. "No, they didn't."

"I realize it sounds too fantastic to contemplate," Worsel said. "But I want to check it out anyhow."

By the time Worsel landed on Dyaddub and settled in at the underground Patrol station, he had worked out his plan for helping 24of6. However, his first task was to review what Kallatra had been doing with Tong.

When he Lensed Kallatra, the *Dauntless* was well over halfway on its own trip to Dyaddub. Kallatra had begun his work with Tong as soon as Kinnison's personal dreadnaught had gone into inertialess drive. He was ready with his first report, and he told the crucial phase as it had happened.

"After all the other tests I could make, I wanted to try hypnotism to produce the catharsis but Tellurians aren't very good at it with Velantians. So I gave Tong a shot of medical bentlam. He was instantly stupified, but instead of an ecstasy of joy, he was filled with dread. I said 'Tong! Show me your evil side!' and kept repeating that. After a minute, he replied, 'It's Worsel, it's Worsel, it's Worsel!' He mumbled it over and over, but I disputed that and told him that it wasn't Worsel. 'It's not Worsel!' I kept saying. 'Who is it? Who is it really?' Then he went berserk. He was tied down, but he darn near snapped the metal straps."

"What did his eyes look like?" Worsel asked.

"They came out on their stalks to fullest extension, turning purple all around the lens, and slowly twisted into knotty cords."

"Great Klono's Ghost!" Worsel said, his thoughts shaky with Velantian understanding. Kinnison and Kallatra immediately knew from Worsel that Tong had become insane. But the concern of the other two Lensmen was tempered by the hope shown by Worsel who said, "What happened then? Is he all right?"

"He's all right," Kallatra said. "Yes, he's fine!" Kinnison added. "Kallatra did the trick."

"How? What happened?" Worsel said, relieved but intensely curious.

"When he went berserk," Kallatra said, "I drove my mind as deep into his as possible, and I imagined my power of el-sike to be expanding larger and larger in his brain. Suddenly I sensed his psyche, enmeshed in some kind of horrible Velantian evilness. Then I said, with every bit of energy and power, 'WHO ARE YOU!' Tong let out one of those horrible hissing screams, you know—I beg your pardon, Worsel! —and his eyestalks untwisted, he stopped shaking, and he said something. I asked, 'What did you say, Tong?' And I clearly heard him say, 'I am Tong. I am Tong. I am really Tong.'

"It sounds like success," Worsel said reflectively, more for his own benefit than for Kinnison, to whom the thought was directed. Then, with greater assurance, Worsel said, "You did it, Kallatra. I'm certain you did it!"

"Thanks, Worsel," Kallatra said. "I'd like to mention some conclusions concerning the whole event."

"Go ahead."

"The most critical point in Tong's mental breakdown," Kallatra said, "came when he concentrated his will into increasing the energy beam against the pirate ship. That was when he became what he describes as 'sick'. His integrated personality cracked and he went from a state of mania to depression. The situation was stressful, and put his mind in disarray. I think I've made a meaningful deduction."

"It concerns the difference between Tellurians and Velantians," 24of6 continued. "You're a cognitive psychologist, essentially, heavy on Gestalt doctrines, but you also understand behaviorism—you usually think in terms of Velantian minds. Velantians, and so many of the best minds, the greatest thinkers, have compartmented brains. Tellurians and other humanoids have a brain with specialized parts, but it is not compartmented; nerve activities can't be isolated into tight compartments—the humanoid brain is too tightly integrated to be able to drop partitions as you can do, Worsel. I think Tong lost his ability to stay compartmented. The partitions went down, and he disintegrated into basic fear and terror."

"In that case, all his logic and reasoning became contaminated with the rawest of emotions, I suppose."

"Yes. And, to prevent utter madness, his rational mind picked you, Worsel—because you were near and in his thoughts—as the evil influence, rather than himself."

"And the visions of the poisonous Lens?"

"Symbolic. For Worsel, meaning Tong, to do what he was doing—equating weakness with evil—meant the Lens was flawed, that the Lens had to be diseased."

"Well," Worsel said, a bit apologetically, "it seems to me there's nothing new here, although you've confirmed what we earlier thought had happened. Did you find anything new?"

"Yes, I did."

"Then what is it?"

Kallatra's feelings came through strongly embarrassed and Kinnison entered the exchange of thoughts. "Kallatra has already spoken to me about this. He says he has something vital to reveal. But he feels that he must first tell you in absolute confidence. Then you are to decide if you wish to reveal it to others."

"Highly unusual," Worsel said. "Do you wish to follow this procedure, friend Kinnison?"

"If you will, Worsel. Kallatra doesn't say so, but I believe it must be something extremely personal about you in particular or Velantians in general. I guess that's all for the moment..." Kallatra's weak agreement came through, "...so we'll be seeing you in a couple of days. Anything before I clear ether?"

"One thing. Prepare the *Dauntless* for something special —for the worst, whatever that might be. I think we'll have to take a close look into Zebub. And in the meanwhile, too, if you and Kallatra—and Tong, if he's up to it—will get together and probe Zebub with everything you can muster, maybe that will help our preparations."

"QX," Kinnison said, adding diplomatically, "Have your little secrets now, boys, I'm clearing ether." Kinnison signed off, his spirit radiating pleasure at the prospect of some physical action. Worsel waited patiently for a moment until Kallatra said, "What I have to tell you is not about you, Worsel, its about Kinnison—I've deceived him. Actually it's about Clarrissa MacDougall Kinnison. I think it should wait until we're together with plenty of time. It's nothing that can't wait." Kallatra was acutely ill-at-ease, but Worsel deeply sensed that the young Lensman's problem was painfully personal and not sinister, and that delay was of no importance. He said, "That's for you to judge, Kallatra," but he couldn't help being intrigued about what the boy might reveal concerning the Red Lensman.

When Worsel had signed off, Kallatra and Kinnison scanned Zebub at long range, several times dropping out of free travel into inert to take measurements. They discovered nothing unusual. When the action did come, however, it was when least expected, just after arrival on Dyaddub.

The *Dauntless* had settled in a hollow between some jagged hills, filmed over by the fine reddish dust which the large ship had stirred up. A landing party of fourteen, including Kinnison and Kallatra, stepped out into the thick sand. Ten of the men, one hand each gripping the handles of a Velantian litter, five men to a side, were carrying Tong. Two others transported Vveryl the Chickladorian in an oxygen-bag litter. After twenty yards, halfway to the blue tripod marking one of a hundred cave mouths, the litter bearers were gasping for breath from their slow trudging through the slippery grit in such thin air.

Unseen behind them a dark mist rolled up over the line of hills at the stern of the *Dauntless* and covered the ship with an utterly black cloud. Within seconds it had reached them. One moment the reddish sunlight of Ekron was warmly lighting the sand of Dyaddub, and the next moment there was absolute darkness. The Lensmen, even with their senses of perception, were as blinded as the ordinary Patrolmen.

"Kinnison!" His name exploded in his mind. It was Tong, and he sensed him, in his medical gown as large as a tent, springing unsteadily to his hind legs from the litter. "There are creatures surrounding us!"

Kinnison, reacting to the warning even as he received it, tuned his Lens to the maximum, racing his mind up and down the entire mental frequency scales, searching for the enemy's thoughts and found—nothing! Not even a thought screen excused the emptiness. He encountered Kallatra's own probes and worried thought: is Tong hallucinating again?

"The enemy!" Tong was frantic. "They're all three-legged and four-armed machines—they're all robots!"

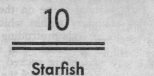

10

Starfish

Worsel was at the foot of the elevator shaft, stalking aboard the large platform with a half-dozen of the black-tired, barrel-shaped robot workers, when he heard Tong's warning. He shoved the last pair of workers out of the way to close the telescoping gates with a crash and pushed the top button. His mind flew upward to meet the other Lensmen —one, two, three—four? The fourth was Vveryl, drugged senseless for the transfer. Kinnison and Kallatra were pictorially completely blind, although they mentally saw vague outlines of the mechanical creatures Tong saw. As Worsel's mind joined theirs, the pictures sharpened clearly within their heads—they vicariously recognized the same robots which 24of6 had described as having reconstructed. Two or three dozen in various sizes became distinguishable as thirty-three units, evenly ranging from two-and-a-half to five feet in height.

Kinnison's mind was filled with words and images. The ship commander was telling him how powerless the *Dauntless* was to help. The blackout was so effective that there was nothing which the *Dauntless* could do without jeopardizing the safety of those under attack. There was so much magnetic interference that friend could not be distinguished from foe on the ship's screens.

Kallatra felt a steely tentacle slide around his waist, but he could see absolutely nothing. He tore at it with the fingers of his left hand, his blaster silent in his right. Nothing was visible to fire at. He heard the many thoughts of his comrades as they sought to group themselves shoulder to shoulder to form a defensive ring. Kinnison's thoughts pierced through the din "Quiet! Everyone quiet!" Instantaneously the Patrolmen blanked their minds. "Worsel and Tong! Take over and scan! Sort us out!'

Kallatra immediately felt the Velantians at work, reinforcing his and Kinnison's minds. Only Worsel, out of the target area, seemed effective. The youth saw in his head, as though a thick smoke were being blown back and forth, shifting now to reveal and now to conceal, the thirty-three robots. Five of them seemed to be on their backs, forming a rough five-corner boundary within which the action was happening. At the ends of rods protruding from their round bodies poured the now-wispy smoke—but it was pouring not out, but inward, as though being sucked up by a cleaning tube. The others were dancing around the Patrolmen, grabbing them with tentacles and pulling them, feet dragging, through the sands. But the tentacles overlapped, and one would tear away another's hold. Tong was on his knees, batting robots right and left. Vveryl was a limp form spilled on the ground, knocked from his plastic cocoon, bright pink face mashed into dull pink sand.

"Steady on, Worsel!—Tong!" Kinnison was hurling orders measured by split-seconds. "Patrolmen! I'll put your hands in touch. Hold fast when I do." Even as Kinnison told him the strategy, Kallatra was following suit, grabbing the dimly seen hands of men through Worsel and Tong's perception and bringing them together, forging some kind of organized unit. "Give me a weapon!" Tong begged. Kallatra, through Kinnison's mind, saw Tong reaching out to the nearest Patrolman, trying to pull out the gun, which had been returned to the holster at Kinnison's order. Then Tong went down, with tentacles wrapped around his arms and legs. The Velantian was so much bigger than the others that the writhing tentacles were not interfering with each other. Or was it because—? Yes, they were after Tong primarily, while they merely kept the others occupied. "Right, Kallatra!" Kinnison had noticed too and flashed his analysis. "They know Tong is extra perceptive and they have to stop him projecting to us." That idea was confirmed by some sudden jabs of the jointed metal arms, punching round, bloody holes in Tong's tough hide.

Worsel's thoughts came through then. "They're injecting him, drugging him. The trauma's bad. The stuff is deadly."

Eight of the men were now in touch with each other, drawing themselves into a compact knot. "Lock elbows," Kinnison commanded. "Blasters out. Fire four or five feet in front of you. Into the ground." The remaining four men had been separated and were being pulled back and forth between several robots. Kinnison was battering his way into the robots nearest him who were making Tong's left thigh and leg one ugly red wound. With his heavy left forearm he knocked spindly arms away and the blaster in his right hand burned into the body joints of the stabbing appendages, skipping from one joint to another as a limb retracted. The smoky darkness was thickening as Tong got weaker. It was Worsel's mental presence which gave Kallatra some perception of the battlefield. The boost in his mind arrived at the very moment that Tong lost consciousness. Like the snap of a camera's shutter, Kallatra's understanding was lit up with a stark vision of the real violence: that the attack was more psychical than physical. Sub-etheric forces? Not a mere robotic attack? That would explain the blocked powers of the Lensmen.

"Salgud." Kinnison called his captain. Worsel's extra mental help strengthened Kinnison's perception. "Salgud! Spray the black cloud with searchlights." Kinnison and Kallatra both sensed that the message got through, but Salgud had no Lens to push back a clear answer through the interference. "Light quanta," said Kinnison, mostly as a quick explanation to Kallatra's puzzlement. "Five of those machines are sucking up photons like water. No light reflects to permit sight—the black cloud, as such, doesn't exist. I think we can overload them. All that energy can't be bottled up for—" Kallatra felt the electric charge of the two Second Stage Lensmen having an inspired thought at the same time. "Worsel!" "Kinnison!" The two called to each other in excited rapport. "That's it!" "You've got it!"

Kallatra got the idea, too, but not on his own, although it was so devilishly simple!

"Salgud!" Kinnison and Worsel were both sending in the order as a joint effort to make sure it got through. "Set up one screen between you and us and beam as much energy into it without breaking through!" Kinnison's expressive command was coming through powerfully, riding Worsel's waves as well, "Salgud! I want the damnedest display of full-spectrum fireworks that you can give me!" Worsel and Kinnison kept repeating the message over and over. In between the message, Worsel's irritability over the progress of the elevator would also come, "Zevz! This soul-wrenching thing's so slow!" and "Don't fold up, Tong!" and back to "This soul-sucking elevator!"

A searing flash of light burst before Kallatra's closed eyes. That every Patrolman had his eyelids tightly shut was due to the Lensmen's forceful warning—all but one unfortunate, however, who had his sight seared into permanent loss. Most of them had also avoided the shock and pain by throwing up a hand or two before their faces. The enormity of the energy before them was like nothing they had ever before experienced so close at hand. The flashing force against counterforce, out in the open, only a few score yards away, was a frightful experience, the white light of many miniature novae bursting into a jagged disc of incandesence.

When Worsel dashed from the entrance tunnel the landscape was a blaze of such dazzling whiteness that he was momentarily thrown off stride and nearly staggered into the blue tripod. All eyes but one were pulled back as far as possible into his head, and even that one merely squinted downward at the glistening sand at his feet. He perceived the scene, the struggling robots being fended off by the Patrolmen with windmilling arms and kicking legs. It was now apparent that the machines were having as much difficulty maneuvering in the heavy sands as the men. Most of the men were bunching up behind Kinnison to aid him in trying to protect Tong, who was snapping his jaws and flapping his wings defensively. A pair of attacking robots had picked up the unresisting Vveryl and were moving to the rear.

As Worsel ran at top speed toward the fight, his wings getting just enough lift to help him skim across the sand, there was a flash of brilliance within the brightness and he felt what he could not hear, a powerful concussion. "There goes one!" Kinnison shouted. "Photonic indigestion!" A moment later there was another disintegration of one of the sucking robots. A half-dozen other machines flung themselves on the ground in a cleaning position, attempting to neutralize the flaring screens of the *Dauntless* as the beams sputtered against resisting fields of energy in cascading showers of white-hot sparks. There was another explosion. "They're licked!" Kinnison yelled in encouragement to the men who were on their knees, exhausted, still weakly flailing. "Every explosion stuffs the others more. It's progressive disintegration. Attaboy, Salgud! Keep it up!" The explosions were accelerating. Almost a dozen machines had become saturated and vanished in the release of immeasurable photonic energy.

Worsel picked up Tong, muscles rippling, legs driving into the ground, and held him out of the reach of the robot arms. "Kinnison! Get Vveryl!" he warned, seeing the robots scuttling back, knocking the Chickladorian to the ground. But Kinnison couldn't see, his eyes still painfully shut. "Salgud! Cut the power! Give the men a chance to see!" The splashing incandesence winked out, but the intensity of the light left the Patrolmen in its aftermath still floundering about, unable to adjust. No more than two seconds passed when one of the prone robots unloosed a bolt of photons at the *Dauntless*. The automatic screens parried the thrust, but not before a scorching scar had been streaked across its side. After the lightning flashes from the tips of a number of metal rods, the absolute darkness descended on them again. It lasted for only a few seconds, but in that brief moment the remaining robots, about fifteen, had scuttled off toward the hills from which they had come. Vveryl was still a prisoner. The *Dauntless* was now in position to blast them, but Vveryl made it impossible. A few expert shots did bring one robot down, but the others continued. Worsel placed Tong on the fallen litter and bounded after them. Two robots dropped to the ground, rods in the air, briefly turning the area into hazy grayness, before exploding almost in Worsel's face as he leaped over them. The big dragon was hurled to the ground, briefly stunned. When he rose, the robots were gone. He dashed over the low ridge of hills fifty yards away in time to see a cave mouth explode outward and crumble closed. The retreat of the robots with a Lensman prisoner had been successful.

For the next ten minutes the *Dauntless,* floating a few feet off the planet's surface along the ridge, searched for the passageway without success. Of the hundreds of tunnels revealed, leading in all directions, there was no indication as to which had been the robots' escape route. As the *Dauntless* scoured the area, scanning as deeply as possible, Kinnison had been sorting out the damage. Tong was in critical shape, Vveryl was gone, two Patrolmen were dead, four wounded with Worsel, Kallatra and himself untouched. One of the Patrolmen had died examing one of those machines disabled by Kinnison's deftly placed shots—while he had bent over it, the thing had exploded in a ball of purplish fire. One by one, the few robots left on the field of battle had done the same until not one machine remained. When the first of three radio-controlled ground cars had whined across the plain from the underground base, Kinnison had barked out orders assigning a pair of Patrolmen to collect any useful fragments around the shallow blast craters. The second car was hastily loaded with Tong and the four wounded crew members and dispatched back to the base, Worsel and Kallatra following in the third car. As they left, the first car returned from its fruitless search and, when the bodies of the two casualties were aboard, it headed back to the ship, with Kinnison in charge. The remaining Patrolmen shuffled alongside to avoid the rearward spray of sand from the tread belts squealing around the large black tires.

Sixteen minutes after the last robot had exploded, when Kinnison was back in his own room and the others were grouped around 24of6's paper-strewn desk in his laboratory, the sophisticated equipment of the *Dauntless* seemed to have located the remaining robots and Vveryl. A Lens was identified and tracked traveling rapidly away from Dyad-dub, in the direction of Zebub, in an otherwise undetectable spaceship. Kinnison personally reviewed the data and had it substantiated by the additional sensors from base head-quarters; it was a certainty, confirmed by the trajectory, that a small spaceship, stripped down to a mere motorized shell, had come out of a cave fed by one of the passageways. The Lens reading indicated that although Vveryl was alive, the Lens was no longer in contact with the flesh of the Lensman. There was no indication from it that there were in-telligent entities in the vicinity, but Worsel's perception amply indicated that there were a dozen or more ambula-tory forms, probably robots, packed around the Chickla-dorian. Because they were inorganic, danger to them from the detached Lens was nonexistent. Within moments after the sighting and analysis, two plans of action were formulated. 24of6 left immediately in his speedster on the trail of the Lens-marked ship in an attempt to get as close as possible, knowing that it carried no armaments. The *Dauntless*, after Kinnison had checked on the hospitalized men while Worsel's speedster was being unloaded, would be right be-hind, ready to close in when able, and from the Dyaddub base Worsel and Kallatra would monitor 24of6's situation constantly.

"I'm visually in contact," 24of6 reported several hours later, "and I'm going to grapple on the blind side of the ship, provided I'm not resisted. I'll chop off their tubes and try to force an entry. My tractors will be directed at you to give you the best chance to snatch us when and if you dash in on us. If Kallatra tells me Vveryl is dead I'll stop my efforts and rely on you." Through their Lensman unity, the others followed 24of6's progress. Without a spacesuit, but with his internal system prepared, 24of6 moved out of his airlock, leaving all doors wide open and his quarters in a vacuum. He had a lifeline clipped to a take-up reel and carried a power cable with a kit of attachments. He magnetically fastened on the larger hull to begin a creeping search for an egress to force. Kallatra, through Worsel, reported no chance in either the substantial or insubstantial, what little existed or could be read, of Vveryl or his captors. 24of6 was dismantling by a flameless torch a supply bay leading directly behind the main compartment.

Kinnison, two minutes behind in the *Dauntless*, had no sooner said, "It's a piece of cake," then he spotted the strangers. Four by four, spaceships were emerging around the crescent of Zebub. Warships. They were forming lines of interception, their speed leaving less than six minutes before 24of6 would have his operation jeopardized. Kinnison informed 24of6, adding, "You have 210 seconds to get in and out. Then the *Dauntless* will act." The enemy numbers had increased to nearly one hundred, and still they came. "Captain!" Kinnison said calmly. "Send out a General Mob call on all Patrol frequencies." Suddenly, the robot ship did the unexpected; it left its curving flight path for a Zebub atmospheric entry and plunged directly downward toward the thick, swirling cloud-blanket.

"Break off, Deuce!" came Kinnison's excited command, expressing a warning about an overly hazardous situation which the other Lensmen also recognized. "Get back in your ship or you'll be swept away! We'll scoop you all up in two minutes." The promise, however, became impossible to keep, for the rapid acceleration of the robots' ship indicated an immediately verifiable new fact: a planetary beam had the coupled ships in its grasp, pulling them downward.

"Be prepared to detach and get out of there, Deuce!" Kinnison cautioned. "We'll risk enemy fire and try something else." Time was running out. The enemy fleet was now nearly three hundred in strength. The question was rapidly changing from one of rescue by the *Dauntless* to one of survival for all.

As the *Dauntless*'s tractors dueled at long distance with the combined force of gravity, ship's propulsion, and planet-based tractor beam, 24of6, now back at his own controls, added his braking power, without effect. The *Dauntless* itself was in a losing struggle, and everyone knew it.

"Salgud!" the Lensman all heard Kinnison say, "there's one last chance. Dash in, slice off the section with Vveryl, and pull it out." The pursued ship was picking up speed and friction. So was 24of6's. "Disengage now, Deuce. Get out now. We can't help."

"I'll stay glued," 24of6 replied. "You'll need me to spot the section for you, maybe to give him first aid if you do pull him out."

The *Dauntless* tested its beams with a few sweeping arcs, dropping its defensive screens so low that the long-range probes of force from the enemy fleet made the ship jerk and shiver. "The plan's dangerous," Salgud said. "My platform's not stable. The cuts may not be accurate."

"We don't have a choice," Kinnison said. "We've got to try. Once into Zebub's atmosphere we'll lose him—maybe for good." Under Captain Salgud's personal control, the *Dauntless* zoomed in and, despite the trembling, cut the ship into three parts, almost exactly where 24of6's telepathic instructions, as relayed through Kallatra-Worsel and Kinnison, were pinpointing the targets. The section came out neatly, spilling out two kicking robots, but was knocked from the *Dauntless*'s hold by tractor beams from the planet. The sections began to burn at the edges. The *Dauntless* was buffeted by some bolts of energy, throwing it a dozen miles out of position.

"Pull out! Pull out!" came 24of6's desperate call. "I'll brake the fall and ride Vveryl's section down. Save yourselves. I'll do my best. Good luck!" 24of6 attached his speedster to Vveryl's section, applying retro power. Twenty seconds later he was swallowed up by the clouds.

The *Dauntless*, all screens up, was fighting to stay intact. The weaponry of the oncoming fleet was increasing in its effective power, hundreds of thousands of miles ticking off as it moved up to maximum sub-light speed. An hour passed before they were out of danger.

The *Dauntless*, while staffed as any Patrol ship of the line, also carried an operations staff for the Galactic Coordinator. This consisted of the traditional four military sections, each headed by a Lensman with the equivalent rank of admiral. So, to his young G-1 staff officer Kinnison turned for up-dating on the progress of the mobilization. A thousand vessels, some independently operating, some knit together in task forces, were on the detector screens. A third of them were already in sub-etheric contact with Kinnison's command post and being fitted into battle plans. Orders had been sent to sub-fleet commanders for relay to the individual captains.

The lenticular tank of the *Dauntless* was a hundred feet long, with a 100,000-plug board capacity for controlling 100,000 Patrol vessels and manning stations for two dozen

Rigellians. The *Dauntless*, however, was not now outfitted for full-scale warfare, with only four Rigellians assigned, enough for the number of battleships expected. They were in position, tendrils outstretched from their huge barrel bodies, and had punched up on their consoles the positions of the ships as they reported in. A mixture of red, blue, green, and orange points of light floated in the tank, all proportionately placed in space and converging on the lights in the center, one small white, one large red. The white marked the *Dauntless*, the red the enemy fleet.

Kinnison was not at the lenticular tank. He was at his own desk, a five-foot tactical tank lowered from the ceiling to hang a few inches above his central core. The three-dimensional image fed from the big display in the tank room below him had all the information he needed. As he watched, a dozen more green lights flashed into position.

Kinnison said, "Give me ten x," and the pattern of dots jumped, spreading out. The white and red lights were farther apart. "Give me another multiple ten." Again there was the shift. Half of the green dots had disappeared from the display, and the red light cluster was discernable as several hundred separate specks. "Give me Ekron, with Dyaddub and Zebub." Immediately several of the almost invisible softly glowing points which were stars and planets brightened. Zebub became a purple light; Dyaddub became an orange one. The red dots were a shell half surrounding Zebub.

"Captain Salgud," Kinnison said briskly, "take us out about twenty mil inert." Twenty million miles was nothing in inertialess flight, but at sub-light speeds it was not insignificant.

"Worsel," Kinnison Lensed over the distance, "what's your evaluation?"

Millions of miles away, the big dragon, coiled in front of 24of6's desk, responded. "I've scanned with Rigellian links and correlated with the *Dauntless*'s and Dyaddub's sensors. There are three hundred eleven enemy. About half are light to very light class. One fourth are medium. The rest evenly divide between heavy and mauler types. You can't engage until you are six-sixty-six of parity." Worsel concentrated on the Rigellian manning the ship's number one position in the tank room, swiftly absorbing information. "Our GP force is about one half assembled." Worsel closed his many eyes and listened for several seconds. "Deuce O'Sx is still QX. He's shaped enough energy to encapsulate

Vveryl, who's still alive but in ninety-nine point nine ninety-nine suspension. His ship can't release the sectional piece because Vveryl is still in it. The robots are paralyzed with the cold; no energy flows in their circuits. Deuce thinks he can stay hidden indefinitely in the lake of chemical slush he's burrowed into. His equipment is barely ticking over but our Lenses cut through the interference, thanks to Kallatra's el-sike boost. Any suggestions?"

"You tell me, old snake. I'm going to have to stooge around this sector of the Purple Veil for at least two days before I have an attack force strong enough to challenge their fleet. What will you be doing in the meantime?"

"Kallatra and I are going to take Flame close in to Zebub, and monitor Deuce real tight."

"What about the Spawn fleet? The rearguard must be anchored where you want to go."

"It is. Flame is up to it. We won't get spotted. And we'll be your O.P. when you finally attack."

As soon as Kinnison had cleared ether, Flame was readied and the Lensmen left. As badly injured as Tong was, he had insisted on being installed in a hospital sling in front of 24of6's console to act as Lensman relay. Worsel was grateful for Tong's presence. Flame would be swinging out and around the Purple Veil Nebula in free flight to come back in toward Ekron and Zebub from the other side; Tong would provide the necessary delicate communications should a crisis develop with Deuce before the circle had been completed. The hours seemed like minutes with Worsel's intricate maneuvering, and they were well decelerated in inert when Tong made contact with the bad news.

"Deuce reports a dragnet operating to find him," Tong said. "Zebub turns out to be inhabited. Self-contained globular cities are numerous and floating at all levels. They can't possibly be native to the planet, he says. They must be Spawn communities."

"Thanks, Tong," Worsel said. "I'm going to Lens him now and inform him that in a few more hours we'll be in position to help him to get Vveryl out."

"Not now," Tong responded. "Because of the spy tracers on him, he's asked for no communications except for emergencies. He's staying silent for at least one full GP cycle. He'll call at 78:15. You're to contact him at 78:20 if you haven't heard from him."

Worsel worked Flame into the periphery of the detector fields of three enemy ships close to the latitude along which

24of6 had entered the clouds. He kept *Flame* undetected and invisible by tampering with the enemy's radiant waves through his balancers. The two Lensmen settled down for a long wait, passively receiving without acknowledgments the frequent status reports Kinnison and Tong were telepathing. There were still several hours remaining to 24of6's deadline when the unexpected Lensed call hit them.

"DXD! DXD!" The red alert code was unmistakably from 24of6.

"Worsel here."

"Kallatra here."

"Lalla, put Worsel on our F-Ultra." Kallatra quickly explained to Worsel that he and 24of6 had a special personal telepsychic frequency through the Lens which had been developed out of el-sike. They had experimented with it and found a potential for tighter security. Using Kallatra as a tuner, Worsel had no difficulty answering, "QX, Deuce."

"The tracers are on me. The trackers are close. I have Vveryl and I have a prisoner—but I can't risk running the tightening blockade." 24of6 was quick and precise, seeming unruffled. "Here's the non-verbal situation."

To Kallatra and Worsel, a recalled memory was reeled off at a speed just below incomprehensibility. The former had little difficulty understanding because of the rapport created by his close friendship with the paraman, while Worsel, his prodigious mind using Kallatra as a catalyst, slipped easily into the new technique.

When the Worsel-Kallatra team vanished into hyper-space to outflank the enemy, 24of6 recalled, he began his efforts to extract Vveryl and bring him aboard the speedster. He put up a pressure along the umbilical cord supplying the stream of energy to Vveryl's capsule, creating a movable bubble-tunnel through the intensely cold liquid-solids, and forced his way through the twisted section, around several frozen robots. The shell of the force containing Vveryl had trapped the limbs of two robots. Noxious gases had formed within the hollow rods from the slight heat of his body, allowing the fumes of the thawing poisons to seep inside. When the paraman's bubble reached Vveryl's, the two melted into one, and 24of6 pumped out the contaminated air from the larger capsule they now shared. A quick medical check confirmed the inevitable; the Chickladorian's condition had deteriorated to critical, his eyes a ghastly white and his skin a sickly pale violet. In contrast, his reddish pink hair looked like a grotesque wig. His Lens was gone, but 24of6's own Lens quickly located it, strapped to the severed arm of a robot lying beyond Vveryl. 24of6 began dragging the unconscious body back toward his ship, the severed arm held like a plug in the end of his bubble of force. As the short gap between the two hulls was being bridged, a large, flat shape smacked the retreating end of the bubble in a swirl of crystals, like a wet leaf blown by a raging slush storm. The thing was heavy and solid, for its impact drove the metal arm forward through the clothing and flesh of Vveryl —and left the Lens, by good fortune, inside the energy shield. The thing was trying to squeeze its center into the bubble along the axis of the rod. Five thick, grayish fingers clamped around the transparent end like a giant hand. To 24of6 it looked like a mammoth starfish, the five triangular sections radiating from a central hump. In the center of the underside was a round hole ringed with spikes which had fastened on the tube end and, under the powerful grip of its five arms and the suction of that mouth, had shaped the end into a nipple which it was trying to bite off. The body squirmed and shifted, allowing glimpses through the cold blue mists of a knobbly, black topside. Its mouth worked with sucking shapes, the inside lighting up and darkening to the rhythm of its movement. 24of6 intuitively understood that it was sucking up energy. He quickened his withdrawal into the ship so that the star shape, ten feet from tip to tip, covered his entry way, its puckering mouth centered on the opening. 24of6 reached across Vveryl's form to pull the Lens off the metal arm whose far end now was pinned by several extensible teeth. As though aware of the prize, the thing pulled back the metal and, with many tongues, fished the Lens into its mouth. The black orifice flashed blue arcs of flame. 24of6 expected the thing to be instantly killed, but the blue arcs ended and nothing happened. 24of6 immediately plastered the creature flat against the hull with a tractor field.

At this point, 24of6's non-verbal recall ceased. There was no need for Worsel or Kallatra to comment; the situation was leading to the inevitable response. The implications of this new life form, impervious to any influence of the Lens, were alarming—the creature had to be placed in proper GP hands and examined thoroughly after the recovery of the Lens.

"I've got to act," 24of6 explained calmly. "I can't wait for the *Dauntless*—Vveryl is on the verge of death." The two Lensmen in *Flame* could feel the fatigue in the flesh of the paraman being swept away as the hatchway closed and the oxygen flooded the control room.

"So here I come! Wish me luck!"

11

Death of a Lensman

For all the power that a Lensman possesses—from the individual super abilities enhanced by the Lens of Arisia to the collective strengths and greatest technical equipment available from the elite corps of the Galactic Patrol—there are times when such incredible power fails. The spontaneous acceptance of the challenge to rescue Vveryl by the paraman Lensman was not a foolhardy decision. 24of6, like most mature and experienced Lensmen, never went too far beyond his capabilities; his judgment had the prime objective always in mind: success. A Lensman did not casually throw away his life, because he knew that his life was too important to be squandered. There was an investment in a Lensman by all who had made him such, from pre-Lens to post-Lens years, from his progenitors, through the Patrol, right up to Arisia, which held the life of a Lensman as one of the most priceless of things. Yet the fact was inescapable, Lensman did die. And Lensman died not by handfuls or scores, but they died—one here, a few there—by the thousands. Never did those of this special brotherhood of Civilization worry about their deaths; they never considered themselves any more in danger than a rank and file member of the Galactic Patrol, but they felt the loss of any one of their breed much more strongly than ever could have been thought possible by such a group of courageous, fearless, adventurous men and non-men. So thousands had dropped from the ranks in the course of duty, and tens of thousands more would follow. A hundred thousand names would go on the rolls of honor, with no end in sight. None, except four, knew this better than those in gray. Gray Lensmen had been tried and tested, and by their extraordinary superior ability advanced to the independent status of Unattached. Of those, the best of the best, the four who were the Second Stage Lensmen, bore the Lensman's Load the most. The Lensman Load was heavy when it was the sorrow of grief at the passing of a Lensman.

The tragedy of the rescue mission of 24of6, Deuce O'Sx the paraman, was not immediately apparent. The difficulties which had been building for him deep down in the churning atmosphere of Zebub were serious, of course, but danger was ever present in the active officer corps of the Patrol, and escape from it was almost always the reward for the fighting qualities of the endangered men. Except once in a while ...

24of6 did not expect Worsel and Kallatra to come after him in *Flame*. Worsel's speedster was a ghostly wraith amidst the enemy, a shifting staging area for the Velantian's mental thrusts and parries. But it was not an invincible *Dauntless*. Nor did Worsel think of doing so, although if he had even half anticipated what was about to happen he might have made the attempt. No, it was just within Worsel's capabilities to keep *Flame* invisible, a spy within the ranks of the enemy, ready for the moment when the *Dauntless* would use *Flame* as the gunsight for a devastating attack.

So, 24of6, closely monitored by the crew of *Flame*, drove his ship upward through a web of enemy beams, as fast as the thick atmosphere would permit, counting on his daring dash to leave the enemy uncoordinated. That is, he tried to drive upward. He had gone less than a thousand yards when he was jerked to a halt. He was stuck to his bucket seat magnetically and did not lurch forward, but Vveryl's body strained against the buckled straps under the enormous G-stresses and, for the first time since 24of6's appearance, a grunt and a groan came from the young man's purplish lips. In seconds both rescuer and rescued were unconscious.

Worsel and Kallatra experienced the flight of the other two, but there was nothing that they could discover to account for the strange stoppage. They both could only conclude that some unknown natural phenomenon in the planet's atmospheric soup had blocked the escape.

"I'm going down, Worsel," Kallatra announced. He began to release the escape capsule which was built into the top of the speedster, above the ceiling panels of the control room. He rapidly sketched his idea for Worsel: climb in the capsule and shoot away and down with it still compactly folded, Kallatra able to fit into one-sixth the area Worsel would normally need; accelerate into the clouds, the refrigerating system ample to handle the heat generated by the ship nearly one-quarter its usual operating load; attach the capsule to 24of6's craft and either free it of its obstacle or make a transfer of the two unconscious men. It might not work, but it was certainly feasible and worth the try, Worsel had to agree.

Within ninety seconds Kallatra was on his way.

He was halfway to his goal when 24of6's thoughts came back in focus. Still stupefied, the paraman at first protested Kallatra's rescue mission, then, recognizing that it was already being undertaken, accepted the possible help.

The paraman turned his attention to what had happened. At first he had thought he had rammed an immovable object, but some quick reading showed him nothing. In fact, there was nothing at all to be learned from his dials and meters and readouts. Absolutely everything was functioning normally, and no force was being applied against him.

Then he discovered the startling truth. The creature which he had trapped against the side of his ship was actually tethered. A thin black line extended from its bony top down into the blue chemical sea. His ship was held like a slim, deep sea fish on a heavyweight line. And, like a fish, he now saw that he was being reeled in.

Worsel knew as much as 24of6 did, but could do nothing, except to try to learn what might be at the far end. The Velantian's quick probe through the electrical turbulence, at the risk of disclosing his position, discovered a huge globe, information he immediately passed on to Kallatra and 24of6. It seemed to be similar to the floating cities 24of6 had earlier reported. And it also seemed to be covered with starfish. For simplified communications, Worsel immediately dubbed the starfish "Asterias" and the globe "Cheenus," from the old Greek word *echinus*. "Cities those Cheeni might be, but weapons they certainly are," Worsel rapidly sent to the others. "The Cheeni are power plants, and the Asteri are cable-fed terminals. There must be an enormous energy potential in the combination. Break away, Deuce, before others latch on to you." 24of6, however, needed no urging; he was trying every possible trick. There was no doubt in anyone's mind that if 24of6's ship was covered with the Asteri or pulled up against the Cheenus it would be absorbed into atomic particles.

Worsel couldn't restrain an emotional cry of alarm. "A dozen of those things are flying your way, Deuce! Cut loose, cut loose!" Kallatra was still many minutes away.

What happened then could never be satisfactorily explained; only Vveryl could have done so. The Chickladorian opened wide his peculiar eyes, the irises completely filling the large triangular area between the three eyelids and con-

123

tracting the tri-segmented blue-green-red pupil to a black dot so that they looked like two huge pink owl's eyes. They were clear, bright and steady. He stared at the metal head of 24of6 and into the glowing sockets. His voice, though low, matched his eyes—alive and vital. "I am dying, Lensman. When I die, so does my Lens die. But I will not just let it fade away. I will command it to go all at once, at the moment of my passing. In a micro-moment—from its stressful instability—I'll release all its dormant power. And as I go free, so will you."

The message was felt by 24of6 even as it was spoken, and he could do nothing to stop Vveryl's sacrifice. He and Worsel and Kallatra all felt the last great surge of life force flow telepathically into the Lens which was still part of him, the Lens which lived, quiescent, within the head-body of the Asterias.

Vveryl the Chickladorian, the young Lensman on his first adventure, died. And with his death there came to Worsel and to Kallatra the sadness of the Lensman's Load. Even far-off Kinnison felt the terrible pain of loss that marked the passing of a Lensman.

And the Lens which was Vveryl exploded with all the unfulfilled potential that Vveryl, in life, had once promised to give to Civilization.

With the extra-dimensional blast the hatchway buckled and the Asterias was blown into shreds. With the release of the creature, the spaceship leapt upward through the hungry arms of the first dozen of its kindred, up, up, beyond the planet, out of control, with 24of6 once again unconscious.

Within one hour 24of6's ship was being gathered in by the tractor beams of an enemy warship, a quarter of a million miles from Worsel and *Flame*.

But nearby, still invisible because it was so small, was the lifeboat with Kallatra in it, quietly tracking his prosthetic friend.

The death of Vveryl cast Kinnison into a melancholy moment filled with painful rebukes of himself for having allowed it to happen. The ambush on Dyaddub was stupid, careless. But Kinnison could not dwell on what had happened; he had the immediate future to worry about.

"What's our strength?" he asked for the sixth time in an hour, his eagerness now built up into the hair-trigger tension of a runner awaiting the starting pistol.

"We're topping point six," Ckawa, his G-1, said.

Kinnison touched a button on the chest plate of the combat unit which he was wearing around his neck. "Check their flight pattern," he said, his words barely audible but amplified by the tiny transmitters pressed against his throat. The Rigellian-in-charge answered, his mental response coming not only in Kinnison's head, but through the ear-plug inserted in his left canal. When the battle got heavy, Kinnison would be using his chest plate, with its score of buttons with as many different shapes, and his ear receiver, to channel certain bits of battle information which might be muddled together in the mass of thought waves which his mind would be filtering.

"Double check their flight pattern," Kinnison countered, to confirm the fact that the enemy fleet was in part holding back, in part retreating. He stared at the tank display, but the colored lights, in their reduced scale, showed no movement.

"They *are* moving back," Kinnison said to anyone who may have been listening. "Captain Salgud. We can't wait to form up completely. We're over point six and climbing—we'll go after them now!"

Kinnison stepped back from his console and dragged his heavy, padded bucket-chair over a circular plate in the floor centered in front of his desk. Manipulation of a knob on the instrument bank brought a metal rod vertically up into the bottom of the chair. A few pushes, a click, and the coupling was made. Kinnison leaned back in the seat, half enveloped by it, and opened up the top of the armrests. From the front almost to the point of the elbow, there were revealed buttons and switches, flickering numerical displays, and blinking colored lights. The Galactic Coordinator was ready for action.

"Worsel!" Kinnison got the Velantian's attention immediately. "We're coming in!" Deliberately avoided, although the intense feeling was there, was Kinnison's sorrow for the fate of Vveryl and concern for 24of6 and Kallatra. "However, I have a request, big fella—be the head man for this operation."

Kinnison's decision to make Worsel commander-in-chief was no whim; the logic was sound, the choice was obvious. Never was an opportunity more golden than the one offered by having the commanding general in the heart of the enemy forces. With the two greatest minds of civilization linked by their abnormally enhanced mental abilities and so strategically placed, the leadership would be the ultimate. Worsel was surprised by the unusual proposal, but he accepted it with supreme assurance.

"Did I hear you say 'head snake'?" Worsel chided, much to Kinnison's amusement. "Naturally the head snake accepts. What's the chain of command?"

"Work directly with the Rigellians at the tank—they'll pick you up easily, they're the best. In fact, I think you worked with them at Klovia. Just keep me informed as your chief of staff."

Worsel wasted no time. He surveyed the enemy forces with lightning speed. "Fourteen battle cruisers, seventeen heavy cruisers—about ten percent to the head-count." For the tank he visualized each ship in its coded color and mentally placed it in its relative position in space. "The ratio is extra high in scouts and auxiliaries," and he ran those off for the Rigellians to add to the display in the *Dauntless* tank. "Four large ships, capital class plus one point two rating, that's about one percent, abnormally low, not at all a battle fleet. Their tactics don't make sense, either. Note the capital ships: still close to the planet, out of supportive position. All this time their fleet has hung back, in distorted formation, instead of taking out after the *Dauntless*. While they've held back we've been allowed to build up reinforcement. But though they're not on the offensive, they're not on the defensive, either—assuming they're not stupid. Conclusion? They're waiting for something to happen. I'm certain the engagement will be entirely in standard inert mode. My decision is to attack immediately in a pentagonal column, sweptback, cone formation 5B-3-2X, doubling on every third ring. That will give us at least four complete rings, the fourth at 72 ships. The fifth can expand as more GP ships come in. Center the thrust on *Flame* and I'll direct the fire power."

Under the Pentagon-B formation, the GP ships tiered themselves like the candles on a tapering birthday cake tilted on its side. The heavier classes assembled on each third ring, but the great preponderance of craft was the fast, light to medium, independent star rovers. One ship, alone, was at the apex, the *Dauntless*. As the charge progressed the *Dauntless* would slow, in effect retracting, and, as the pressure mounted, each five-sided ring would slip back inside the next, telescoping the formation into more and more of a units-in-line pattern.

When Worsel deemed the moment right, he ordered the firing of the beams of the first three rings, deliberately held short to deceive the enemy. In his invisible position, he again adjusted his balances to distort the radiant waves of the enemy. This time he managed to reach out and affect nearly fifty ships in his vicinity. With the *Dauntless* speeding in on him as a bulls-eye, that meant the fifty ships were the ones which should have been most able to concentrate their deadly beaming right into the incoming Patrol. But the guns of the fifty enemy vessels were somehow missing their targets, no one knew why—except Worsel, because it was his doing. His wave-balancing act was throwing off the spotter instrumentation of the foe just enough to make the aim inaccurate.

"All elements!" Worsel's command instantaneously went to and through the Rigellian to all captains. "Do not fire within the dead ahead arc of five degrees. Concentrate your fire left and right on all ships adjacent, moving your beams outward as appropriate." To Kinnison alone he said, "The fifty enemy in my area can be ignored" and explained why the ones on the periphery were more dangerous, having a true picture of the GP locations. "Besides," Worsel added, "this new tactic I've thought up is untested for side effects— it's possible that our aim will be erroneously calibrated, too. We'll get them as we go through."

The GP fleet, now telescoped into one huge disc, ceased firing and passed through Worsel's zone. Worsel's distortion became ineffective, but the enemy ships had very little target, viewing the inside edge of the disc of ships. As the GP vessels began to leave the area, they reversed their formation, telescoping in the opposite direction. Worsel directed fire on the core of enemy vessels and the destruction was complete. Half of the entire enemy force had come under fire with a fifty percent success score—about seventy-five of 350 ships were badly disabled or destroyed, with virtually no damage to the Patrol!

"Now all ships follow the *Dauntless* in a sweeping 360 degree circle for another attack." Worsel mentally calculated the flight path for Captain Salgud and passed it on in seconds. "Kinnison!" Worsel gloated, "Half their ships don't have inertialess drive. We'll cut them to pieces, and they know it! Watch out—this is one time we might get a white flag from a ship or two." Worsel's moment of exhilaration was dampened by an unexpected sight. As the GP fleet swung around in a graceful curve away from the system, the ships of the enemy in optical sight as tiny flecks of light against the nearly starless emptiness of space beyond the nebula, the surface of the nearby blue-white planet began to grow large black spots. They were the black globes which 24of6 had encountered and had printed as an image on Worsel's brain. As Worsel saw them now first-hand, he quickly perceived them in depth. They were all of the same size, perhaps each a mile in diameter, and they came surfacing through the clouds of Zebub, to float there on the turbulence. The Cheeni were covered with patches of dark gray, which were the Asteri, thousands on each globe. When first he noticed them, there were only three, becoming six, then eight. Now there were several dozen bobbing below, revolving slowly, solid black balls spotted with gray stars, with no marks or traces of structuring. The first few Cheeni now were releasing their Asteri, which waved lazily like a species of underwater plant. His perception indicated that they were filled with thousands of moving forms, but he could feel only a few hundred humanoid minds. They indeed seemed to be what 24of6 had judged them, floating cities, although perhaps the term might better be industrial units or some such other kind of unified society. Worsel was dividing his attention between three events, the path of the GP fleet, the position of the remaining 230 of the enemy, and the growing numbers of Cheeni. Even his exceptional multi-compartmented mind was not able to probe the Cheeni as thoroughly as he would have liked. His observation indicated that most of the ambulatory figures inside the globes were mechanical, mostly suggestive of the warrior-robots who had captured the late Vveryl, and the feeling grew for him that these globes were self-contained experimental stations, a combination of laboratory and factory. He decided that their principal function were the manufacturing of the robots and a controlled evolution of the Asteri for some future project.

The *Dauntless* had led the attacking force around in its circle and the second assault was about to begin. The black globes, assembled into a polygonal pattern and hovering in a fixed position just above the cloud banks, with the planet slowly sliding beneath, began, one by one, to rise toward the protecting fleet, condensing into a polyhedronal shape. Just how dangerous those thirty globes might be Worsel had no way of judging. The second assault might have to be executed differently. The polyhedron was now complete, accentuating the fact that the globe which marked its geometric center was different from all others; it was slightly larger, had neither fixed nor waving Asteri on its surface, and had some slight bulges that suggested special properties. A quick scan determined that this globe most certainly had inertialess drive, whether or not the others did.

Suddenly one of the uppermost globes disintegrated with a flare of light—shrinking rather than expanding—and immediately blinked out into nothingness, followed by a black after-image of such a short duration that Worsell did not really perceive it. Another flash of light, then darkness came. And another and another. The black after-images, like negative reflections of some sort of hole in space, were now clearly fixed in his mind by their repetition. The globes were blowing up so quickly that half of them were destroyed before Worsel's analytical mind could determine that the energy was being absorbed by the central globe. The process was a duplication of the photon-absorbtion which had recently happened on Dyaddub. The globes were not being attacked; they were simply destroying themselves. Then one broke ranks and moved swiftly down toward the clouds. It had gone barely ten thousand miles when multi-colored beams shot simultaneously from a dozen different warships and it, too, exploded. The self-destruction was being allowed no exceptions! In a burst of atomic energy, so intense that the protective alpha and gamma radiation screens of *Flame* could not block all the harmful rays from briefly bathing Worsel, the remaining globes were destroyed, leaving the single central sphere remaining.

Worsel took a moment to dig out three anti-radiation pills the size of gytczl eggs, and to wash them down his throat with a long pull on his water tube.

"We're coming in!" Kinnison, observing the fireworks through both his and Worsel's minds, was principally concerned for the organization of the new attack. "Take over, Worsel!"

Worsel came to a split-second judgment. "Keep all defensive screens up at full power. Fire no weapons. Use every resource to throw a tractor-net around that remaining globe. Execute a telescoping Pentagon-5 and capture that globe. Right now it's about as dangerous as all the other Spawn ships combined. Be careful—but capture it!"

A slight correction in the angle of attack put the *Dauntless* on collision course with the Cheenus, the rest following a distorted pyramidal form because of the proximity of Zebub.

The unexpected happened. Instead of the enemy rallying around the single Cheenus, every vessel with the capability went into free drive and disappeared, every inert ship moved into a direct confrontation with the GP formation—and the Cheenus simply disappeared in a stupefying nova.

Worsel's instantaneous query to the Rigellian-in-charge confirmed his deduction. The one hundred nineteen enemy ships in inertialess flight, many times the speed of light and accelerating, were going off in one hundred nineteen different directions within the 360 degree sphere, less the eight degree radius blocked by the bulk of Zebub inself. Worsel decided that pursuit of them was impossible. His first concern was to keep track of the Cheenus and to take with him the bulk of the Patrol ships in pursuit of it like starved gners after a fat abbet. But the Rigellians could not fill in the blank in his own perception on ship's instruments; the Cheenus had simply disappeared, with no trace.

"That's tough, Worsel," Kinnison commiserated. "I know we could have learned a lot from its capture. It must have been so important that they blew it up, instead of taking it into free evasive action." A quick understanding of their minds put Captain Salgud in charge of disposing of the weaker, smaller force which was engaged in a suicidal assault against them. "Congratulations, old snake! Great job! The victory is yours! They're scattering to the four winds, but there'll be another time."

"Thanks. But that Cheenus didn't destroy itself. The tactic was so damned clever—it discharged all its stored-up photonic power in that huge flash, and simply destroyed all trace of the path of its escape. It's credits to crullers that the globe gave one huge shot of free drive, and is now coasting undetected through this arm of the galaxy—every trace muddied by the paths of the other ships. We had the thing in our grasp and I muffed it."

"No way could you have prevented that, Worsel," Kinnison said. "Enjoy the victory. We came through that fracas with no more than a couple of superficial burns on a couple of our ships. Want to put in for Admiral?"

"What!" Worsel relaxed and enjoyed making his sardonic reply more than savoring his victory. "Call that a reward—turn me into a desk-bound button-pusher like you? No thanks!"

"QX, you irresponsible adventurer," Kinnison fired back, still riding an emotional high of pleasure at the outcome. "I get your message. You've got another job to do. You're flitting after Kallatra and Deuce."

"Right you are, my friend. Kallatra's sending back a perfect trace. It was fun, but I'm on my way the instant you give me my release."

"QX, Worsel. The *Dauntless* and the fleet will mop up here—in twenty minutes to two hours we'll annihilate the remainder, although it may take us several days if there's apt to be many prisoners. Then we'll survey Zebub. Good hunting. Clear ether." *Flame* immediately vanished from Kinnison's tank, off faster than Lensed thought with only the faint trace left by Worsel ticking off on the sub-etheric monitor assigned to keep as close tabs as possible on the Velantian.

Kallatra's deliberate spoor was almost unrecognizable, even for Worsel who was concentrating on following it. Kallatra was taking no chance on giving his stalking position away because he was so very close behind the enemy ship. It was fortunate that he had been so close when the heavy battleship drove out of the system under full inert or Kallatra might have lost it completely. Although he didn't have the power plant to keep pace with the battleship, he did have the inert capability and sufficient tractor efficiency. As that ship went free, with 24of6's speedster caught and held just aft of the engine room, so did *Flame*'s lifeboat match the same power phase under Kallatra's synchronous response. At the moment of acceleration Kallatra fastened on to the larger vessel with an unbreakable tractor clamp and became an integral part of the other's mass and movement.

After several hours of cautious probing during the flight, Kallatra's consciousness suddenly bumped into 24of6's, much to the paraman's surprise. 24of6 was aware that he had been unconscious for a long period of time, and his exploratory mental inspection had fully expected a complete absence of any friendly thought, especially as the vacuum of a million mile range had become immediately apparent. The two Lensmen quickly reviewed the situation.

Trapped by the enemy warship as an interloper, 24of6 had been held near the cargo ports. Only after the ship's escape had the speedster been pulled inside an airlock, but even then the huge doors had been left open as a precautionary measure, with a cupped force field around the speedster to absorb the shock of an unexpected explosion.

No thoughts were to be found on any frequency by 24of6 until he picked up Kallatra's, but he had been able to use his Lens to search through the ship. The crew was nonexistent, the vessel being run by a computer brain which virtually filled the control room, all systems being integrated into it and all decisions coming from it. There were hundreds of warrior-robots of various sizes walking about, waving arms and rods, having no tasks to do, but in compulsive, meaningless motion. There was an eerie sense about the whole scene, as if time were limitless or did not exist. 24of6's ship was ignored for an unreasonably long period of time, almost as if forgotten, before the paraman noticed any evidence that the brain was undertaking some new initiatives. 24of6 felt spy-rays sweeping through him, and he screened his Lens in his head and disguised the organic parts of his body as chambers of fuels and lubricating oils.

A half-dozen robots, looking sinister because their actions were purposeful and controlled, entered the cargo airlock through a portal in the force field. They started to force an entry into the speedster by ray guns and drilling tools, so 24of6 simply opened the door to prevent damage, ready to paralyze them with a strong magnetic charge and attempt an escape with them at the first sign of serious trouble. Only one robot entered and immediately took hold of Vveryl's feet, dragging the body out and laying it on the airlock floor. 24of6 was ignored, as if he were merely a robo-pilot. The robots stood around the corpse prodding it and waving their arms. With no telepathy possible, 24of6 could only deduce by surreptitious inductive circuit tapping and gingerly operated spy-rays that the brain and the robots were examining the Chickladorian body. The uniform made it apparent that they had a dead Patrolman, but there was no evidence to show that he had been a Lensman. The obvious conclusion was that the Patrolman had died in his craft, which had been operated by a robo-pilot. At least, that was what 24of6 hoped would be believed. The force screen came down completely, and they carried the body into the main part of the ship. By spy-ray 24of6 watched them inject fluids into the corpse, swathe it in a mass of fusing transparent bandages, shove it in a corner, and then leave.

Again 24of6 felt the spy-rays on him, scanning both him and his ship to make certain it was not an explosive device. Again they seemed satisfied that it was no threat, although they still left the cargo door open. 24of6 assumed that his organic material had been successfully masked, but perhaps they may simply have disregarded it, much as an organic creature might disregard the artificial parts in the serious study of an organism's structure.

"Thought waves are alien to this ship, Lalla," 24of6 said, "so let's communicate freely. Let's call Worsel, who's already on his way, and plan on capturing this ship. This crowd's pretty stupid—I think all I have to do is blow the brain's fuses. The robots can be stopped easily with solid projectiles; they can be knocked off like tin cans. When Worsel is in visual touch with you, we'll coordinate an attack and then swing into action. Meanwhile, we'll just wait."

Kallatra, in his indetectable lifeboat, was scanning space with his simple electromagnetic detector, worried by the growing number of enemy ships showing up on his screen. They were coming in at all angles, probably fleeing the *Dauntless*-led fleet. It was the spectacular appearance of the principal Cheenus which most upset him. It materialized in a blaze of light on the other side of the warship he was tracking, and within moments the two ships were attached. He immediately began figuring out a plan to dash in and out of the cargo area of the warship, picking up 24of6 or perhaps joining him in the speedster. One of the special bulges in the equator of the Cheenus opened and the warship nosed into it. In the midst of this activity an alien thought suddenly was in his head: "You have a Lensman there! Kill the Lensman!" Kallatra then saw Worsel's image, grotesquely distorted, and felt his el-sike powers warning him of unimaginable danger and evil. He sensed 24of6 saying, "Lalla, what is—?" and then sudden silence, as two slicing beams within the cargo area cut the paraman's speedster in half, top to bottom, and again in half, front to back. The longitudinal slash also severed 24of6 right through his heart, the moment that his thought to Kallatra was interrupted. 24of6 was technically dead, but through his el-sike Kallatra heard 24of6 clearly but weakly saying, "Get out! Get out! Lalla, get out!"

The alien thought came again. It described the young Lensman's location in a flash of coordinates and the brain acted within micro-seconds. Kallatra was held in a tractor beam. "Kill the Lensman!" the voice thundered. "The Lensman is a woman!"

Again Kallatra saw what appeared to be Worsel's face, a double image which kept merging and separating, merging and separating.

"That's a lie! That's impossible!" came one thought. "That's a fact! The Lensman is a woman!" came another thought to Kallatra, this now apparently emanating from the tortured mind of an insane Worsel.

Kallatra's boat was drawn rapidly toward the cargo area where the destroyed prosthedon that had been 24of6 lay in two pieces on the deck of the speedster's control room. As he slammed to a halt against the inner hull of the warship, his wild probes detected the popping of the computer-brain's fuses.

Lalla Kallatra lay in a heap on the ceiling of the upside-down flimsy lifeboat stunned senseless. The unthinkable thought which was torturing the sane Worsel was a reality. Kallatra was a woman Lensman.

12

The Worst Kind of Traitor

As Worsel's mind reached out over the light years and touched Kallatra's, the inexplicable, like a terrible, persistent nightmare, happened again. The evil face of himself formed in his head, image upon image, one for each of his eyes, then doubled, then doubled again. His teeth showed white and sharp, his lips curled, his tongue flicked wickedly, a leer, a snarl; the horror was again complete. There was no Tong to share this vision; it was all his. Worsel, the schizophrene, was worse than ever—the dual personality of himself was alone, mismated, in hyperspace, conjured up by a young Lensman with psychic powers, accompanied by the weirdest of fantasies. "Kill the Lensman!" Kill himself? Kill 24of6? Kill Kallatra?

The Velantian dragon was coiled in a tight ball, frozen to his pilot's cage. The outrageous thoughts—"Kill the Lensman!" and "The Lensman is a woman!"—tightened the cable-like sinews of his arms and legs so convulsively that the claws of his hands slipped around the control bar on which they rested and punctured the soft heels of his palms while those on his feet unsheathed and hooked into the mat flooring.

This time the tidal wave of emotion which surged instinctively over him did not submerge his rational self. It was no longer the shock it had been the first time he had experienced it, and now he had two ways to resist. The first way was through instrumentation; he sat before the most elaborate mind-oriented equipment that could be expected of a renowned psychiatrist of his peerless ability and reputation. The second way was through a fellow Lensman who had special talents in mental frequencies which suggested new and better opportunities for greater understanding, Lalla Kallatra. To him Worsel sent out at once an urgent command: "Monitor me!' and was surprised and worried to find that his objective was unconscious, mind screen up and tight.

135

The nightmare vision was fading.

Worsel switched his complete attention to his activated telepathic scanner-analyzer, a bilaterally integrated mechanism which located, identified, and examined both internal-external ethereal and sub-ethereal emanations registering within the brain. There appeared to be nothing unusual. And yet there was a hint, a subtle suggestion of an unidentifiable signal coming from an untraceable direction in to his sub-consciousness, a unique phenomenon he had never noticed before. No frequency was indicated by any of his gadgets; there was merely the disturbance on his own brain patterns by *something*. There was nothing against which he could re-act and drive a thought. He was helpless.

The ugly vision, however, was almost gone.

For many seconds Worsel sat immobile, his perception sweeping across the enormous range of frequencies, always with one section of his mind watching for the slightest devia-tion of his brain pattern as a clue.

He caught many thoughts far and farther away, even be-yond the Milky Way, but nothing which he sought. From time to time he would call Kallatra and, though there was no conscious response, he was reassured by the sense of personal peace in which that Lensman's mind drifted. On the other hand, he was puzzled by the ever fainter thoughts from 24of6 which seemed to be reviewing that paraman's entire life. From a great distance there was an unaccountable *blip* in his pattern and he tried a deep space probe with his mind tuned as high as it would go. He held the probe steady for nearly two full minutes before he had to drop his intense concentration under the excruciating strain.

With his release from his self-imposed task and the end of the final ghostly vision, other thoughts were coming in to Worsel. He picked up Kallatra's mind, and he read what had been happening for the past handful of minutes. There had been a flurry of activity. What he read was incredible. For the briefest moment he thought he might be hallucinating about Kallatra. Then there were more images. They came from 24of6—and they were even more incredible!

Kallatra had come to full consciousness just as Worsel had isolated himself with his deep space probe. Kallatra had wasted no time, vaguely hearing urgent orders from 24of6. There was no chance of help from Worsel—in a split second she had realized Worsel's temporary absence. The young female Lensman accomplished her objectives almost before she thought of what she was doing: she had scooped up the top portion of 24of6's dissected body with a tractor beam and, englobing it and fixing it fast to the hull of the lifeboat, accelerated away toward Worsel's *Flame*, slipping through a concentration of pencil-beams following in her wake.

Worsel read no crazy thoughts. No one was insane. The brain of 24of6 still lived, its metabolism suspended by the absolute cold of space. Kallatra was racing to *Flame* for shelter and help. *Flame* would be a galactic super-ambulance to carry the essence of 24of6 to Dyaddub for salvage. Worsel read the plan in Kallatra's mind: there was that new, nearly-finished prosthedon on Dyaddub ready as a life-saving support system.

Worsel instantaneously became part of the rescue effort. He fastened his own tractor on his returning lifeboat and was already dragging it into inertialess drive toward Dyaddub. He sent two messages: one went to Kinnison with the position of the two ships—the warship mated to the Cheenus —and the other went to 24of6's laboratory on Dyaddub to alert the staff of the emergency. What he did not tell even Kinnison was what he had suspected, now confirmed: that Lalla Kallatra was undoubtedly more woman than man.

His first reaction was simply to dismiss the obvious because it was a known impossibility. No woman could be a Lensman. Mentor had explained that as a fact. The Lens of Arisia was sex-oriented; no woman could be a Lensman because it was a physical and psychological impossibility. But, Worsel realized, even as he rationalized that dismissal, it was not true—for the Red Lensman herself was a woman, the most womanly of women. And there was evidence. The dying thoughts of 24of6 could not be dismissed. Worsel considered himself released from the human code of ethics in this case; he felt it was logical to listen in on the last thoughts of a dying Lensman when valuable knowledge might otherwise be lost forever. The phenomenon of a mind approaching death was of intense interest to him, and so he soaked up the unreeling history, with its disclosures. In them Worsel was picking out all pertinent material, including the strange story of Lalla Kallatra: a girl prodigy whose father was a Lensman named Samuel O'Stead and who was, despite her natural super powers, barred by the destiny of the Red Lensman from becoming one herself. And so, when her father had raised his motherless daughter and tutored her to the limit of his ability, he had surrendered her to the custody of the prosthedon 24of6, who officially became her foster father. With a new name—Lalla Kallatra—the girl had become a boy for all planetary and Patrol records. Worsel wasn't sure if the girl actually had become a boy—perhaps the youth was half and half, for humans and the like sometimes slipped into unusual states. At any rate, it was inevitable that he or she should become a Lensman. If she were actually female, then secrecy would be expected, and her mind would have to be kept inviolable.

Worsel now suspected that Lalla Kallatra might be bearing a terrible burden, the concealment of her sex. Such a possibility put Worsel in a perplexing position. What could he say about it, especially to Kinnison, his friend? There was only one woman who had ever been or who ever would be such a unique person in the Patrol, in Kimball Kinnison's conviction—or, for that matter, in the presumption of all Civilization. Worsel decided not to worry about it now; he made a quick decision. Until he had further evidence and Kallatra's sanction, he would speak of Lalla Kallatra as the male she pretended to be, and see her as a female only in his own thoughts. Perhaps in the near future Mentor would have to be consulted for clarification.

As for 24of6, Worsel was now convinced he wouldn't die. The trip would be successful, and 24of6 would live again in an even more bizarre and different form. There was the other unresolved problem. "Kallatra," Worsel said evenly, seeking to be precise in his basic facts, but elaborate in the sketchy thoughts which rose around and surrounded them, "I've had my schizophrenic symptoms again. I've reason to believe there's an outside force at work, a telepath of unusual power. Just before you rescued Deuce I had a brief trace on it. I think I actually poked the source. There was something at the other end, something unseen, like a phantom. The frequency is measurable, although only in half-waves as reflected by my brain. The other halves are simply not there, completely missing, undetectable, scientifically unexplainable. Such mental frequencies are not only beyond my experience, they're even beyond my knowledge. Sub-etheric, perhaps. It's something in your line. It's akin to your description of electro-psychic communication."

Kallatra was, Worsel keenly noted, as self-possessed as ever, her mind screen on guard as always, exhibiting no elation at her rescue and escape, nor any anxiety about the devastating misfortunes encountered.

"You can also consider the occasion of the robots attack on us on Dyaddub," Kallatra said. "I felt an outside force at work there, too. At the time I thought it might be, as you say, sub-etheric."

Worsel was aware of a change in the young Lensman. Although her comment was as sharp, punctilious, and unemotional as ever, her thoughts were less ingenuous, as though bracing herself for some sort of trial. In this, Worsel was right.

"I'll open my mind to you, Worsel—so you can couple your mind to my electro-psychic energies. Concentrate on those visions you've just had. *Think* yourself into union with this, this evilness. Keep your thoughts in union, but not in harmony. Be an unsympathetic enemy, not a sympathetic friend. If you can, Worsel, *hate* what you saw, *hate* what you see, try to project that hate toward it."

Worsel found himself mentally gliding downward, the descent rapidly becoming steeper, until he was plummeting down a dark tunnel. The sensation weirdly reversed itself; he was shooting upward, not downward, a typical vertigo of deep space. The mind he was traveling through had no gender; he had no inhibitions against looking because he expected to find no clues and he found none. He heard Kallatra saying, far, far away, "You *hate* the thing, Worsel! *Destroy* the thing, Worsel!" And Worsel *hated* and wanted to destroy. With all the power of his mighty mind, he drove a shaped thought like a spear into the ugly shimmering vision of himself. *I hate you,* he projected. *I'll kill you.* He saw a reflection of his Lens buried in his forehead. The clean, crisp rainbow flashes were not mirrored there; the innumerable tiny, crystal-like gems so harmoniously united within a Lens were here, instead, crude, furry things of disorder and turbulence. The pulsating power which he felt and perceived was a peculiar, leprous *squirming.* He projected: *I hate you—I'll kill you—WHO ARE YOU?* The ugly vision vanished and Worsel was alone in the black emptiness of another space or dimension. He heard a voice calling him, a silent whisper which was saying his name "Worsel" and telling him to return. Reluctantly, because he was so at peace, so tranquil, he did.

Worsel snapped back into Kallatra's mind and immediately sensed the young Lensman's difficulty. Kallatra was semi-conscious, her mind wide open. Worsel was so taken by surprise that he glimpsed the hidden corners before he could stop himself. He saw now what Kallatra had so dreaded to reveal, why the young Lensman had been embarrassed with Kinnison, what Worsel had almost been honestly told but put off. The veil was drawn away at last, the mask was removed: Lalla Kallatra was a fifteen-year-old girl!

And Lalla Kallatra was dying!

Three neat microscopic holes had been driven completely through her left shoulder, left lung and behind the left ear, coming out the right temple. Kallatra had not escaped, after all, from the frantic firing at the time of escape. Only the warping effects of acceleration and the inertialess boost of *Flame*'s engines had kept the wounds from becoming instantly fatal. But those minute punctures should not be leading to death—it was Kallatra's sapped spirit that had brought her life forces so low. It was the result, Worsel knew without question, of the confrontation with Worsel's alter-ego; the similarity to a Delgonian malignance which he knew so well gave him the wisdom to apply mental resuscitation, to strengthen the ego and to revive the will to live.

Kallatra grew stronger with the infusion of the Velantian's own enormous energy. By the time they reached Dyaddub, Kallatra was coming back from death, and 24of6's continued existence was also assured.

He made contact with their minds, individually, to hearten them as they received medical attention. He was aware of the touch of apprehension they each had about hiding their innermost secrets and he blanked the knowledge he had from his mind and attitude.

Many hours later, when Kinnison arrived at the underground laboratory, Kallatra was virtually healed and 24of6 was on his way to being better than ever. They all were in the living quarters discussing the paraman's makeshift housing, the new, not-quite-finished body with the temporary attachments. His frozen remains had been speedily encased in it. Hardly much more than his brain remained. His brain had been removed from his old head casing, all nerve connections at the top of the spine cut away with a laser, and submerged in a synthesized protoplastic colloid. The biggest worry had been the danger of character change; it wasn't just life that was being conserved, it was his distinctive ego which they sought to preserve. The key had been the delicately blended molecular formula of artificial blood, with its enzymes and bio-chemicals and nutrients so peculiar to the paraman. The remnants of his organic body were virtually gone now. They saved and relocated the glands, but he no longer had his heart and one lung. The technicians had improvised with an awkward hodge-podge of paraphernalia projecting out of the modified chest area. During the entire process of emergency engineering, as the brain was transferred from its temporary tank to the new skull, 24of6 kept in close communication with Kallatra, and also with Worsel. He even offered advice on his own reconstruction.

As messy as his chest was, his back was just as bad. He had tanks and tubes at the base of his skull, and boxes and power packs connected to a sort of spinal column. Less fluid circulated now to support his life; electrical circuitry had replaced the liquids where possible. Only the environment of his exceptionally convoluted brain remained as it had been. A tiny chemical factory within the tank at the back of his neck vitalized and fed that which was 24of6.

His face was the same. With his long, flowing robe hiding the crude improvisations, he seemed unchanged.

Kinnison, in his supple gray leather harness and lustrous boots, was dressed in the traditional "grays," a deliberate symbolic expression of the war he was now fighting. He put his hands on his hips and leaned against one of the crystal columns in which exotic plants grew, a picture of self-assured power. "The enemy has abandoned the Ekron system," he said. "We tried to capture some of the inert warships, and although some even did try to surrender they all were blown to atoms. Maybe most were courageous suicides, but with that number I'm certain a lot were involuntary victims. Anyhow, we've just completed a preliminary reconnaissance and survey. Zebub is deserted. Obviously, as there's really no land mass, no continents to build on, those Cheeni were the only habitable places, sort of oases in the frozen clouds. The fleet's assembling. We should be ready in a few hours." He turned to Kallatra and with a brisk gesture of his open hand indicated his turn to speak. "Now, what have you guys cooked up?"

Kallatra, still in his role of young boy, was clear-eyed and unmarked by the pencil-beam burns, even stiffer in his posture of respect because his left side was still sore. He had a data-receptor lantern in his right hand. He raised it and projected a three-dimensional picture cube into the center of the room, displaying a star map of that sector of space very similar to a tank projection. A brightly blinking red light marked the edge of a system of suns and planets whose area was indicated by a pink stain.

"The flasher," Kallatra explained to Kinnison, "marks the location of the warship which captured Deuce O'Sx. We assume the Cheenus is still attached. The locator-signal comes from his disabled speedster. We assume it's an oversight on their part, so we've a direct line on the ultimate direction. The mated pair has pursued an erratic course of evasion for some time, but the current movement has been such a steady line for such a long period that we can further assume that we now have its destination identified as the Ranggi System."

The picture cube disappeared, and Kinnison said, "So, friends, that's what we're after. Reports do confirm scores of enemy vessels, probably those from Zebub, converging on this system. My goal is to destroy those ships. I'd like Worsel to attempt the same tactic so recently successful—speeding into the heart of the enemy formation in his indetectable ship. However, I know you want to capture one robot, not the Cheenus itself, by following the locator signal. That's a priority objective set by Deuce." He looked at them. "Can Worsel mastermind both at the same time?"

Thought waves came strongly from 24of6; the quality of the mental sounds different, but the mannerism was the same. "I've studied Worsel's plan—even helped a little. Yes, he can do it." There was absolutely no movement or gesture; the only sign of life was the pulsing of the tube entering his chest from the box at his side. "It's important we make the attempt. We know the warrior-robots are highly dangerous. They are independently intelligent, yet they radiate no thoughts, a disturbing characteristic. We don't know how they are manufactured or maintained and repaired. I believe the Boskonians or their Spawn or whoever are responsible have made a break-through—it could revolutionize our galactic security as well as our tactical warfare. It's vital to capture at least one of them. Also, an Asterias—if there is one—for they seem to be another artificial, if radically different, life form weapon."

"I want to know why the Patrol exploration team was chopped up into little pieces," Kinnison said.

"Kallatra has a feeling about that," the paraman said. "He senses that the men were engaged in hand-to-hand combat, probably in space, and simply hacked to pieces, then not too well buried to hide the evidence. The real mystery is why there are thousands and thousands of robot sizes."

"We *must* capture one—undamaged," Kinnison concluded. "The only course is for Worsel and Kallatra and Tong to make the try."

"I hope we'll get the entire Cheenus." 24of6 seemed quite hopeful. "We need its papers and documents, too. Remember, a long time ago, before my assignment to Zebub, I reported to headquarters about possible sentient machines. I suspect some of my own theories are being used. I think the Boskonians and their Spawn stole my reports—may still be stealing my reports. They knew when to attack you on Dyaddub. They evacuated Zebub with bewildering speed. There are spies around—at high level."

"It's true," Worsel said, "that Boskonia is dead at the top, but in some sectors the Bosko-Spawn are worse than ever. However, spies may not be the trouble. We may have communication leaks."

"I said the schizophrenia case was closed until we had cause to re-open it," Kinnison pointed out. "Well, we've got to reconsider."

"My new visions were a repetition of the earlier one," Worsel said. "But this time they seemed outside myself—the alter-ego generator shrinks before my scrutiny."

Tong, the veteran Velantian, closely following the discussion, interjected. "And yet, this time I was unaffected. I didn't receive, and I evidently didn't transmit such visions." He shifted his weight to his huge, plastic-encased left leg, his movement and his mental attitude showing his concern. He feared Kinnison or Worsel might exclude him from the forthcoming action.

"That underscores a fact," Kallatra's sharp thought wave had extra emphasis. "My explanation now is not satisfactory. It was logical then; in fact, it's still logical. But I don't myself believe it any longer. Consider this: back on the *Hipparchus* I reported Tong being delirious and mentioning a 'wood house'. I now know what Tong meant. Can you recall it, Tong?"

"Wood house?" Tong shook his heavy head. "No, I don't. Let me run that episode through my head—let's see— I said 'wood horse'. But I don't know why I said it."

"Wood horse!" The minds of both Worsel and Kinnison simultaneously flashed understanding and they looked at each other, Kinnison's eyes wide and Worsel's all extended.

"It's easy to see it now, isn't it," Kinnison said. "Wood horse—wooden horse. Somebody coming into our network like a Trojan horse—accepted as a Lensman, but not one."

"Or a traitor," Worsel suggested.

"A bad apple?" Kinnison was shocked. "We've never had one."

"He could be sick or insane," Worsel persisted. "I can see some circumstances. . ."

"So can I," Kinnison agreed. "It's possible, but highly unlikely. A traitor . . ." He ran his fingers through his hair and shook his head slowly, more in wonderment than in denial.

"There are many Lensmen missing, unaccounted for," Worsel continued.

"Such a Lensman could have gotten into my Lensed conference," Kinnison agreed, reconciling himself to the idea. "I thought something like that, I must admit, after the repercussions. The reports of dark shadows and shapes and all that stuff. . ."

"The puzzle is why Worsel and Tong were affected," Kallatra mused. "I feel it has something to do with my psychic powers. Yet Vveryl felt nothing."

"I agree, Kallatra," Worsel said. "I think it does have something to do with your el-sike. Perhaps, though, it was *you* who were the target—and we didn't recognize the fact."

"That makes sense," Tong said. "I almost destroyed *Hipparchus*. If I had, it would have destroyed you."

"If Tong and I were only incidentally involved," Worsel said, "or maybe secondary targets, then what made us so susceptible?"

"I can guess," Kinnison said sadly. "The traitor is a Velantian."

For a long moment everyone was quiet, transmitting no thoughts.

To break the tension, Kallatra tried a side issue. "Why don't we brainstorm this problem by freely jumping back and forth into each others' minds? I don't mean all shields down, but more like a common corporate mind?"

"No good," Worsel said. "We've found that individual discussions with independent thoughts produce a greater variety of ideas when each one can pursue his own thought lines. There's the additional danger, now that we are more susceptible to eavesdropping."

"Worsel," Kinnison said, his thought coming out as slowly as speech, "can you consider that there is a super Overlord behind all of this? Or perhaps that the Velantian traitor is under supervision of an Eich survivor, bearing in mind the frigid, poisonous planet of Zebub?"

"That horrible possibility has crossed my mind."

"Then that could mean," Kallatra added, much concerned with his theory about el-sike's involvement, "the use of the hyper or fourth or some other dimension—perhaps even on the edge of the plane of existence? All these suggest a problem so complex as to be nearly impossible to solve, or even to comprehend."

"You're right, Kallatra," Kinnison agreed. "Let me call Nadreck immediately." He wrinkled his brow in deep concentration and held it for a half minute, the others respectfully silent, until he relaxed and reported, "Nadreck has observed nothing in hyper dimension or in any other spatial or temporal dimension." Kinnison looked at 24of6 and added, "I told Nadreck about your misfortune, and he sends his condolences and best wishes. He also remembered your original name from a long time ago when you had your initial misfortune—Samuel O'Stead. That seems to ring a bell with me. Anyhow, I'll be sending in a request to headquarters to review your files in all your names, to see if we can find a lead toward finding who or what may have stolen or copied your research reports."

By the emerald-filled gizzard of Klono, Worsel thought to himself, *that makes Deuce O'Sx Kallatra's real father! The conspiracy against Kinnison's knowing about another woman Lensman was extensive. It could not go on this way much longer.*

"Your work, Deuce," Kinnison was continuing, "must somehow be related to Worsel and Kallatra. Why did the Lensman-traitor, if there indeed is such, give *thought waves* as orders to robots who can't receive? It might have been to provoke Worsel or Kallatra or somebody unknown. But I agree it's probably that the computer-brain is hooked up to a thought projector-receiver—specifically designed for communication or control by the traitor's Lens. Why did the mysterious mind say 'The Lensman is a woman'? Was the Red Lensman being threatened or somehow warned? If there's a connection here someplace between your work on robotics and the robots and the work of a Lensman-traitor, perhaps your files and reports might reveal something significant. Even Arrow-22 might be involved. We've *got to try* to capture that entire Cheenus. The medics on *Dauntless* have QXed Deuce for the trip—capture even one robot and he'll be handy for a quick evaluation. Well, I guess that covers everything. Let's go, Deuce. I'll see you three later, after we've whipped their tails."

Tong looked at Worsel, grinned and winked one eye, his tongue flicking out several times in unrestrained pleasure. Not only he—even Deuce—everybody—was going to get into the action.

"Lensmen," 24of6 said. Worsel could sense what was coming. Electricity was snapping in the thought waves of 24of6 and everyone winced at its unexpectedness. "Lensmen. You must be told what friend Kinnison will soon find out. Lalla Kallatra is my daughter."

Tong was greatly surprised, but Kimball Kinnison was utterly flabbergasted.

The face of the Galactic Coordinator looked like stone; there was not a flicker of any emotion on it, much to Worsel's amazement, expecting, as he did, a tumultuous flare-up. The Lens on Kinnison's wrist, however, was like a fierce fire under glass and everyone noticed it.

Kinnison's private thought was so powerful that Worsel, who knew what to expect, caught it: a flashing wave charged with emotion propelled like a missile to far distant Arisia, directly at Mentor.

"What kind of deceit have I been subjected to? What's the meaning of this—this trickery?"

Worsel wasted no time. He threw an arm around Tong's shoulder and quickly walked him out of the room.

Kinnison told him later what had happened. Mentor, in his slow, measured way, had patiently explained about the Cosmic All—that there were now appearing, in the ranks of the Patrol, members of the humanoid female sexes. The long-range plan of the Arisians which had culminated in Kimball Kinnison's marriage had been completely in accord with their visualization of Civilization's destiny. The psychological importance of the one, the ultimate, woman in Kinnison's life had been nurtured and fulfilled. The Red Lensman had pioneered the way; there would be more women Lensmen; the Red Lensman herself would now breed some females who would far transcend the ordinary rank of Lensman. The status of Clarrissa, Kinnison's bride, was not being diminished; on the contrary, it would soon be greater than ever.

After the shock of the disclosure had been dissipated by Mentor's calmness, Kinnison accepted the reality of the situation and recognized its inevitability. Just before his departure in his own speedster to join the *Dauntless*, he had a brief word with the girl. "You'll have to give me a break, Lalla—that is, if you'll let me use your first name. Kallatra seems so d-darned stiff for a young 'un like you." She smiled her assent. "I mean, forgive me, let me get used to the idea. What tore it was getting it sprung like that on me. You know. Well, anyhow, Lalla, you're doing a—a heck of a job. Cris, my wife, she'll be real pleased."

Kinnison left, still feeling awkward about it, but much happier.

Soon afterwards Worsel sped away in *Flame*, dragging his expanded lifeboat, which now contained the massive bulk of Tong crowded in against Lalla Kallatra, plus the special equipment which had been improvised and prepared. The sudden change of sex of the young Lensman made hardly any difference in their attitudes toward Lalla—she was as good, bad or indifferent now as she had been before—and they liked her neither more nor less.

Worsel's plan was extremely simple, but far from easy to execute. First of all, *Flame* and its lifeboat were inherently indetectable to electromagnetic detectors, being completely non-ferrous and utterly non-reflective. Secondly, the intrinsic velocity of the enemy pair was constantly known by the transmitter still operating from the warship's airlock. Worsel simply matched intrinsic velocity with his target *before* he went inertialess with *Flame;* then he went free, and, up-dating his readings with his onboard computer, came right in against the hull of the warship at the end of the cargo port, unseen, his speed far in excess of light—and stopped instantly. The calculation had been within centimeters. The maneuver was a masterpiece. The lifeboat was quickly swung around *Flame* and into the empty cargo area not far from 24of6's ruined speedster. That was phase one.

Phase two began with the discharging of the special equipment, three pre-stressed metal nets lined with tough black plastic carrying electrical charges. Each was inverted into a small volume, so that when triggered it would unfold itself inside out against a robot and thus enmesh and trap it. Tong, suited up in the heaviest of dureum armor, was assigned the actual kidnapping of one, two, or three robots, should phase three fail completely. With traps sprung and victims held fast, unable to absorb any outside energy because of the opaque covering, Tong would be flipped away from the ship and far into space by Worsel's tractor beam, to be picked up later.

Phase three was Kallatra's. She would probe for the thought-receiver aboard the warship and attempt to take control of the central brain; with no trouble expected, there should be no impenetrable safeguards operating. If Kallatra succeeded, the ship would be immediately immobilized, and she would proceed with the same stratagem against the Cheenus. Success against the Cheenus had to be accomplished within ten seconds; otherwise they would abandon it and hurl the captured warship—including Worsel, Tong and all—toward the protection of the incoming GP fleet.

Worsel had a dual function, as strategist in command and as the reserve force.

With Tong outside, Kallatra sprawled on her back and began her mental probing. In the Universe there is an infinity of vibrations and she knew and could utilize all those that were known by Civilization. She also was finding and exploring, especially through her electropsychic powers, vibrations which seemed likely to be classified as comprehensible frequencies. Her probes were along two lines: one followed the standard mental frequencies which the evil entity had used for his piercing commands; the other went into the mysterious areas of el-sike, hyper dimensions and planes of existence into which Kallatra had projected thought without being able to firm up any measurements. She immediately located the battleship's thought-receiver, which was directly integrated with the computer-brain. With a lightning thrust she issued a deactivating command which left the computer helpless; in effect, she had pulled the master switch and the warship was captured. There was no activity on the el-sike level. Within seconds Kallatra had launched another mental assault at the computer-brain she found in control of the Cheenus and, because of the link between the two ships, she had an equally quick and easy success. The Cheenus was also captured! It had been so easy! So easy, in fact, that they felt that the real struggle somehow had yet to begin.

Lalla Kallatra stepped out of the lifeboat in her light-weight armor holding an auxiliary thought-projector and gestured to Tong to discard the nets and return to the controls. She wanted to enter the warship and manually disconnect the computer controls, but she needed Worsel to keep the barrier around the thought receiver while she strengthened her el-sike defense. She tossed a request to Worsel to take over the barrier. She took only a millisecond, but brief as the moment was, the strange mental entity struck her. The hand-held projector blew up before her face in a blinding flash.

Worsel and Tong both felt the devastating blow. Because they had so many eyes, some kept as spares during dangerous moments, and because they used perception as much as sight for sensing, they didn't really appreciate how devastating the effect was. Lalla's eyeballs had been burned from her head, mentally from the back as well as physically from the front.

The left hand which had held the projector was completely gone.

But she did not lose consciousness. In fact, she did not lose the concentration of her psychic powers, for Worsel's take-over had given her that surge of released energy which had blocked the foe's killing blow and ricocheted out her eyes. Her own considerable mental powers were wrestling for survival with another super entity.

Another Lensman!

This was no GP hierarch gone wrong! This was not the traitor they had all dreaded and half-expected. This Lensman was more incredible than ever dreamed, utterly Boskonian . . .

. . . a Black Lensman!

13

Threat from Beyond

Into the Ranggi system came 10,000 Spawn ships and 8,000 of those of the Galactic Patrol. The *Dauntless* was in the vanguard, its automatic pilot fixed upon the sub-etheric waves broadcast from the belly of the enemy warship. At first the Ranggi system was merely a wave reading on the screens of the *Dauntless* and a spot of light in the larger tank, an uninspiring representation of just another astronomical cluster to be found in the galaxy. But when the *Dauntless* shifted from free travel to inert, the unique beauty of the new sector instantly struck the eyes of Kinnison and his fellow Patrolmen. Ordinary vision could see the small bright discs in the star-sprinkled sky like variously colored jewels, but the telescopic augmentation was truly dazzling.

Nearly one half of the stars in the Milky Way are in multiple systems—three or more clustered together. Only one out of four stars are solitary, and one third travel as double stars, all in a rich variety of blues, yellows and reds, normal or giant, pulsating or exploding or dead. The Ranggi system was a stellar triplet consisting of a normal white star paired with an orange giant, around both of which orbited a yellow star. Kinnison was struck by its similarity to the familiar Zeta Cancri, in which the interior pair revolve every sixty years and the outer one orbits as their satelitte every 1,150 years. There were eight major planets and thirty-two minor ones. The battle zone was shaping into an oval area between the eccentric orbits of Ranggi planets IV and V as they approached conjunction.

When Kinnison sent out a line to Worsel, he instantly recognized the crisis in its climax: a wounded Kallatra was being strangled into oblivion by a super mentality. Only the bolstering powers of Worsel and Tong were staving off the titanic force crushing the young Lensman.

The renegade Lensman! Kinnison thought, imperfect in his impression, but close enough to the truth to have a basis for action. And he acted instantaneously.

Kimball Kinnison, at that moment the most powerful mind in two galaxies, ground his teeth and projected to the utmost of his will power. To the last microwatt of his mental energies he drove in behind Tong and Worsel like a fullback hitting the line of scrimmage to break the opposition and drive the ball carrier forward. His sudden presence was as effective as a pinprick into an overinflated balloon. The alien entity simply vanished, with a mind-shattering bang.

Out of their disordered thoughts left by the sudden victory, their first concern was for Kallatra. Her mind block freed her of her pain, but she needed immediate medical attention. Promptly and efficiently what had to be done was done.

The others were also somewhat the worse for wear, exhausted and too weak to comment, but Kinnison had read their relief and the knowledge, with gratitude, that it was he who had so unexpectedly joined them.

"By Klono's claws!" Kinnison exclaimed, able now to take time to express his feelings. "By Klono's cantankerous claws, you fellows met something there!" He searched their minds. "You all right?" he asked again, although they had signaled that they were.

"So," Kinnison said, summing up what was in everyone's mind, "there is a false Lensman on the prowl. Too bad, too bad; in fact, it's terrible! Still, I'm damned pleased you haven't uncovered a traitor, after all. I knew Mentor couldn't have made such an error. No Lens of Arisia, this. Boskone born and bred, eh? By all the purple hells of Palain, it's far worse than we imagined!" They had a mental picture of him sadly shaking his head. "Of course, Military Intelligence has always worried about such possibilities. My Kinnison ancestor, Rod the Rock, worried about Black Patrolmen. How much more awful he'd find Black Lensmen. Now that we know our enemy, we can take steps."

Kinnison was ready to turn to other problems, with the moment of adjustment over, but he felt moved to say something to Kallatra. "You were great, young 'un!" He almost added "... for a girl," for old attitudes died hard. Mentor had changed the rules and he would live up to them—he vowed henceforth to overcome his prejudices.

Again he asked them if they were all right, and when again he had been reassured, he asked about the ships they had been stalking, read the situation and said, "How long can you hold out? We've got a major enemy fleet blocking our way to you."

Worsel replied, "We're holding on indefinitely, but any moment something could bust loose. The sooner you get here the better is our chance of keeping these prizes."

"There are," Kinnison informed him, "more than ten thousand fifty ships organizing into a three-D X-formation on a longitudinal axis. Are you going to be able to move in closer and run the show like the last time, Admiral? Or does this Black Lensman . . . ?"

"I'll move in, Kinnison. I'll help in the strategy, but I'd better keep my mind concentrated on the problem here. Kallatra's our watch dog. She knows now she has the special ability to warn us about a reappearance of the Black Lensman. But she'll need all the help she can get. These prize babies are just what we want, and the other side must know it. They'll try to take them back, one way or another, or attempt to destroy them. There's no doubt at all that you've got to pull us in, or defend us as soon as possible."

"QX. I'll see what I can do." Kinnison hesitated for a moment. "Just one thing, Worsel. I read your mind clear as crystal. But Kallatra has a mind screen up. Now I know she's a peculiar one, and the situation's mighty touchy—but this Black Lensman seems so damned insidious. Is there any chance she's under his power—maybe even *is* the Black Lensman? I'm not questioning your competence, Worsel, old friend, I'm just seeking more reassurance."

"Now that you ask—she's permanently blinded and has lost her left hand. But mentally she's QX—stronger than ever. I know you worry about these things, my human friend, but don't worry now—Lalla Kallatra's a real Lensman."

A shocked Kinnison swore and, to cover his emotions, curtly said, "I'll be back." Ten minutes later he was. "The fleet's not all here. Even then we'll be outnumbered. We're not properly organized for our most effective attack. The captains have not all been briefed. Our reconnaissance hasn't been completed." Worsel could almost hear Kinnison's big, frustrated sigh. "We will attack at once."

Worsel wasn't surprised. He said, "QX. Who's in command?"

"It will have to be me, Worsel. The *Dauntless* is going to lead the attack. My job is to secure the ships you're holding. Your job is to feed the Rigellians information, and me advice. QX? Clear ether."

Worsel literally girded himself for action. Around his hard belly, as much a magnificent example of physical power as the hard pectoral muscles of Kinnison, he tightened his leather-covered mesh-dureum belt from which hung his various items of equipment, including a hefty Velantian blaster. He hunkered down in his split-seat chair, tail sticking up behind him. The tail muscles were relaxed now, but when the situation got tense they would stiffen, the tip of his scimitar tail would swell to expose the horny, razor-sharp edge, and the entire length of it would sway and quiver and sometimes twitch. He threw a quick double examination by telepathy and perception on Kallatra; the girl was fine, just as he had told Kinnison, not that bad off—a new hand could probably be regenerated, though the eyes might not. He didn't feel sorry for Kallatra—that was not in his nature—but he did feel a bit angry that such a young Lensman should lose physical perfection so soon in her career.

"You QX?" he asked, taking some effort to pierce even the lowered top part of her mind shield, and, when she said she was, he told her what he must do to begin her chance at a regenerated hand; he had to pare a complete cross section from the stump of her arm two or three millimeters thick. She reasserted her mental block, barring all pain as he did the minor surgery. The flesh he wrapped in sterile film and slipped into one of his smallest specimen cryostats from his gadget-box for indefinite preservation. At the first chance it would go by courier to the Medon Institute for tests and, with luck, the growing of another hand. In six months it would be full size, ready for grafting. The new technique guaranteed no deformities, for it could be regrown in the laboratory until it was just right. When he had re-bandaged her arm, he told her of the developing attack plans by himself and the Patrol.

"Go ahead, Worsel," she said, "and don't concern yourself with me. I'll keep an open terminal tied to your mind. I'll keep you posted, so you won't have to divide your attention. If the tie-line snaps, then you can jump right into my mind and help out."

Worsel scanned space. With his lightning perception he classified each ship as to class and armaments even as he signaled its location to the *Dauntless*. As he placed the ships in the visualized tank he always personally liked to run in his head, other parts of his brain were shaping up strategies to be considered. It was immediately apparent that the enemy had no new or complicated tactic with which to confront the Patrol; they were going to rely on their superiority in weaponry. Whereas the enemy had only one primary objective, to destroy the other fleet, the Galactic Patrol had two, to destroy the Spawn, and at the same time complete the capture of the two Spawn ships.

Worsel's flow of information to the Rigellians in charge of the tank now was being interrupted with his advice to Kinnison. Even if Worsel, freed much more by Kallatra's suggestion, had wanted to develop the battle plan, as he had done the last time, it would not have worked. Worsel saw that Kinnison's strategy was a simple dogfight and no time wasted starting it. One by one the GP ships peeled away from their flight lines and went into intricate maneuvers at conventional, inert speeds. Flashing specks seemed to be a concave hemisphere approaching from the direction of the Purple Veil Nebula, growing larger and larger, until the concavity curved inward behind him. The entire Ranggi system was surrounded by GP ships darting along the edges of the enemy formations, twisting in and out, precision firing only when on an individual target. At first there were a few red rays shooting out and fading, then there were blue ones, then green, until a network of all the colors of the spectrum were interlacing in every direction. Occasionally there would be a flare as a hit was scored and atoms disintegrated. But there was very little of the traditional concentration of firepower and the steady growth of sparkling defensive screens typical of a battle of this size. It was rapier thrusts, hit and run, with pencil-beams pricking away at the foe. Worsel realized now how brilliant Kinnison's strategy was; the superior piloting of the Patrolmen gave the Spawn no advantage in its overwhelming firepower. Half their guns were useless because they couldn't locate the GP ships quickly enough, and the other half couldn't focus together for the most effective punch. True, the Spawn began to pour all their power into only half their guns, to increase their efficiencies, and, unfortunately much too true, they began to puncture or slice an increasing number of Patrol ships, though for their numbers they were being outfought.

Slowly and inexorably the pattern was changing. The Spawn were grouping together more and more, blocking off the individual penetrations of the GP ships, forcing the GP fleet into a wheeling glove, like Indians around a wagon train. The pivotal point was Kallatra and the deactivated ships, Worsel sitting off only a few thousand miles away from them. He could see the *Dauntless* now. Although it looked like the rest—a streak of light among the many other streaks—his mind picked it out. The clues were many—Kinnison's mental line of thought, Deuce's Lens keeping track of the three of them, the Rigellians in strong link—but, most spectacularly, the driving twists and turns at breakneck speed by Captain Salgud, Kinnison's protege using Kinnison's distinctive slam-bang style.

Kinnison's mind impacted on Worsel's "Worsel! Kallatra! Tong!" and in a flash he gave them his new strategy with the reasons behind it. As the Spawn condensed into an organized defense, their strength grew; the Patrol would soon be suffering prohibitive losses. A damaged Spawn ship could still hover behind the front line, contributing its power to the enemy net, while a GP vessel would have to drop out of the racing attack. The Patrol would soon be throwing itself like ocean waves against a cliff, with as much chance of sweeping the enemy away. At any moment the foe could retake the two captured ships or, if desired, simply obliterate them. So Kinnison was making one final thrust, directly at the other three Lensmen, a spearhead leading, in nose-to-tail file, the entire GP fleet. The attack would carry into the heart of the enemy formation and Kinnison's force would surround their interlocked prey in an impregnable defensive ball until the steady build-up of the Patrol on the outside could crush the enemy like a hammer against an anvil.

In a flashing arc the maneuver was brilliantly executed and the tables were turned. The Patrol ships had curled inward before the Spawn had recognized the threat. Too late, the enemy re-grouped and counterattacked. Their battle was lost. Even as they milled about, uncertain of their next formation, the incoming GP ships were hitting them from the other side.

Kinnison was prepared for the suicidal counterstroke, even as Worsel saw it developing and telepathed a warning. Every enemy ship turned and dived directly into the heart of Kinnison's tight defense. One by one, faster and faster, the attacking vessels exploded—not disabled, as almost all the casualties had been up to this point, but completely, irretrievably snuffed out. The destruction continued; the penetration, however, deepened. One of the Spawn, masked by the explosions of its companions all around it, plunged to

155

its goal—it speared the docked warship and they both blew up in a gigantic soundless flash. Only the quick reaction of Worsel salvaged the Cheenus as a prize; he had seen the inevitable and he had instantaneously ordered the Rigellians to direct the *Dauntless*'s tractors and snatch the Cheenus out of harm. Within minutes the assault was over, the Spawn annihilated, space filled with incandescent bits of debris and tenuous, glowing clouds of many-colored gasses.

The planetary system was now vulnerable to conquest and occupation by the Patrol, although that might take many months. The information and data about Boskonia and the Bosko-Spawn would take years to evaluate, and Kinnison issued the orders to begin the tasks. There was, however, the immediate reward: the search through and the examination of the Cheenus.

Paraman 24of6 was hurried aboard, as if at any moment it would be recaptured or disappear, and 24of6's anxiety, first for the injured Kallatra, and then for the Cheenus's robots, contributed to that feeling. Kallatra had applied her own first aid, her Lens pushed up her left forearm out of the way and the stump neatly bandaged at the wrist. Her blackened eye sockets, however, were a horror to behold. 24of6 gently put a padded plaster across the injured area from temple to temple, like a white mask, and ordered her back to the *Dauntless*.

"I can't leave, Deuce," she said. "You know that. I have to stand guard against a reappearance of the Black Lensman." The fact was irrefutable; even Kinnison back on the *Dauntless* with his compassionate concern for any injured Lensman saw there was no alternative, and agreed to that. Her mind was sound, Worsel verified that fact. She was, by her uniting of the senses of perception of Worsel, Tong and 24of6 with her own Lensed-powers, as mentally capable as ever, and thus indispensable.

An inventory was quickly made by 24of6 of what had been captured; there were surprisingly few different items. There were three hundred and three warrior-robots of Ekron, of varying sizes, and not a trace of the star-shaped Asteri. Every one was perfect—yet none contained a single measurable erg of energy. The computer-brain was not simply disconnected; uncountable millions of chips and transistors had been fused mysteriously, perhaps by the Boskonian Lensman's bolt of energy which had maimed Kallatra. There were no living beings. There were no files or records. There was no equipment to repair the robots. The Cheenus seemed more like an empty shell, conventionally powered and automated, than an important enemy vessel customarily stuffed with alien technological and scientific secrets. But the robots themselves were enough to make 24of6 rejoice—and to reveal to him their fantastic enigma.

The paraman, his gown disarrayed so the temporary tubes and wires hung openly from his chest and stomach, was so excited that his not-so-smoothly-functioning prosthedon shook and made his non-mental voice quiver. He had gathered his Lensmen comrades and Patrol co-workers together in one of the less garishly painted rooms he had chosen to be his lab, with Kinnison Lensed in. He displayed two robots, one two feet high, the other twice as large, otherwise identical. Through a power rheostat he made first one, then the other, stand up on its three legs, waving its four arms, unreeling and retracting its three tentacles, raising and lowering its spindly rods. Then he had the two in operation at one time; their movements were uncoordinated and they kept accidentally bumping bodies and striking each other with their appendages. The conclusion was inescapable that their independent reasoning was impaired, either by the disruption of the computer-brain or the intervention of the Black Lensman.

"These two mechanisms," 24of6 said solemnly, "have measurements of every part in direct ratio to their size. Such is the case of the other hundreds of them. Every one, every part of every one, are identical in design—yet no measurement, no size matches. The explanation is so simple—and so beyond belief." The hollows of his eyeholes were radiating now; specks of lights and pulsating flashes grew in intensity as his Lens within his head registered his fervid mood. "They are different ages, so they are different sizes."

"Are you telling us these robots grow?" Worsel said incredulously. "Show us your mind, Deuce!"

There flashed within the minds of the other Lensmen the incredible deduction of 24of6. The warrior-robots were not constructed, not manufactured, but grown like animals from metal-based seeds. The fundamental building block was a semi-liquid or pseudo-cell. The biochemical reactions of the crystals came from electron-transport chains. This was not the "spontaneous generation" of the ancients, but a contrived system of synthesis of inorganic compounds. An inanimate-animate world of replication had been created in order to destroy. This miracle of invention had only one ignoble purpose, to forge a more efficient weapon of war. Warrior-robots were to have been copiously cultivated in the nurseries of the Cheeni in the cloud-shrouded planet of Zebub.

"Mechanical cattle grown for slaughter!" Tong said, intrigued, as Worsel's mind filled with theories and Kallatra merely accepted the whole idea quietly, her own mind preoccupied with her concern for another manifestation of the Black Lensman.

"Semi-liquid crystals I understand," Worsel said at last, "but metal-based seeds—what kind of metal?"

"It's an unknown alloy, Worsel, undoubtedly isotopic or with some obscure, rare elements. I don't have an analysis."

"Much carbon?" Worsel hinted at the possibility that 24of6 was jumping to biased conclusions, that it was really a form of carbon-cycle organic matter.

"Some carbon, I'd say, yes," 24of6 silently fired back at him, "but not organic cellular construction, which is chemical in nature, but inorganic, which is electrical in nature."

"And what's the energy carrier within the crystals?" Worsel asked.

"It's a substance much like the adenosine triphosphate of animal life."

"ATP. QX," Worsel said, "and for a communication system, such as DNA is at the heart of life and growth, what do you think this inorganic life form has?"

"A replicator or arranger very much like deoxyribonucleic."

"Hmm. Well, what about sex? How do they make the seeds and the fruit? Oh? No sex?" 24of6's explanation came rapidly to Worsel. Or rather, it was a lack of explanation, for 24of6 didn't know and had to confess that he was guessing about the seed. In fact, he had to admit that the "seed" he had identified was not a liquid crystal, but a hard crystal, evidently dead. Worsel could see now that the capture of the Cheenus and its mindless robots had produced few answers. Instead it had raised questions, many questions. There were clues available, but the secrets might take years to uncover.

Worsel took charge then. The threat from the unknown was now the paramount problem. The Boskonian Lensman had been driven off, but he had not been killed. Worsel was completely convinced of that fact. They were four Lensmen on the spot—they had to draw the enemy into mental battle before time and space moved one milliminute or one centimeter more. All of these thoughts he pressed upon the minds of the others. They all agreed: the Boskonian Lensman had to be confronted again, soon—if possible, as Worsel wanted, now.

"Deuce," Worsel ordered, "leave us. Scour the Cheenus. Collect as much information as possible, but be prepared to join us mentally at any moment." 24of6 was eager to get on with his research and scurried out at once. "Kallatra, prepare to open your mind to Tong and me." Worsel next called Kinnison, informing him of their findings and discussion, most of which he had already picked up, and the action they were forced to take.

"Good luck, old snake," Kinnison said, "and to all of you, and good hunting. I'll alert Nadreck and Tregonsee. We'll all be ready to help the instant you call." Without another thought they cleared ether.

"Ready, Tong? And you, Kallatra, ready?" Worsel's thoughts were like whispers. He felt Tong insinuating himself into the one compartment of his mind which was psychologically ready, like a launch pad, to beam into Kallatra's. The girl's mind was drifting closer and closer to theirs, taking split-seconds which seemed like minutes, offering itself like a living funnel for the beam of mental power Worsel had shaped from the two Velantian brains. Worsel for a moment felt his inner self being siphoned out of his head and into Kallatra's until the Velantians' accumulating power backed up and filled the vacuum. Now, paradoxically, instead of his mind being emptier, it was fuller; together they were far stronger than a mere sum of three; Tong and Kallatra and himself were one functional unit, a gun in which Kallatra was the barrel, Tong was the double charge of powder and Worsel was the bullet.

The electro-psychic energies of Kallatra again seemed like a dark tunnel into deep space of another kind. Through it—going not upward, nor down, nor out, but *inward*—sped their mental projectile, elongating more and more until it had the shape of a javelin rather than a pellet. Worsel didn't need the girl's urging to focus on the target—the ugly lizard face of the Boskonian Lensman—and to concentrate on developing one raw emotion: hatred, spiked with detestation and saturated with loathing. The tunnel ended. Suddenly, preposterously, the hurtling javelin was not deep down, but far out, beyond the end of the Universe, where it disappeared like smoke into and among, not one, but a billion billion billion figures—an infinity of creatures.

Their consciousness was back on the Cheenus and the mental gun was gone.

"Obviously we missed," Worsel said simply. "But what did we expect to find? A body? Or a spirit? A Black Lensman? Or perhaps something worse—a mastermind behind a Lensman pawn?"

Kallatra was too tired to reply.

"Can we try again, Kallatra?" Worsel asked. All his eyes studied the perspiring face behind the bandage in search of her emotions; his disengaged mind gently brushed the tumultuous unreadable thoughts of a drained and exhausted young girl.

"Not now," she said. "Perhaps soon—perhaps never." Though he could feel her strength gently rebuilding, he sensed fear, but not for herself.

"What did you see?" she asked.

He told her his impressions, of the trip and of the vague vision of infinity. So did Tong, identical in every way. And she herself confirmed what they had all seen.

"What do you fear?" Worsel asked.

"I don't know," Kallatra said in an unruffled, matter-of-fact way. "We were some place I've never been before. It is not bad—it is not good—I simply know it is *wrong*. I also know it is a place of danger."

"Another dimension?" Worsel suggested, and an alarming image of billions upon undetermined billions of creatures invading the galaxy swept like a lightning flash across his mind.

"Possibly another dimension," Kallatra replied. "But not a physical one."

"Not physical?" Worsel snorted in instinctive denial of a supernatural phenomenon. "A dream world?"

"We had a psychic encounter," Kallatra said, in shock. "The realm we saw is not a dream. It is real, inhabited by a multitude of non-existent entities."

"A spirit world?" Worsel said, thunderstruck. "That must be where the Black Lensman dwells."

"No, no," Kallatra protested. "That can't be. You must be wrong, Worsel. Perhaps his psyche travels there, as ours just did, but his body must be somewhere along the line we traveled."

"I hope you're right, Kallatra. Otherwise we'll never catch him. If we missed him in our headlong pursuit, then the only way we can catch him is to make him come to us."

Worsel, without warning or invitation, suddenly pressed into the young Lensman's upper brain, as tightly as possible for utmost security. "Perhaps it's not the Black Lensman we

160

seek! It may be his master we fought and pursue! You're close to death, my young friend. Examine yourself. This is no simple Black Lensman we're fighting—it's a demon or a fiend. It's like a ghost from the worst of the nine hells of Valeria. You're the exorcist it has to fear. It will—I'm utterly convinced—it will come back and strike at you any moment now. You're marked for death."

Kallatra's mind blazed high in a surge of energy, with an intensity Worsel had not felt before. "You're right, Worsel! I'm vulnerable now! Look at my Lens!" The appearance of her Lens of Arisia was startling. Instead of the lustrous, gleaming wholesomeness of crystals rippling with pseudo-life, there were sullen purple patches over half the surface. "Life has been drained from it despite the transfusion of our combined life-forces. Beyond some point the crystals will wither to death. And you others may soon afterwards be destroyed, too."

"Lalla Kallatra." The big, solemn Velantian hesitantly spoke. "We must risk our lives here and now. We've broken through to a place of death. It has touched us, especially you. All who wear the Lens of Arisia are now threatened by an immaterial force. All of Civilization is exposed to destruction."

"You are right, dear dragon," Kallatra said, choking with emotion, which she always so determinedly avoided. "This fiendish Boskonian thing stalks us. I don't fear death for myself, but for you and Deuce and the others. My death will take away from you the best weapon Civilization has, my el-sike power. I sense that if we fail and fall, each and every Lens could become a sinkhole into another dimension and drain away the vitality of the Patrol and Civilization itself."

The agony in Worsel's mind was great, intensified by the unexpected sentimental youth. To think that even the Lens might fail!

"Mentor is here!"

Mentor!

There flooded into Worsel's mind the calming presence of the Mentor fusion, so high in frequency and so finely tuned that the others, not even Kallatra, suspected it was there. "So, Worsel of Velantia, your foe draws you into its web."

Worsel's spirits rose; Mentor had come unbidden, all-knowing the moment of greatest need.

"And now," Mentor continued, unruffled, "you distrust the Lens. Be reassured. The Lens of Arisia can never, even

161

unwittingly, harm you or Civilization. As for your foe, you will find it because it will find you. You are right about it. It is not a Black Lensman whom you fight. You fight a Lensman illusion. A lensman-Fiend. It is a frightful force for evil from a realm where even we cannot go. Wearers of the Lens and all of Civilization are indeed in great peril. As for help from Arisia, Mentor can give no special help because it is not within our plan or scope. Frightful things are destined to happen, so be it. You will, of course, confront and fight again because you must. Kallatra the psychic, in our trust, will find the way. Indications are that a costly victory will be yours."

The deep, soundless voice was gone. Snap! without a further thought or word, so typical of the Arisians.

"Kallatra," Worsel said, "I've heard from Mentor. Our Lenses will not be the means of our destruction. We're not fighting the Black Lensman, we're up against the real Boskonian power, that which Mentor calls a lensman-Fiend."

Kallatra had been slumped against a headless robot, on guard, but as Worsel turned to her she roused herself to blazing life, nodding as if she knew now that Mentor had been there. They exchanged quick thoughts and began the vigil which they knew would not be long.

Worsel contacted Kinnison and briskly reported the recent events including Mentor's disembodied voice. Kinnison, upset by the idea of a lensman-Fiend manipulating a Black Lensman, nevertheless, because he understood the stress the Boskonian-hunters were undergoing, made no comments and asked no questions. Instead he casually mentioned that he had contacted Nadreck and Tregonsee, who were ready to help, and skipped on to say that exploration of the Ranggi System was underway. Perception-sweeps indicated that there would be much information about Boskonia and the Bosko-Spawn. Moreover, several score of Patrolmen had surfaced, spies with much to tell about old mysteries and ship disappearances, and the unhappy news of Patrolmen missing in action who were dead. Kinnison made one oblique reference to the Black Lensman affair "There's a sense of strange, intangible mental optimism among the minor leaders we've captured. I suspect your quarry is responsible. I hope you get him—or it—sooon. Better luck this time."

As Kinnison's mind departed Worsel's head, 24of6, who had returned to the room, himself mentally entered Worsel. "Kallatra's had it bad. I'll join with you this time. My psychic powers are latent, but their potential is enormous.

162

Now I will release them. Remember, I'm more pure mind now than any of you. Let's entice our opponent back to face us." The paraman had straightened his clothing and stiffened his posture in the manner of a recruit reporting for duty.

"QX, Deuce. Let's see if Kallatra is willing."

Worsel bent down and studied the girl's tense face. She gave a start but didn't break her mental concentration, unconsciously touching the bandage with her hand. "I understand, and I'm ready, Worsel," she said. In a gesture not expected of him, he picked her up with his gigantic hands and set her on her feet.

The four of them stood in the center of the alien room. A dozen warrior-robots, their heads disconnected, were scattered about the floor. The two robots 24of6 had demonstrated were seated on opposite ends of the low black table, like mismatched bookends, their chests open, parts missing. 24of6, the newcomer, stood on one side of the table, the other three together on the opposite side, a strange sandwich of a petite girl between two tall dragons.

Kallatra pressed her hand to her forehead and the link-up began. In her one hand she held a thought projector. The others knew she was using it like a lightning rod, offering the same situation as the last time the Black Lensman, or lensman-Fiend, had struck them, but although they feared for her safety they made no comment.

The thing unquestionably was lying in wait for them. It immediately launched its assault. The projector in Kallatra's hand burned like a fireball, spinning Worsel around, dropping him to one knee. He heard Tong's distorted, gurgling hiss through Kallatra's ears and the soundless cry, "The Black Lensman is here—in this room!" And then he felt a blow on his head which further stunned him; his consciousness was slipping away. But a voice within his brain said, "Wake up, Worsel, or you will die!" Worsel, clearing his head, rose and turned.

He saw Kallatra attacking Tong. The incongruity of their sizes did not, at that moment, appear ludicrous. It was the giant Tong who was in trouble. Lalla had her left wrist against her bandaged forehead, Lens pointing at Tong's Lens in his own forehead. The power she was emitting was so intense that little worms of fire crept along Tong's crystals and made his long head jerk convulsively, banging his slack jaws against his chest. His arms flew up across his face to fend off the scalding pain.

"Worsel!" Tong's call was feeble. "She's possessed! Save

me, save me!" Then Worsel, his mind touching Kallatra's, saw the real enemy: it had sharp red teeth, bright green scales, large black wrinkled wings—a Velantian? A Delgonian? An Overlord? No, none of those—it was more like a spiny, many-tentacled octopus. A winged, reptilian spider? The pictures flew through his brain cells in a milli-second. And then he knew: an Eich! From the hierarchy of Boskonia came a defeated enemy who had not been destroyed. Evil personified. As ruthlessly cold as its frigid body. An Eich!

Tongs arms flashed down as he tottered one step forward, his taloned claws, with the speed of desperation, raking across the slender body of Kallatra. The girl staggered back, almost severed across her slim waist by the slicing blow. Tong tottered one more step toward Worsel, pitifully begging, "Help me, Worsel!"

Worsel was frozen by the vision of the Eich. Kallatra had struck him down with the force of her mind when his back was turned, possessed by the Eich. So it seemed. Struck him down? Mentally? That had been a *physical* blow. From a human female whose left hand was gone and whose right arm was now gone to the elbow? "The Black Lensman is here —in this room!" Tong had said. "Wake up, Worsel, or you will die!"—Tong had not said *that;* Kallatra had!

Lalla Kallatra was lying on the floor, her blood already soaking into the gown of her paraman father, who had been knocked down and unconscious, spattered by the exploding flesh of his daughter. Lalla Kallatra was dying. Poor girl, commented one part of Worsel's compartmented mind; poor girl! There's no hope for her—will the Black Lensman die with her? But the other parts of his mind were racing to make a judgment and to formulate an action—so they instantly acted upon the thoughts that came through: Tong had known better. Mentor had told them that it was not a Black Lensman they fought. Mentor said they fought a Fiend. Worsel saw the great bright Light of Understanding . . . *Tong is the one!*

Worsel saw the Lens in Tong's forehead squirming now, under the relentless pressure of the dying Lensman. *Squirming.* He threw every electron of his power, magnified by his own Lens, into Kallatra's courageous mind. He felt his projection slide once more, as if along a tube, and strike Tong's Lens in a crushing blow. There was a soft and feathery sensation and there was the Eich, a huge grotesque face inches away from his.

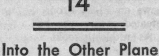

14

Into the Other Plane

Far, far away in the depths of the Second Galaxy, on a planet defiantly called Je-Jarnevon, or "Jarnevon Again," a number of Eich, as was their wont, had formed a council. They were not survivors of their home planet of Jarnevon, which had been so ignominiously crushed by Kinnison between two colliding planets in his famous nutcracker weapon. They had been away, bent on fomenting evil, when the calamity took place. So they survived. But they had crept away into the far reaches of their Second Galaxy and vowed to continue the destructive work of Boskone. They were not discouraged, although they had lost an entire galaxy—the Second—just as they were about to capture, so they thought, another—the First. They would start over, and it might take a few thousand years, but they would win again. They were ruthless and cold-hearted in their attitudes as well as their blood; their ethics were as twisted and bizarre as their multidimensional bodies, a mixture of loathsome serpent and obscene vulture somewhat resembling a siphonophorous purple-bladdered man-of-war. They would never believe that Boskone could go on without them, despite the fact that it seemed another echelon of control, the Ploor, had taken over. They had, in short, arrogantly formed another Council of Boskone, which had no real power but which served to make their ambitions seem logical and real. But they did have one important ally—a secret weapon which, conceivably, could turn their humbling defeat into a genuine struggle and, doubtless, devastating victory.

The hope of the New Council of Boskone was a ghost.

The ghost was an Eich, disembodied and supernatural and claiming to be the spirit of Eichlan, the former First of the old Council. None of the New Council believed the lie or cared. They had no concern that Eichwoor [the Woor of Eich, or the Ghost of Eich, as they chose to call it] main-

165

tained he came from another existence, or, more correctly, was suspended between this existence and the next, a purgatory in which so many Eich and others from Boskone seemed to have found themselves. They neither cared, because of their pride and vanity, from where he came, nor the circumstances of his situation. They cared only that he could help them. Actually they believed he was a gifted Eich living on some uncharted planet, who came into their thoughts because eventually he would try to assassinate one of the New Council and offer himself as a replacement, perhaps even as the First. All Eich had extraordinary mental powers. All Eich were expected to be able to manipulate other creatures mentally without any physical contact. But Eichwoor was certainly exceptional. Lately his exploits, if they were to be believed, and there was good evidence that they should be, had been very remarkable.

Eichwoor had nearly destroyed several Lensmen. And he had wrestled down a Second Stage Lensman. He had eavesdropped into a galactic-wide Lens-to-Lens conference called by the coordinator of the First Galaxy, Kimball Kinnison himself. Now he was about to switch from the one Lensman who had harbored him to that Second Stage Lensman called Worsel. With him in the Galactic Patrol as one of the elite officers, the New Council would not find it too difficult to recover some of their lost worlds.

Eichwoor explained how he was so fortunate as to be able to come back, at least to some degree, to a temporal existence. He had been locked in a deathly struggle with a Lensman called Samuel O'Stead—a very distant relative of the very First Lensman!—and they had both died, killed by each other's tenacious savagery of mental power. But by a strange quirk, and a bit of help from another Lensman who was Second Stage, the Lensman O'Stead was brought back to life, what was left of his body encased in a series of mechanical containers. An ethereal thread between them had been spun at the moment of their simultaneous deaths; by this thread Eichlan had become Eichwoor, able to drift through the real plane of existence and touch the minds of those whose psyches were most susceptible. O'Stead never knew of his shadow, the evil which came and went like a devil's halo above O'Stead's boxed brain.

Eichwoor had no limits in time or space. He claimed the New Council of Boskone as his kin and adapted to his new existence of the spirit by adopting their goals—and he was equally involved with O'Stead's activities, worrying for a while that the thread would be broken each time O'Stead underwent another operation. He was relieved and exultant when O'Stead improved enough to become both 24of6 and Deuce O'Sx with the regaining of his Lensman status.

The Woor of Eich had grown more knowledgeable and bolder with the passing years. More and more confidential papers were passing into his possession and on to the New Council. It was unfortunate that the New Council of Boskone was so pitifully weak and ineffectual, unable to make good use of such material. He had contemplated leaving his Eich kin to cooperate with others more capable, but the pride and arrogance of a true Eich would not let him. Things were bound to get better; his evil deeds certainly would begin to prosper and magnify.

That feeling was strengthened by his greatest achievement: slipping into Kimball Kinnison's Lens-to-Lens conference and embarking on his carefully nurtured plan to take over and possess a Lensman. His present host, the paraman 24of6, would not be risked; that Lensman was his guarantee of continued subsistence among the living. Using 24of6 as a base, he could seek and find someone important to appropriate. At first he might share its possession, but eventually he would completely occupy and own both mind and body. However, there was first one creature who was a threat and needed to be destroyed.

Lalla Kallatra, daughter of O'Stead-24of6-O'Sx, was of great concern to Eichwoor, because she possessed a power which could track him down and destroy him. Her father was a latent psychic whom, by great good fortune, no one recognized as such, but she had the active power, and was trained to use it. As long as she did not suspect the Eich's presence, he was safe. And as long as he hid within and around the unknowing mind of her father, whom she would never suspect or violate with scans, she would never suspect his presence. The risk, however, was an intolerable burden— Lalla Kallatra had to be destroyed.

The opportunity came when she went to Pok. He tried to kill her then. It was easy to steer the Boskonian warship against the Pok supply ship. [He would never use the defeatist term of Spawn.] He experimented with Tong, and found the Velantian could be taken over by him for a period of time, although he was not skilled enough to be able to remain. He was even able to move in and out of

167

the mind of the famous Worsel without revealing who he was, for the pathological fear of Overlords was enough to mislead the Second Stage Lensman. His attempts to kill Kallatra with the pirate ship, and then through Tong, were done without disclosing himself or his true objective. His involvement with Worsel thrilled him, but it also shook his egotistical confidence, for he recognized that Worsel had the power of mind to destroy him—and Kallatra could be the catalyst. And so Eichwoor had little choice, as he saw it, to undertake nothing less than the destruction of both—Kallatra first, then Worsel. That was what he now spent the time brooding over. He didn't care that 24of6 suspected the truth about his theft of the paraman's research. He found it unimportant that a project of warrior-robots whose development he had subtly influenced in the Ekron system had been wiped out. He found no significance in the spontaneous generation of robotic intelligence on Pok, because there was no connection with him so far as he could see, and, besides, the unliving Arrow thing had left the galaxy and disappeared. He worried only that the hour of reckoning with the psychic Kallatra was inevitably approaching.

Eichwoor was a ghost who was doomed to haunt the temporal plane, and saw only the life he had lost. He did not see the other opportunity because he did not look that way. It was providential for Civilization that he did not. It was likewise providential that the race of Eichs were one level removed from the all-highest evilness of the galaxies, the implacable enemy of the Arisians, the ruthless Eddorians. The Eddorians, therefore, were not aware of Eichwoor, although even if they had been, it is possible—because of their obsession with mechanisms—they may not have looked that other way, either. In Arisia, however, there was a discomforting awareness of Eichwoor's ghostly potential. It was theoretically possible for that abominable spirit to be the funnel down which could pour, into the Civilization he hated, all the evilness of the purgatory he partially inhabited. If he ever found that he had that power . . . ! It was all Mentor could do to keep from losing his composure, to keep from violating his rule against psychological meddling, and thundering, *Lensmen, the Universe is on the razor's edge of disaster!* Mentor did not, because Mentor—omnipresent, virtually omnipotent—expected Worsel to destroy the threat, to render it unbegotten, and therefore null.

And so the supreme moment had come. Worsel confronted

the Eich spirit. Two divergent existences clashed as two super powers dueled. Worsel instinctively comprehended the enormity of his role, and the absolute necessity for success.

Worsel of Velantia, Second Stage Lensman, unsurpassed High-Tension Thinker, now the most powerful mind of Civilization, stood rigidly in the center of the Cheenus room, his teeth glinting between thin lips frozen into a snarl. Only one tiny part of his brain was in touch with his surroundings. The only movement detected by his perception and his eyes, extended for full sphere vision, was from the mammoth room next door visible through the archway. There, beyond the huge, transparent cargo door against the far wall, a sky of stars and sparking wreckage rolled steadily sideways. The cluster of three Ranggi suns, white and orange and yellow, slid by slowly. Everywhere, mechanisms, robots, and robotic parts littered the glossy floors. The figures of the paraman and the wounded young Lensman, soiled machine bending over torn flesh, were a soundless, motionless tableau to his eyes. Stale oil vapors tickled his nostrils and contaminated the protruding tip of his sensitive tongue. The one tiny part of his brain registered all this. All the rest of him was fixed on the specter which seemed to dangle, disembodied, inches from his nose.

The hideous face of the Eich was as sharp as a hologram, but its equally repulsive thoughts were amorphous and unclear. Worsel had the mental sensation of drowning in a bubbling vat of putrescence, prevented only by the unyielding, shielding, psychic umbilical tube which was Kallatra's own spirit. The battleground was the empty shell which had been Tong's brain. Tong, the ego, was gone. The Eich gloated with the knowledge of Tong's destruction. The Eich had leapt in and overpowered Tong because it had already been in the room, invisibly interfused with the aura of the paraman Lensman. It had mutilated Kallatra, but not destroyed her. Tong's ego had been dispatched to the next plane of existence, but his life force had been absorbed by the ghost, much as an Overlord might do. And yet Kallatra had not succumbed. The Eich had smashed down Worsel with one of Tong's great hands, attempting to neutralize Worsel physically, using every mental quality to annihilate Kallatra. Kallatra had not failed; she had, instead, revived Worsel and had counterattacked. Worsel had nearly made the mistake of aiding the wrong entity.

The greatest brain in the galaxy did not make errors;

Worsel had hit the Eich with unexpected suddenness and power. Worsel's irresistible dart through Kallatra's salient defense shook the Eich loose from control of the Velantian body it possessed. It tried to drench and smother Kallatra's etheric needle and couldn't. The stream of force from Worsel burrowed into it and forced it out of Worsel's head. It was floundering, now, in limbo, seeking to make its stand in some other mind or from some other base.

Both Worsel and Kallatra expected it to return to the mind of the Black Lensman, assuming it had such a base. It did not. Instead, like smoke through fine mesh, it slipped into the next plane of existence and hovered there; Worsel could sense its presence, although he could not follow. Kallatra could have followed, but, weakened as she was, it would have been foolhardy to try. The Eich was in its sanctuary.

"It cannot come out," Kallatra said, "as long as I'm on guard."

For a long time Worsel searched the ether. There was no trace of a Black or Boskonian Lensman, evil Velantian or otherwise. There was nothing of significance he could find anywhere, even with Kallatra's weak but still effective help; moreover, he touched Nadreck's and Tregonsee's alert subconsciouses, receiving negative replies. He would have continued his futile probes much longer, but he was drawn back to the little room by the tiny, repetitious shocks emanating from 24of6. The paraman was moaning over Kallatra, in great emotional distress. Worsel was also startled to find that the sense of tranquility and composure which Kallatra had been exhibiting was deceptively optimistic.

"Lalla is dying," 24of6 said when Worsel knelt down beside the father and daughter. Worsel had to agree. The paraman's logic was unimpaired, but the turbulence of his emotions was painful for Worsel to feel, even as resistant as he was to the intensity of human personality. "There's no more I can do for her here, Worsel, beyond my first aid. We must get her back to the *Dauntless*. Or to Dyaddub. Right away." Worsel could read what 24of6 had in mind; freeze her and save her, as the paraman had been saved.

What Worsel was reluctant to say did not have to be said. Kallatra herself summarized the situation.

"You can't freeze me," she said matter-of-factly. "That would let the Eich out. Remember, I'm on guard."

"But you'll die," the paraman protested, arms moving jerkily in gestures of frustration.

"Not before I do what has to be done," she replied. "A psychic force must stay on guard. You, Deuce, can be that force. You have the latent power. I'll teach you my essential techniques. With Worsel's help, you'll succeed. You'll hold back the Eich. And some day you'll cage it permanently."

Worsel wanted not to hear 24of6's thoughts, but it was his duty to listen. Something had to be done with Kallatra and her father, and it had to be done soon. 24of6 seemed paralyzed with indecision; the choice lay between the life of his daughter and the doubtful development of his abnormal powers for the sake of Civilization.

"There's an important fact," Worsel said, "which neither of you know." He gently stripped away the torn and bloody gown from 24of6's mechanical body and threw it into a corner. "Deuce happens to be the unwitting medium for the Eich ghost. The Eich has been Deuce's companion for years. In fact, I believe there is some sort of psychic connection through Deuce's mind which permits the Eich to enter this temporal world of ours."

"By all the Gods of the Ancients!" 24of6 exclaimed in horror. "You must be mistaken, Worsel!" Kallatra protested the charge, too. But then, when Worsel said nothing, 24of6 said, "When I was first killed, the Boskonian who died with me at that precise moment was an Eich. I was returned from the dead. Perhaps something strange did happen." Kallatra fell silent as her father added. "I believe you, Worsel."

"That may not continue," she said, "if Deuce becomes stronger. We have no other choice. I can linger for days, if I'm not moved. I can resist sleep. There's time to train him."

"And perhaps to make the danger greater," her father said. "If I'm not already the Black Lensman, I may become one."

"You're not the Black Lensman," the girl said. "I've no doubt. We must get started. We've very little time. There is no other way, is there, Worsel?"

Worsel surprised them both by saying, "There is another way." After some silence, he added, "I'd rather I didn't suggest it."

"Well," said 24of6, "if we can't move her, if we can't get her to a life support machine—" He broke off, an idea sharp in his head. So sharp that Kallatra cried out, "No!"

"Yes," said Worsel. "That's a way."

There was much rapid discussion between father and

daughter on a very emotional level, but they came to the conclusion that Worsel knew was inevitable. The father would give up his body so that his daughter might live.

"Its feasible, Worsel! It will work! The only doubt I have concerns those clumsy hands of yours. But I'll do the surgery, and you can make the exchange and tighten up the bolts." He immediately visualized a detailed plan for Worsel to follow; the way the paraman's brain case should be opened and the fluids drained, the manner in which Kallatra's brain should be lifted with a flimsy, sterile plastic sheet from the medical pack, the positioning and the replacement of the fluids. To 24of6 it was simple, and he made it that way for Worsel.

Kallatra had been patient throughout the briefing of Worsel, her mind isolated from preparations and fixed upon the transmission line she had plotted between 24of6 and the gateway the Eich had used into the psychic plane. But when the preparations were complete for the operation to begin, she spoke into both their minds. "Deuce must not die. It's not necessary. I know you both believe a danger will be eliminated if Deuce does die. It's true he's been used by Eichwoor. But now that we know the danger, Eichwoor will never be able to function that way again. In fact, Deuce can become an Eich detector. Don't let him die." The effort to express herself while maintaining her vigilance was physically overtaxing, and a fit of coughing wracked her mangled body.

"I've no wish to let him die, young one," Worsel replied. "I've been observing him. There's no evilness in him—nor any abnormal weakness. He'd never wear the Arisian Lens if he weren't deserving." Worsel sat the paraman on the floor and wrapped one of Tong's stiff arms around his mechanical body to hold him upright, "As soon as his brain's removed, I'll freeze it. He'll live again in another body." Worsel, all the tools and instruments from the medical chest spread out on a sterile sheet on the floor, gently pulled Kallatra onto the sheet and at the feet of 24of6. He knelt lower, his elbows supporting his body, holding laser scalpels in both hands. "Here we go."

With 24of6's direct guidance of his muscular system, he had Kallatra's brain exposed and severed in minutes. Next, the paraman's own brain was out and wrapped in another sheet. Kallatra's was mounted in the prosthedon immediately, the dismounted Lens crystals pressed against her frontal lobe, and the cover was tightly replaced.

Although 24of6's brain had functioned during the entire

operation and was still awake and alert, conditioned for years to existence without a normal body and able to endure short periods without nourishment or oxygen, Kallatra blacked out.

So, at the moment of her greatest vulnerability, the Eich struck.

Her temporarily suspended consciousness left her helpless. But her father, all his powers intact though limited in his reserves of energy, fought off the thunderbolt which was being driven through his mind to destroy her.

At his first mental cry of anguish, Worsel applied his own powers to blunt the attack. Eichwoor almost possessed 24of6. Almost, but not quite. Worsel hung on, refusing to be driven from the contact with 24of6's ego. Never had the Velantian Lensman experienced more excruciating mental agony. Burning strands of pure energy encircled sections of his brain; hot wires tightened against his membranes. A thousand slasher worms were burrowing into his vital substance, dissolving it from his material body. Worsel's eyestalks twisted in torment from the flames consuming their muscle roots.

A cooling wave of concordant energy washed over him and extinguished the fire—Kallatra was aroused, her mind now supporting his, reviving her father's. Worsel felt father and daughter blending into a transcendent psychic force, two disembodied minds united in an extraordinary mental phenomenon. No physical limitation held back either Lalla Kallatra or Deuce O'Sx. The Eich was outmatched.

With a swiftness which Worsel had hardly hoped for, the struggle was over and Eichwoor retreating. The combined minds of Kallatra and 24of6 were in full pursuit. Worsel followed close behind, now only an observer.

Once more, in an infinitesimal tick of time, the galaxy was crossed and the void of the Universe penetrated almost to the end of infinity, where the curtain of the next existence hung. Once more Eichwoor, like smoke blown through gauze, slipped beyond and hovered there. Kallatra halted on this side. 24of6 did not. He did not hesitate; he glided through and struck Eichwoor, floating on the other side, and they both vanished.

Worsel's mind whirled backward in a long, spiraling return journey, sucked along in the wake of Kallatra. He was again in his body, eyestalks relaxed, muscles soothed, all pain gone.

"Deuce is dead," Kallatra said, listlessly. "He crossed over.

His life force is gone from our world. He'll never be back. But neither will the Eich." Kallatra moved what was now her prosthedon, her Lens flickering through the transparent window in the domed casing. Kallatra's transference was entirely successful, but she wasn't jubilant. "It's all over."

"Not quite," said Worsel. "There may be a Black Lensman."

"I think not,'" Kallatra said. The girl ceased all transmissions, totally exhausted. Worsel listened to the unaccustomed silence in the room and felt at peace for the first time in a long time.

"No, I must agree, there isn't," Worsel told himself. He let the compartments of his brain argue the idea until he finally decided upon his conclusion "There is no Black Lensman. There never was such a forthright enemy—understandably misled, misguided, mistaken. That was our imagination. A Black Lensman was our attempt to explain the inexplicable. And Eichwoor fed the delusion. There was only the Lensman illusion of the lensman-Fiend—vicious, depraved, evil." Worsel played back that statement in his mind, reviewed it, and decided it was right. During this time he had gathered up the remains of the girl's body, shaped it and wrapped it in one of the sheets. He did the same with the lump of flesh that had been 24of6, checking to see if the Lens was dead to confirm that 24of6 had not somehow survived. That Lens indeed was dead and disintegrating. He left it alone to vaporize into nothingness. He stowed the grisly items in his speedster and called Kinnison.

The good news far outweighed the bad news. Kinnison was sorry to hear about Deuce O'Sx. He was astounded to hear of a ghostly Eich. But he was elated about the banishment of the Eich and the fact that there was no such a thing as an enemy Lensman, be he Black, Boskonian, zwilnik or otherwise. He wanted to convey his personal thanks and good wishes to Lalla Kallatra, but her brain was dormant in its shell, still in a recharging state of sleep.

"Deuce's death knocks me for a loop, Worsel," Kinnison said. "I liked that bucket of bolts for the genuine human qualities he somehow managed to retain. As for Lalla, by Klono, she may not be the youngest Lensman, male or female, around, but she'll be the youngest around with Patrol Honors, you can bet! We'll fix her up with the finest new body we can make, that's a promise."

"Speaking of bodies, Kinnison, my friend," Worsel said. "It will take a while, but we'll see Lalla Kallatra again as we know her. She would have had a hand regeneration. Instead, there's a more ambitious opportunity. With the Council's approval, I propose to clone a body for Lalla Kallatra."

"Wow!" Kinnison exclaimed. "What a superb idea! That means a future brain pattern transference. Has it ever been done? Who will do it? Who will grow the clone? Does Lalla approve? I would think so. Can the Red Lensman be of help?"

"Hold on, hold on, Kim," Worsel said. "I don't know all the answers yet. But I think a body can be grown without another brain, as one would grow an organ or an appendage. It could be engineered, improved. Male instead of female. Then there would be a brain transplant. Or perhaps there could be a more direct symbiotic growth, old brain blending into developing body. The time factor can be reduced to maybe a year or two. I'm sure the Dyaddub lab can handle either case."

"Count on me," Kinnison said. "We'll do the best for her, based on her choice. The important thing for everyone is to keep that brain of hers alive and healthy and well guarded. We need her psychic mastery. The welfare of Civilization may depend on her. And, personally, I'm rooting for her to be a lovely young lady again. Meanwhile, Worsel, all this is under Lensman's Seal. You, me, Kallatra, anybody connected with this project. QX?"

"Agreed," Worsel said.

"Only two others ought to know right now, Treg and Nadreck. Do you agree with this, too?" Within minutes of Worsel's approval, Tregonsee had responded with an acknowledgment, congratulations and good wishes.

Nadreck was next, with his typical impersonal, all-business attitude. "I have attempted to trace Eichwoor's frequency, but it does not exist. I am sure you had this remarkable experience, Worsel, and that it was not one of your hallucinations. However, nothing I have been asked to check out leads to anything. I can register no facts. Naturally I cannot verify that there was no Black Lensman. I cannot verify that there ever was or will be one. I cannot find a lensman-Fiend and respectfully point out that you initiated the term, not Mentor. I am happy, however, to be able to report thus in the negative.

"As for your psychic activities," the Palainian Lensman said, in his peculiarly gloomy way, "they intrigue me. As I cannot prove such a place exists, I do not believe a threat can come from there. Nevertheless, I will do some serious thinking about it. Personally, I do not believe in ghosts. This is especially significant, may I point out, inasmuch as so many of your fellow oxygen-breathers keep mistaking me for one."

Kinnison laughed at the humorous idea.

Worsel wondered.

Kallatra, who was just stirring to wakefulness in an unfamiliar body, caught the drift of the discussion. She didn't wonder about the reality of ghosts—she wondered about how one went about killing a ghost when a ghost is already dead.

ABOUT THE AUTHOR

DAVID A. KYLE's experience in writing science fiction goes back to the "Golden Age" of the late 1930s when "Doc" Smith's works were setting the style for all others. For some years, Mr. Kyle confined himself to radio broadcasting (he owns one New York State station and is associated with several others), and then lived abroad. He has now returned to writing full time. His most recent book is *Science Fiction and the World*. Mr. Kyle was a close personal friend of "Doc" Smith. During Smith's lifetime, the two discussed future stories in the "Lensman" series (considered the most famous series in the history of science fiction). Some of the concepts discussed are embodied in *The Dragon Lensman*.

FANTASY AND SCIENCE FICTION FAVORITES

Bantam brings you the recognized classics as well as the current favorites in fantasy and science fiction. Here you will find the beloved Conan books along with recent titles by the most respected authors in the genre.

☐	01166	URSHURAK	
		Bros. Hildebrandt & Nichols	$8.95
☐	13610	NOVA Samuel R. Delany	$2.25
☐	13534	TRITON Samuel R. Delany	$2.50
☐	13612	DHALGREN Samuel R. Delany	$2.95
☐	12018	CONAN THE SWORDSMAN #1	
		DeCamp & Carter	$1.95
☐	12706	CONAN THE LIBERATOR #2	
		DeCamp & Carter	$1.95
☐	12970	THE SWORD OF SKELOS #3	
		Andrew Offutt	$1.95
☐	14321	THE ROAD OF KINGS #4	$2.25
		Karl E. Wagner	
☐	14127	DRAGONSINGER Anne McCaffrey	$2.50
☐	14204	DRAGONSONG Anne McCaffrey	$2.50
☐	12019	KULL Robert E. Howard	$1.95
☐	10779	MAN PLUS Frederik Pohl	$1.95
☐	11736	FATA MORGANA William Kotzwinkle	$2.95
☐	11042	BEFORE THE UNIVERSE	$1.95
		Pohl & Kornbluth	
☐	13680	TIME STORM Gordon R. Dickson	$2.50
☐	13400	SPACE ON MY HANDS Frederic Brown	$1.95

THE FANTASTIC ADVENTURES
OF THE LENSMEN CONTINUE...

They're legendary star warriors whose fabulous exploits
have made them elite guardians of the galactic empire.
Their most potent weapon is the mysterious force of the
crystal embedded in their flesh — a force that binds alien
adventurers from every corner of existence to the cosmic
brotherhood of the lens.

The entire planet was an awesome time-bomb set to explode at the slightest provocation. Worsel's first blunder
was merely lethal. His next promised to be positively
catastrophic!

An astounding new novel in the
magnificent tradition of E.E."Doc"Smith

13741

0

76783 00195

ISBN 0-553-13741-7